The Harbor of Lies

Debra Burroughs

This is a work of fiction. Names, characters, places and incidents either are the product of the author's imagination or are used fictitiously. Any resemblance to actual persons, living, dead (or in any other form), business establishments, events, or locales is entirely coincidental.

Lake House Books
Boise, Idaho

First eBook Edition: 2014
First Paperback Edition: 2014

THE HARBOR OF LIES
by Debra Burroughs, 1st ed. p.cm.

Visit My Blog: www.DebraBurroughsBooks.com

Contact Me: Debra@DebraBurroughsBooks.com

ISBN-10: 1502832143
ISBN-13: 978-1502832146

DEDICATION

This book is dedicated to my amazing husband, Tim,
who loves me and encourages me every day to
do what I love – writing.

TABLE OF CONTENTS

ACKNOWLEDGMENTS

I would like to acknowledge my awesome Beta Readers, Cathy Tomlinson, Janet Lewis, and Buffy Drewett, who inspire me and help me with their words of encouragement and critique.

I want to also acknowledge my brilliant Editor, Lisa Dawn Martinez.

"Oh, what a tangled web we weave when first we practice to deceive."
~ Sir Walter Scott

PROLOGUE

Sometimes people will tell themselves little lies, hoping they will help them cope with difficult things— hard truths really—that they'd rather not think about. Sometimes people harbor lies, protect them at all costs, for fear of what unleashing them will do.

In the end, the real question is: Without truth, is it really a life worth having?

~*~

"YOU DON'T UNDERSTAND," the man cried. "I'm in too deep."

His eyes glistened in the moonlight as he stood at the top of the steps, on the front porch of a big yellow house. He was illuminated only by a single bulb near the front door and the warm glow emanating from the large, living room windows. His voice was tight and raw, filled with desperation, as he spoke to another man who stood on the lawn, darkened by the shadows.

"Giving up is not an option. I've got too much at stake."

"They'll come after you for sure," the second man cautioned. "It's not safe for you to keep going the way you are, all the secrets, all the lies. People are going to get hurt—and I'm not just talking about you."

The first man glanced over his shoulder at the front door, then his gaze flew back to the other man. "I can handle it."

"Fine," the man on the lawn snarled. "Have it your way. But remember, when it all comes crashing down around you, I tried to warn you."

"It won't." He ground out the words of assurance, but he didn't sound convinced.

"I hope that young woman you're so fond of doesn't get hurt because of all this." He turned sharply and stomped off to his small SUV, parked at the curb. He looked back at the house, seeing the man still standing there, arms crossed, watching him as he got in and began to drive away.

"What an idiot!" He slammed his hand against the steering wheel, then hit the gas and sped out of town.

The road began to wind as it climbed up into the mountains. He peered into the rearview mirror, noticing bright headlights behind him. They stayed on his tail for a few miles. He was going the speed limit. Was the other guy in a hurry or something?

He slowed a bit, rolled the window down, and stuck his arm out, motioning for the other vehicle to go around him.

But it didn't.

"Oh, jeez...come on, fella," he groaned.

Maybe the other driver didn't feel safe passing on this mountain road. So, the man did the only other thing he could—he sped up. But the bright headlights kept pace with him.

Apprehension started to set in. He felt around on the dark passenger seat for his cellphone, thinking maybe he should call his friend at the police station and ask for some help, but as he went around a tight corner it slid onto the floor and out of reach. "Shoot!"

His chest began to tense and an eerie chill slithered down his back. His fingers wrapped tightly around the steering wheel. Was the other driver bearing down on him on purpose?

He drove this stretch of road often, there was a bridge over the ravine up ahead. He stuck his arm out the window again, encouraging the vehicle to pass him, hoping he would do it before they reached the bridge, but the driver hung back.

Oh, come on!

His knuckles were turning white as the roar of the tailing vehicle's engine grew louder. Maybe he was working up speed to pass. The lights intensified as it drew closer. He could make out that it was a pickup truck. It drifted toward the center line.

Finally, it was going to pass him. He breathed deep and allowed his hands to relax around the steering wheel.

Wrong move.

As they approached the bridge, the rumble of the truck's engine reverberated and echoed off the mountainside, drawing closer. Too close. The man had no time to react as the truck rammed into him, sending the little SUV careening off the bridge and into the ravine.

CHAPTER ONE
Lights Out

COLIN ANDREWS—THE SEXIEST MAN alive. It didn't matter that he wasn't on the cover of People Magazine. Hers was the only vote that counted anyway. And right now, Emily Parker gazed with adoration, across the candlelit dinner table, as her sexiest man tenderly held her hand.

In the flickering candlelight, his hazel eyes met hers and it stirred something warm and delirious in her. Though their whirlwind romance had been fraught with turbulence, Paradise Valley's handsome police detective had managed to win her heart and convince her to accept his proposal of marriage.

Now, if they could just make it to the altar unscathed.

He was dressed in a black suit and crisp white shirt that enhanced his broad shoulders and slim waist. His dark hair was trim and neat, his smile sexy and engaging.

Her heart was full as she gazed across the table, thinking how far they had come since they'd first met and how many times they had ventured too close to losing each other. Tonight she simply wanted to enjoy a romantic evening with him.

Colin had taken her to a late supper at the elegant new Brickyard Bistro in Paradise Valley. "You know, Babe, I love everything about you." He ran his thumb playfully over her engagement ring. "Your smile, your mane of blond curls, the feel of your soft skin."

"Oh stop," she said, rolling her hand in a motion that told him to keep going.

"I love how your blue-green eyes turn bright turquoise when you're really mad and how you don't think twice about doing something dangerous. Shall I continue?"

A small giggle escaped her. "I think that's quite enough." His compliments were verging on the edge of cheesy and she suspected he knew it. They would have a good laugh about it later.

Dinner had been fabulous. The food, the service, and the atmosphere had all been first-rate.

In the middle of the elegant dining room, an impressive young man, dressed in a black tuxedo, had played beautiful, romantic music on the grand piano as candlelight had danced across the shiny ebony surface. It could not have been a more perfect evening—that is, until they were driving home.

Colin began to press Emily about nailing down a wedding date, something she'd been finding increasingly difficult to do, and, from that moment on, their conversation downgraded from gloriously romantic to slightly contentious.

"We were having such a nice evening. Why do we need to spoil it by arguing about setting a date?"

"Because we've been engaged long enough, Babe. I want to be married."

Her little black dress suddenly felt too tight. "But how can I pick a date? Every time we do, something terrible happens." Beside him, in the Jeep's front seat, Emily twisted to face him. "Our wedding plans are cursed, Colin. They're cursed!"

"Don't be so dramatic, Babe. They're not cursed." He flashed her a patronizing grin.

Huffing, she tugged at her skirt. "What would you call it then?" Frustrated, she crossed her arms tightly over her chest, pressed her back against the passenger door, and groaned. "First the groom is arrested for murder—"

"Yes, but he was exonerated." Colin winked at her. "Don't leave that part out."

"Granted, but then our wedding planner disappears into thin air, leaving us high and dry."

He flashed a glance at her. "You know we had no control over that."

"My point exactly."

Colin reached over and gently pried one of her hands loose, wrapping his around it. "As hard as it was losing her, we can always get another—Camille, for instance."

"They say bad things come in threes, so what's next?" She moaned, exasperated with herself. It wasn't like Emily to be so negative. Even to her own ears she

7

sounded like a whining child. What was bothering her so much? Could it be the ominous feeling that another catastrophe was looming around the corner? Or the thoughts of her late husband that had been plaguing her recently?

Colin downshifted and brought the Jeep to a stop at a red light. "Nothing else is going to derail our wedding plans, Babe. I promise. I won't let it."

"I know you'd like to believe that, Colin, but you have no control over—"

"Attention, available units," a strong, female voice crackled over the police radio in Colin's dash. "Burglary in progress at forty-three sixty-six Evergreen Way. Adult male, Caucasian, twenty to twenty-five years of age, last seen wearing a blue t-shirt and jeans. Long blond hair and beard. Unit to respond?"

Colin shot Emily an I-have-to-take-this-call look, then answered the radio dispatcher. "This is Detective Andrews. I'm almost twenty-three that location. I can respond until uniform personnel arrive."

"Copy. Detective Andrews, twenty-three. Unit to assist?"

Another voice came on the radio and confirmed their assistance.

The police call reminded Emily who she was—no longer merely a woman in love, it was a call to action. She swiveled straight in her seat and adjusted, first her safety belt, then her skirt. "Let's catch this guy red-handed."

"Not you, Emily. You are going to stay in the Jeep."

He should know better than that by now. Emily had

been a private investigator for over a year. As a consultant for the Paradise Valley Police Department, hired by Police Chief Nelson himself, she had helped Colin solve several cases during that time—occasionally, or frequently, despite his objections. Did he seriously think she would sit quietly in the car while he investigated the break-in?

"I mean it, Emily. You stay put."

She crossed her arms and pursed her lips. Two were better than one. What if he needed her help?

Approaching the subject property, Colin turned his headlights off as he rolled the Jeep to a stop at the curb. He clicked his seatbelt off and reached for his gun.

"Please," she cooed.

"Not a chance. You stay here."

He climbed out and quietly closed the door.

Emily rolled her window down and watched Colin cut across the driveway and disappear around the brightly lit side of the house. As soon as he was out of sight, a noise issued from the opposite side.

"Colin," she whispered loudly out the window, hoping to get his attention, but he was long gone.

He's not going to like it, but I've got to check it out. She dug her pistol out of her purse, slowly opened her door, slid out, and gingerly shut it behind her.

She crept across the lawn in her high heels, transferring the weight to her toes to avoid sinking into the ground. Emily made her way toward the darkened side of the house, where a window stood partly open. Keeping her gun low, she pushed up on her tiptoes and peeked inside. She saw no movement.

A couple of quick footfalls behind her drew her

attention and she began to turn. Before she made it all the way around, searing pain shot through the back of her head and she collapsed down onto the hard, damp earth. Then, everything went pitch-black and silent.

~*~

Colin rounded the perimeter of the house from the backyard. A light came on in a small frosted window on the side of the house next door, faintly illuminating the area between the two homes.

No! Not again.

There, reflected in the glow of the dim light, Emily was slumped on the ground, motionless.

Colin's heart skipped a beat.

Why didn't she stay in the car?

He checked her pulse, then raised his eyes to the sky, thanking God she was alive. Colin glanced around for the perpetrator, but there was no sign of anyone. He whipped out his radio and called for an ambulance, a sick feeling swirling in the pit of his stomach at the sight of her.

The roar of a car engine at the curb told him backup had arrived. He hurried to the front of the house and waived his arm in a wide sweeping motion, gesturing to the officers.

They jumped from their cruiser and hustled over.

"I assume the suspect fled on foot. I didn't hear any vehicles. He clocked my girlfriend before he got away."

"She okay?" one of the officers asked.

"Unconscious. You two start scouring the neighborhood while I radio for more officers." Colin reiterated the brief description of the man. "Get going and let's find this SOB."

As soon as the officers took off, Colin made the call as he raced back to Emily's side.

Within minutes the ambulance arrived, and Colin waived the EMTs over. When the additional officers showed up, Colin gave them directions and sent them off, keeping a close eye on Emily.

"Her vitals appear normal," one of the paramedics explained after he checked her out. "Hopefully she's only temporarily knocked out, but let's get her to the hospital ASAP. A possible concussion is nothing to take lightly."

This was not the first time Colin had watched the woman he loved being loaded onto a gurney and put in the back of an ambulance. He wished he could say it would be the last time, but he knew his fiancée better than to think such a thing about this beautiful, sweet, fearless, stubborn, exasperating, yet totally lovable woman who had agreed to marry him…if only he could get her to the altar in one piece.

Another squad car pulled up and Officer Ernie Kaufmann climbed out. Ernie was not only Colin's right-hand man, he was almost family. "What's going on, Detective?"

Colin explained the situation. "Not again," Ernie moaned.

The ambulance pulled away, lights flashing and sirens blaring, whisking Emily to the nearby hospital. Leaving Officer Kaufmann in charge of the crime scene, Colin followed the ambulance in his Jeep.

Was this the third thing Emily had been afraid was

going to happen?

~*~

Emily smoothed the soft, sheer layers of her flowing white gown as she waited for the wedding to begin. The organ music started and the double doors to the chapel swept open for her grand entrance.

There was Colin, standing down front, beside the minister, wearing a black suit with a white rose boutonniere. Her gaze drifted over the small crowd of her friends and family, rising to their feet on both sides of the aisle, smiling at her.

She took her time floating through the white rose petals, which were strewn down the aisle. She wanted nothing more than to run to Colin before anything, or anyone, got between them, but her feet wouldn't move any faster. An ominous feeling washed over her.

With an encouraging smile, Colin held his hand out to her. She was about to take it when a collective gasp rose from the crowd. In her peripheral vision she caught heads whipping back, toward the doors.

She glanced over her shoulder. What were they staring at? There stood Evan, her late husband—at least she thought he was dead—dressed in a black tuxedo. Her heart began to hammer. She glanced quickly at Colin, then her gaze flew back to Evan.

Evan held his hand out to her. "Come back to me, Emily."

Her gaze fell to his hand, then rose to his face. *What do I do?*

Her focus whipped back to Colin, his hand

extended to her as well.

"Come back to me, Emily."

Warm lips touched her forehead and she heard the words again. "Come back to me, Emily."

She woke and her eyes fluttered open. Colin was leaning over her as she lay in a hospital bed. The corners of his mouth tugged upward and a spark of relief flashed in his eyes when she came awake.

Her gaze flitted around the room. "Where am I?"

"St. Luke's Hospital." Colin pulled up straight and lightly grasped her hand. "You took a nasty crack on the head tonight, and you've been out for a few hours. How are you feeling?"

She felt her head and winced. "No wonder it's throbbing." With her hand to her head, she noticed a monitor wire dangling from a device on her finger.

"You have a bit of a concussion, the doctor said. What's the last thing you remember, Babe?"

Emily grabbed the control hanging on the side of her bed and raised the head so she could sit upright. "Well, I remember we went to dinner—which was wonderful, by the way," she paused and flashed him a grin. "Then a call came over the radio for a B and E. We responded. You went around one side of the house—"

"And you took the other, even though I told you to stay in the car."

"I tried, but I heard a noise on the other side of the home, so I snuck around to see what it was. That's the last thing I remember."

"That must've been when the perp got the jump on you and smacked you on the head with something." Colin kissed her hand. "I'm just glad you're okay. You really scared me. Again."

"Sorry." Emily pouted and attempted her best guilty-puppy-dog look. "Really, I am."

"Next time I tell you to—"

"Oh, Emily!" Maggie gasped, running into the room, with Camille close on her heels. "Are you okay, girl?" Leaning down, she gave Emily a quick squeeze.

"Yes, Em, are you okay?" Camille repeated. "We heard you were attacked by some deranged maniac."

Maggie Sullivan and Camille Hawthorne were part of Emily's close circle of friends. Any time she needed them, they were there, no matter what.

"It's not that bad," Emily said.

"You poor thing." Camille squeezed in and gave Emily a quick hug too.

Maggie turned to Colin. "Did y'all catch the criminal who did this horrible thing to our Emily?"

"Yes, my men found him outside a house, a couple of blocks away, hiding in some bushes."

"Paradise Valley used to be such a safe place," Camille lamented.

"This guy made a twenty-mile commute—he was from Caldwell," Colin replied. "A meth addict looking for something he could sell to make another score."

"How bad is it?" Maggie asked.

"I haven't talked to the doctor yet, but I'm sure I'll be fine. I'm pretty hard headed." Emily flashed a hopeful smile.

Colin chuckled. "I'm glad *I* didn't say that."

Camille frowned at him before returning her attention to Emily. "Anything you need, Em, we're here for you."

14

"Has Isabel been here?" Maggie asked.

Isabel was another girlfriend in their group and an FBI agent.

Colin cleared his throat. "She called, couldn't make it for a while, working a big case out of town, she said. I filled her in on what the doctor had to say. She'll check back in the morning."

"How about filling me in?" Emily raised her brows slightly.

"Like I said, the doctor explained you had a mild concussion and they're monitoring your condition through the night. She was in here checking on you right before you woke up, and she'll be back in a couple of hours to check on you again."

"What's going on in here?" boomed a big burly voice. Officer Ernie Kaufmann filled the doorway, wearing a wide grin. He was like an uncle to Colin and had become a good friend to Emily. He stepped to the foot of the bed. "I got everything buttoned up down at the crime scene and the paperwork's done, so I thought I'd check up on our girl."

Emily smiled. "Hello, Ernie. You didn't have to come and check on me."

"Of course I did."

"Excuse me, people." A frumpy middle-aged nurse with a halo of gray curls bustled into the room. "There are far too many bodies in here and it's way past visiting hours." She flitted to the machines to check on Emily's vitals. "I'll have to ask you all to leave."

A wave of protests arose from the visitors, but the nurse wouldn't have any of it. "Now, now, I'm sorry, but this little gal needs to get some rest."

"You heard the lady." Ernie lumbered out, first to comply.

Maggie and Camille each snuck in a quick hug with Emily before making their exit. "We'll get your house ready for when you get home."

Colin bent down and planted a long, soft kiss on Emily's lips. "I love you, Babe. I'll be back later."

She grabbed his hand as he stood up. "That's it. That makes three."

"Three what?"

"Three bad things happening in a row. Now we don't have to worry. There shouldn't be any more catastrophes to stand in the way of our wedding. Right?"

"Right." Colin kissed the back of her hand and smiled. "Should be smooth sailing from here on out."

~*~

The next morning Colin brought Emily home from the hospital. Maggie and Camille were already at Emily's little bungalow, fluffing pillows and preparing snacks, getting ready to fuss and dote over their friend until she was back to normal.

Maggie, a fitness trainer, was also somewhat adept at massage and offered to give Emily a good neck and shoulder rub, while Camille, a caterer and event planner, whipped up Emily's favorite foods.

"It looks like you ladies have things well in hand. I should head down to the station," Colin said. "I've got a couple of cases to work on, including the guy who assaulted my fiancée."

"You go on ahead," Camille told him. "We'll take

good care of our girl."

Emily reclined on the sofa with Camille stuffing a couple of pillows under her head. "Don't worry about me, Colin. I'll be fine. You go catch some bad guys."

He chuckled as he bent down and kissed her good-bye.

As soon as Colin was out the door, Camille asked what really happened the night before. "Don't spare any details."

"It's not a big deal," Emily moaned. She explained how they went to dinner and talked about choosing a wedding date—well, argued about it really. Then he got the radio call of a burglary in progress. "When we got to the house, Colin went around to the left and I heard some noises to the right, so I went to check it out."

"Colin had you checkin' out a dark yard all alone?" Maggie drawled in her southern accent.

"You're not a cop, Emily," Camille pointed out, as if Emily didn't already know that. "What was that man thinking?"

"I know I'm not a cop." Emily rolled her eyes. "But as a private eye, I am not without skills."

Maggie and Camille nodded.

"That's true," Maggie agreed.

She, along with Emily and Isabel, taught self-defense classes for women, not to mention their routine practice times at the firing range.

"Don't be too hard on Colin," Emily said. "He actually told me to stay in the car."

Camille's blue eyes rounded. "He did? So, then why—"

"When I heard something on the darkened side of

the house, I couldn't just let him walk into danger, not when I could help him."

Maggie perched on the arm of the sofa. "Sounds like you were the one in danger, my friend."

"Okay, so let's get back to what you said earlier," Camille cut in. "Did you two pick a wedding date? There are still so many details to pin down. You really need to reserve a venue soon."

"We were thinking, maybe, about six weeks from now."

Camille frowned. "That's not long enough to make all the arrangements, Em."

"Camille, Camille, Camille," Emily moaned, laying her forearm dramatically over her eyes. "Colin and I have told you all along that we only want a small wedding. Just close friends and family, maybe in my backyard. You know I have a beautiful garden with the deck and the ga—"

On second thought, maybe she shouldn't mention the gazebo Evan had built for her. Perhaps that was a bad idea. "Anyway," Emily continued, "there's more than enough room for a small wedding in the backyard."

"And I've told you, Emily," Camille countered, "a small wedding just won't do. There are simply too many people in this town that will expect to be invited, and we'll need a large enough venue for the reception to serve dinner, a place for the band and dancing, and—"

Emily's cellphone rang. She shook her head at Camille as she snatched the phone off the coffee table. Checking the caller ID, she saw it was her sister in Maine.

"Hello, Susan."

"Hello, Emily. How are you?"

Had Colin phoned her about Emily's little mishap?

"I'm doing better," Emily replied.

"Better?" Susan paused, clearing her throat. "I'm afraid I have some bad news about the wedding."

CHAPTER TWO
An Unusual Proposal

BAD NEWS ABOUT THE WEDDING? They had already suffered through three bad things that could have derailed the ceremony. It should be smooth sailing from here on out, Colin had assured her. Now what?

"What are you talking about, Susan?"

Susan lived with her husband and children on the coast of Maine and was Emily's only sibling. She was a take-charge, first-born child, and much older than Emily.

Their mother had passed away years ago, and, with the distance between her and Susan now, the sisters had rarely seen each other since Emily had married Evan and moved west to Paradise Valley, Idaho. With their father in an assisted living facility for patients with Alzheimer's, Emily was grateful for phones and Skype—otherwise she would feel like she had no family.

"Well, Sis, I'm afraid we won't be able to come for the wedding."

"Why not?" Emily wondered, now, if her sister even knew she had been attacked and had spent the night in the hospital with a concussion.

"Brian's been in a terrible car accident and he broke both of his legs when he flew off a mountain road."

"Oh, Susan, I'm so sorry." Emily's concussion didn't seem so important anymore. "What happened?"

"The details are kind of sketchy. Brian said someone was following him too closely and, next thing he knew, he was in the ravine."

"You don't sound convinced." Emily's suspicious senses tingled.

"It just seems like there's more to the story. The doctor thinks he'll likely remember other details as time goes on."

"Is he going to be...*okay*?" Emily didn't want to ask directly, but she wondered if he would be able to walk again.

"Eventually, yes, the doctor said, but it'll be a long recovery. His legs were badly broken, in multiple places. Once he's out of the hospital, he'll be in a wheelchair at first, and then on crutches for a while. Between that and all the medical bills, well, there's just no way—"

"But we haven't even set a date yet."

"I know, but you've been saying it was going to be this fall and it's already the end of September. I assumed you just hadn't gotten the invitations out in the mail yet."

"My wedding planner and I were just talking about picking a date before you called." Emily glanced up at Camille. "We were thinking six weeks from now, but we could postpone."

"Oh, Emily, I appreciate that, but with Brian's condition, and the cost...there's simply no way we can come."

"I understand," Emily muttered sadly. "Poor Brian—I hope he's up and around before too long."

"It'll just take time," Susan said. "But..."

"But what?"

"I may have come up with another way to be at your wedding, and you won't have to postpone."

"What is it?" Emily asked, with a hint of skepticism in her voice. *Skype the wedding?*

"Now, hear me out first, and then take some time to think about this before you respond."

"Think about what?" Emily's gaze flew to Maggie, who returned her stare.

"As I'm sure you remember, I've been working part-time at the Rock Harbor Inn as their wedding consultant. Oh, Emily, we have the most beautiful weddings on the lawn overlooking Frenchman's Bay."

"Yes, I know. What's your point?" Emily hadn't meant to sound so impatient, but her sister was taking too long to finish her thought.

"Well, we're nearing the end of our tourist season. We only do weddings until the middle of October. I've just had a cancellation for that final Saturday. It would be in two weeks, which is too soon for anyone else to book the place, so I thought maybe—"

"Anyone else?" An uncomfortable chill slid down Emily's back. "What are you trying to say?"

"Here's what I'm thinking, if you guys agree to come to Rock Harbor, I will handle all the details from this end. That's the only way I can think of to still be part of your wedding. Is that something you might consider?"

That was a lot to take in—a logistical nightmare in the making. Emily's thoughts were a jumble and no words would come.

"Sis? Are you still there?" Susan asked.

Emily blinked a few times, trying to absorb the information. "I'm still here." She looked down at the phone, then up to Maggie and Camille, who were both gaping at her.

"What do you think?" Susan asked.

Emily stuck the phone up to her ear again. "I...I don't know what I think."

"What is it?" Maggie whispered impatiently.

"You want me to have my wedding in Rock Harbor, Maine, in two weeks?"

"What?" Camille and Maggie gasped in unison.

"Yes, silly, that's what I said." Susan breathed a laugh. "Weren't you listening?"

"It's just kind of hard to wrap my brain around right off. Give me a minute."

"I'd be thrilled if you'd say yes."

"I'll have to talk it over with Colin and get back to you."

What would he have to say about this hair-brained idea?

"Now, don't take too long," Susan warned. "Like I said, it's only two weeks away."

~*~

Once Susan had hung up, Maggie and Camille

pelted Emily with a barrage of questions.

"Have your wedding in Maine?"

"Travel all the way to the other side of the country?"

"Do you know how much that will cost?"

"Put on a wedding in just two weeks?"

"What about all the people who were planning to attend your wedding?"

"What is Colin going to say about all this?"

Emily raised both hands in surrender. "Calm down, you two. I only said I'd think about it."

The doorbell chimed. "Saved by the bell." Emily rose from the sofa and stumbled slightly. "Whoa." She put a hand to her head and sat back down, feeling dizzy from getting up so quickly.

"I'll get it." Maggie smiled. "You just sit there and rest." She went to answer the door and swung it open to find their friend Isabel.

Isabel stepped into the entry and gave Maggie a quick squeeze. "How's Emily?"

"Better," Maggie replied.

"You're not going to believe the latest," Camille called from the living room.

"The latest?" Isabel asked, as Maggie linked her arm through Isabel's and walked her into the next room.

Camille settled on the arm of the sofa. "Emily's sister can't come for the wedding and—"

"Oh no," Isabel said.

"That ain't all," Maggie continued. "She suggested we all go to Maine and have the weddin' there, at the inn where she works." Maggie planted her hands on her hips. "What do you think of *that*?"

"Well…" Emily stepped in, "she didn't exactly say we should *all* go."

Maggie sat on the sofa beside Emily and rested a hand on her shoulder. "I'm sure that's what she meant, Em. She certainly wouldn't expect you'd leave us all here."

Isabel pushed her long, dark curls over her shoulder as she took a moment to let it sink in. "When?"

"In two weeks," Camille huffed. "Can you believe it?"

Isabel rubbed her jaw and pursed her lips as she thought about it. She was the logical one in the group and preferred to think before speaking. "I think it sounds like a wonderful idea."

"It does?" Emily was a bit surprised by her practical friend's response.

"Oh, Isabel, you can't be serious." Camille crossed her arms for emphasis. As a caterer and event planner, her experience would say that it would take weeks, maybe months, to pull together such an affair.

Isabel settled on a chair near the sofa. "Emily and Colin keep saying they want a small wedding, but you two," Isabel wagged her index finger between Camille and Maggie, "keep trying to make it the event of the year."

"Well, um, we just want the best for Emily," Camille muttered.

"Emily, if you go along with Susan's suggestion, it would be almost like eloping," Isabel grinned, "like Alex and I did."

"Eloping?" Emily echoed, remembering back to a spat she and Colin had had over that very subject. He wanted to elope, but she wanted to be surrounded by the people they loved.

"Only it would be better," Isabel crossed her arms and sat back in the chair, "because you'd have your friends and family there."

Camille popped up off the arm of the sofa. "But what about the cost?"

"The cost?" Isabel asked. "Hmm. Didn't you tell us that you and Jonathan have been saving up for a vacation, but you couldn't decide where to go?"

Camille nodded that she had.

"And with all Jonathan's business trips, I'm sure he's got tons of frequent flyer miles saved up," Emily added.

"True, but—"

"And, Maggie," Isabel cut Camille off, "didn't you tell me Peter wanted to take you away for a long, romantic weekend?"

"Yes…" Maggie seemed to wonder where Isabel was going with that.

Could this really work? Emily ran her fingers through her tousled curls, letting the possibilities dance in her mind. "What we save in not paying for the wedding would cover our airfare, plus airfare for Colin's parents."

Camille bolted out of her seat. "But what about the other people in town—the police chief, the mayor, and your other friends, like Ernie and Marge?"

"You're right," Emily nodded sadly, "they would be pretty upset if we left them out."

A bright smile spread across Isabel's face. "What if we have a big celebration when you two get back from your honeymoon? Alex and I could host it at our place."

Isabel lived in a sprawling, two-story brick home with her lawyer husband, Alex. It was surrounded by expansive, manicured grounds and a large, stone patio, the perfect setting for the event.

Camille's expressive blue eyes widened. "Then all those that would have been invited to the wedding can come to the reception." She seemed to be getting on board with the idea. Her hand waved through the air and her gaze followed, as if she were visualizing the entire scenario. "Oh, I can just see it now. A big white tent on your lawn, little twinkle lights everywhere. I'll prepare the food. We can hire a band."

Maggie's face lit up and she clapped her hands. "Like a big ol' party!"

~*~

The women bounced ideas off each other, and the excitement grew, at the prospect of having a destination wedding in picturesque Rock Harbor. Camille made some snacks while they sketched out plans for the trip. Without having spoken to any of the men yet, Emily was reluctant to call Susan back to tell her they would come to Maine, but it looked more and more like a real possibility.

"I've got to get going," Isabel said after the table was cleared. She hugged the girls good-bye and went to the front door.

She opened it to leave and met Colin, climbing the few steps to the porch. "Hey, Isabel, what's up?"

"Oh boy, you have no idea." She laughed a little as

she passed him.

"What do you mean by that?" he called after her.

Isabel kept walking to her car and waved a hand in the air. "You'll find out."

CHAPTER THREE
A Shift to Maine

COLIN CROSSED THE LIVING ROOM and leaned down to kiss Emily, ever-so-briefly. Even so, the soft warmth of his lips lingered on hers. "How's my girl doing?" His sultry eyes searched her face as he sat on the sofa beside her. "Feeling better?"

She nodded and smiled. "A lot better."

A small crease formed between his brows. "I ran into Isabel on the porch. She sounded like she was trying to warn me that you girls were cooking something up. What's going on?"

With Camille's and Maggie's help, Emily excitedly explained Susan's surprising proposal for their wedding. "It will almost be like eloping, which you said you'd like to do."

"But I thought you hated the idea of eloping. If I remember correctly—"

"I know. I know." Emily recalled the argument

they'd had about it at the time. "But that was different. This way, we're not running off by ourselves."

"Yeah, but—"

"We'll be married in two weeks, and that means less time for anything else to get in the way of our wedding."

"Good point," Maggie added.

Colin took Emily's hand. "We'd better think this thing through, Babe." He lifted his eyes to the two other women standing in the room.

Camille took Maggie by the arm. "I think that's our cue to leave. Let these two lovebirds hash things out."

As they left, Camille gestured to Emily, raising her thumb and pinky to her ear and mouthing the words *call me*.

Emily smiled and waved her off. Leave it to Camille to pick up on Colin's hint to give them some privacy yet be unable to resist urging Emily to call her with the juicy details.

Colin rested an arm on the back of the sofa. "Now, tell me again, what happened to Brian that they can't come here?"

Emily repeated what Susan had said, including her suspicions that there might be more to the car crash than a simple accident taking place.

"Was she hinting we should look into it if we decide to come?" he asked.

"I'm not sure, but if it was you," Emily laid her head on his chest and Colin draped his arm around her, "I'd certainly want to know."

~*~

By the next day, Emily had convinced Colin they should take Susan up on her offer, using many of the points the girls had bandied about the previous day. As well, the other three women spoke to their men about the adventure and, eventually, all of them were on board.

When Colin phoned his parents and told them about the plan, offering to pay for their flight back east, they were thrilled at the idea of being able to go to Maine at the peak of fall colors, in addition to the wedding, of course.

Now, what Emily had dreaded—the logistical nightmare.

Last-minute air fares were tricky. The four women would fly out on Tuesday, before the wedding, while Colin and Alex would follow on Wednesday, after tying up the separate cases they were working on. Jonathan, Camille's husband, would have to fly in from a business meeting in Chicago, and her daughter, Molly, from college in Florida.

As well, Peter, Maggie's boyfriend, who also happened to be Camille's brother, would be coming in on Friday from his television reporting job in Seattle. Then, lastly, Colin's folks were scheduled to be traveling from San Francisco on Friday as well.

The closest airport was in Bangor, an hour away, so arrangements would have to be made for several rental cars. If everything went like clockwork, the entire guest list would be in Rock Harbor for the rehearsal dinner on Friday night—fingers crossed.

~*~

The day of the trip, Emily was up at four in the morning, scurrying around, doing last-minute packing, rushing to be ready for Alex to take the girls to the airport for a six am flight. She hadn't slept well the night before. Her dreams, which had been filled with visions of her late husband, Evan, had unnerved her.

He had plagued her dreams for months following his murder, but eventually their frequency had subsided. Although, around the one-year anniversary of his death, the dreams returned, haunting her for weeks. That had been more than six months ago and she thought she was finally over them, but these last few days before the trip to Rock Harbor, they were back. A few mornings, she actually would have sworn she awoke to the scent of Evan's aftershave.

She had moved on and was totally in love with Colin. So why these painful dreams of Evan and why now?

Emily remembered being fresh out of college when she had given her heart to Evan. They had been happily married for five years. But even if the dreams had come back, it didn't mean Evan could. He was dead now, and she had grieved for him. She had also solved his murder and learned the surprising truth of who he really was. But she'd come to terms with all that, using the painful realization to push herself to move on and begin a new life.

No. Evan was her past. Colin was her future.

As she gathered her toothbrush and makeup bag, Emily paused and stared at herself in the bathroom mirror. The whites of her eyes were flush with red. Maybe she could get some sleep on the long flight to

Maine. She tipped her head back and squeezed a drop of Visine into each eye.

Emily took one last look at her wedding dress. For a moment, she saw herself wearing the lovely gown, standing with Colin and the minister beneath an ivy-covered arch on the sprawling lawn, between the inn and the bay.

She carefully tucked the dress into the wardrobe bag and zipped it up. The wedding would be perfect. Colin was all she could ever want in a man—smart, strong, protective, kind, honest, and so handsome that he made her heart melt and set her body on fire.

Although, she had to admit, Evan had been all of those things too—except the honest part.

Emily threw the last of her toiletries into her carry-on bag and zipped it shut. She was done grieving over Evan. She had to let him go, once and for all. She would not let those wretched dreams ruin her wedding to Colin.

After a quick glance around the room for anything she might have forgotten, Emily dragged her wardrobe bag, carry-on, and suitcase out to the entry to wait for her ride.

Alex Martínez got his wife and the other girls to the airport in time for them to catch their early flight.

"Guns, girls?" Alex asked as he unloaded all their luggage from his vehicle.

All heads snapped in his direction.

He lowered his voice. "Sorry, just wanted to make sure they're not in your carry-ons."

"I'm a professional. I think I know the rules," Isabel said softly.

"Me too," Emily whispered.

"Call me when you arrive," he told Isabel.

She gave him a quick kiss. "I will, and don't worry."

The four checked in at the ticket counter and breezed through security. Before long, the announcement was made to begin boarding. Camille and Maggie were seated together and Emily and Isabel were a couple of rows behind them.

After getting situated and strapping their seatbelts on, Emily leaned back against the headrest and closed her heavy eyelids.

"Everything okay?" Isabel asked.

"Just tired."

"Didn't sleep well?"

"Not really."

"Me neither. Anxious about the trip."

Emily opened her eyes and turned toward Isabel, grateful there was no one sharing their row. "I had another dream about Evan. I don't know why, but it's a bit unnerving."

"It's probably because the wedding is getting so close. Maybe deep down you feel a little guilty about remarrying—subconsciously I mean."

"Guilty?"

"Not that you should, Em. But maybe, subliminally, you think you're betraying Evan somehow."

"Well, someone should tell my subconscious that Evan is dead. It should move on and be happy for Colin and me."

"The only one who can tell it that is you, Emily."

~*~

After a long day of traveling, the girls finally reached Bangor, Maine, where they rented a car for the last leg of their journey. With Emily behind the wheel and Isabel manning the GPS, Camille and Maggie happily chatted in the back seat.

They ventured off for picturesque Rock Harbor, perched on the edge of Mount Desert Island, the sun setting by the time they got on the road out of Bangor.

"I'm so disappointed. It's so dark we're missin' all the fall color," Maggie said, referring to the dense foliage turning rich autumn hues of yellow, orange, and red.

"We'll see plenty of fall color in the next few days," Emily assured them, recalling the times she had come to visit her sister and her family. "I'm glad you guys convinced me to have the wedding here."

"We're thrilled you brought us along for the ride," Isabel stated. "You could have done this without us."

"She wouldn't dare," Camille shot back.

"She's right." Emily glanced into the rearview mirror and peeked at Camille after having heard a frown in her friend's voice. "I would never have done this without you all."

Camille briefly met her gaze before Emily returned her focus to the road. "I was glad to have the two weeks before this trip to get the plans rolling on your reception."

"I meant to ask you how that was going." Emily

kept her eyes on her driving.

"Oh, it's going to be fabulous, Em." Camille patted Emily on the shoulder and went on to explain her plans in detail for most of the rest of the hour's drive.

"Here we are," Emily announced as she pulled into the dimly lit parking lot of the five-star Rock Harbor Inn and Spa. "Isn't it beautiful?"

CHAPTER FOUR
A Taste of Rock Harbor

"OH, EMILY!" MAGGIE GASPED, eying the expansive, three-story Victorian inn through the car window as they pulled up beside the massive french doors and the wall of small-paned windows that fronted the entrance. The lights inside the spacious lobby and front desk area cast a warm glow on the side lawn. "I had no idea it would be so fabulous."

The doorman, dressed in a sharp, dark green uniform, opened the driver's door and Emily swiveled out. "Welcome to the Rock Harbor Inn, ma'am."

"Thank you." Emily smiled, briefly making eye contact before her gaze was drawn away to the beauty of the inn.

The rest of the women exited the vehicle as the man grabbed a wheeled brass luggage cart.

"May I bring your bags in for you?"

Emily popped the trunk with the car's key fob.

"That would be appreciated."

Camille stopped and drew in a deep breath. "Can you smell that wonderful salt air?"

The doorman loaded the luggage as the girls chattered and giggled through the main door and meandered to the front desk, admiring the hotel's lavish interior.

The lobby was like the parlor of a southern plantation mansion, with its high ceilings and ornate support columns. An array of overstuffed chairs and comfortable, skirted sofas were strategically arranged around the large room, set up for easy conversation.

In the center of the far wall, a crackling fire filled the grand fireplace, which was outlined with a massive, white wood mantle, and flanked with tall windows, dressed with floor-to-ceiling floral draperies.

Emily's cellphone dinged and she dug it out of her purse.

"Will your sister be coming to the hotel this evening, Emily?" Isabel asked.

"No. Susan just sent me a text that she'll meet us in the morning for breakfast. The kids need her at home tonight."

"Let's get checked in, girls," Maggie piped up, "and go find somewhere to eat. I'm starvin'."

"Sounds good. I'm dying to have lots of lobster while we're here in Rock Harbor," Camille said. "Fresh out of the bay, right?"

"Only they don't say *lobster* around here, Camille," Emily kidded. "They say *lobstah* from Rock *Haabah*."

Maggie giggled. "As long as it's delish, I don't care what they call it."

The girls crowded around the check-in desk, giving their personal information to the young lady behind the counter and retrieving their room keys.

"The spa is close by?" Maggie asked.

"*Eyah*, to the left of the *pahkin*' lot," the clerk replied.

"I'm sorry?" Maggie frowned, not seeming to understand what the woman was trying to say through her thick New England accent.

"Eyah?" Camille asked.

"Sorry, miss." Emily stepped up to the counter and turned to Camille. "*Eyah* is how they would say yeah. And the *pahkin*' lot is the parking lot. People who are from around here don't often say their *R*s."

Camille's deep, blue eyes flicked to the clerk. "Why is it you don't say your *R*s?"

"It sounds so awful, like a pirate or something. *Arrr.*" The clerk tried to get her mouth around the consonant. "See...awful."

Maggie and Camille chuckled at her attempt.

~*~

After getting a dining recommendation from the desk clerk, the four women checked into their rooms, then went out for a short walk through the quaint little town, headed for a restaurant called McFay's Public House.

The narrow sidewalks on Main Street, adorned with old-fashioned streetlamps, were quite crowded on that evening. Men, women, and children were bundled in coats and scarves, popping in and out of the various eateries and shops, enjoying them before the end of the season arrived. There was a crisp chill coming off the bay, mingling in the air with the salty scent of the sea, warning that winter was on its way.

The girls reached the restaurant and were shown to their table, the savory smells of roasted beef and boiled lobster wafting through the air. Pure-white linen covered the tabletops, and waiters in crisp, white shirts and black slacks carried circular trays overhead, stacked with delicious meals.

Once seated, the hostess handed them each a tall, folded menu and told them their server would be right with them.

In time, a handsome young man approached, his black hair parted and slicked back. "My name is Brett. I'll be serving you this evening. What can I get for you ladies?"

The girls placed their orders, handed him their menus, and he disappeared.

"Was it hard getting away this week?" Emily asked Maggie, who ran her own fitness center.

"No, just rescheduled appointments. I think Camille had a tougher time."

"Camille," Emily said, "what happened?"

Camille had started *Bon Appetit!*, a catering and event/wedding planning company, over six years ago. That was where the four of them had originally met and where they became close friends. Camille had offered cooking classes to get her business off the ground and the other three had shown up, badly in need of improving their cooking skills.

"I had to give up a company party I was catering."

"I'm sorry." Emily patted Camille's hand.

"Don't worry about it. I had another caterer fill in, and now he owes me." Camille smiled smugly. "What about you, Isabel?"

Years ago Isabel had worked at the CIA in Washington, DC and had relocated to Paradise Valley to take a job at the Boise office of the FBI. As the four women became great friends, Isabel, eventually with Emily's assistance, taught self-defense classes at Maggie's studio so they would all know how to defend themselves. With Emily taking over Evan's PI practice, those classes had turned out to be a lifesaver more than once.

"Fortunately, I wrapped up a big case last week and managed to dodge any new cases. I don't think my boss caught on—at least, I'm praying he didn't." Isabel chuckled.

After relishing their various lobster dishes and crab cakes, and exhausting conversation about the wedding and the men in their lives, the girls meandered out of the restaurant, stopping briefly to decide where to go next.

Emily glanced up the street toward the various shops. She startled, thinking for a second that she saw Evan in the moving crowd. She shook her head and blinked a couple of times, her gaze scanning the throng of people in search of a man resembling her former husband. The only one she spotted was a man wearing a coat similar to the one Evan had worn. He was about the same height and build too, but when he turned to face her, he was much older and actually looked nothing at all like Evan.

That must've been who she'd seen. She shook her

head. What was she thinking? The lack of sleep, and the recurrence of her dreams, was playing tricks on her mind. She would be sure to get some rest before the wedding.

~*~

The next morning, Emily spotted Susan waiting in the hotel's restaurant as the four of them came in for breakfast. Susan had let her hair grow out since Emily had seen her last. She had the same honey-blond color as Emily did, but it was long past her shoulders now, cascading in waves and large curls.

Standing a couple of inches taller than Emily's five-foot-six frame, Susan's build was a little sturdier. She was almost ten years older than Emily, approaching forty, and still fairly attractive. She'd been a bit of a mother hen since their mother had passed away, but Emily knew she meant well.

"Oh, Susan, it's so good to see you." Emily gave her sister a warm hug.

"I'm glad you all made it safely," Susan responded. "How do you like the inn?"

"It's beautiful," Emily said with a smile, "and the view from the inn is breathtaking."

The others quickly agreed. "Absolutely breathtaking."

Emily made introductions between her sister and the girls as they took their seats around the linen-covered table, her friends still commenting about the lavish inn and the remarkable views from the dining room.

The restaurant sat on the side of the hotel that

overlooked the water, less than fifty feet from the shore, facing Frenchman's Bay. Massive picture windows on three sides of the restaurant offered stunning views of the sparkling blue waters, dotted with lobster boats moored out in the bay. The dock and marina were off to the left and several larger craft were berthed there— whale watchers, fishing excursion boats, cruising trawlers, and numerous private vessels.

"It's especially glorious on mornings like this, when the sky is clear and bright." Susan's gaze drifted momentarily to the bay as well, then she brought it back to the table. "But it'll be turning gray and nasty soon enough."

Gray and nasty? It was just like her sister to turn something nice into something negative.

"I'm glad we could sneak your wedding in before the first storm," Susan continued.

Sneak it in? Before the first storm? A chill rippled down Emily's back and she reached across the table, toward her sister. "Is there a chance the weather will turn stormy by Saturday?"

"No, not yet." Susan patted Emily's hand, as if hoping to calm her sister's fears. "It's still too early for a storm, but it won't be far off. This whole island will be buttoning up before long."

"Are you certain?" Emily had forgotten about Susan's talent for finding the worst in situations.

Camille and Maggie exchanged nervous glances.

"Don't worry," logical Isabel said. "Susan should know about these things. She lives here."

Emily didn't need one more thing to worry about, one more thing to prevent her from marrying Colin

Andrews. Rain or no rain, she was marrying him on Saturday—*this* Saturday.

"After breakfast, Emily, we have an appointment with Reverend Kinney," Susan continued. "He'll be the one performing the ceremony."

Emily nodded, still unsettled by the storm comment.

"Unless the bride and groom have their own choice, the inn has been using Reverend Kinney, from the Community Church, for all the weddings this past season. I think you'll like him. I asked him to meet us here in the lobby, then we can—"

"Susan." Emily raised a hand, cutting her sister off in mid-sentence. "Why don't we order breakfast first, then we can talk while we eat."

"Sorry, girls." Susan's gaze drifted from face to face around the table. "I'm just so excited to be able to do this for my little sister that I simply plowed right ahead without thinking. Yes, let's order."

The food was delivered and the girls talked of the wedding while they ate. Isabel savored her eggs benedict while she listened to Emily and Susan discuss the ceremony, as Camille and Maggie threw in their two-cents. With all the chatter, Isabel's mind soon wandered off, back to Emily's wedding to Evan.

Emily hadn't known it back then, but Isabel had worked with Evan in Washington, DC. She recalled her fondness for him in those days, even though she knew he flitted from one woman to another as his work took him travelling around the world for the agency.

Though Isabel would never think of herself as a runway beauty, she was aware that she was a good-looking woman. She had been told enough times how her long, brown hair, the color of rich espresso, emphasized her dark-chocolate-colored eyes. And, although she was only five feet five, she had a strong, lean body, which helped in her government job.

One day, she had worked up enough courage to invite Evan to go with her to a concert. She had tickets to see El Divo and thought maybe they could grab drinks afterward, at least that was what she had planned to say. But that day, Evan had waltzed into the office, all lit up. He had met the girl of his dreams, he had said, a woman who turned out to be Emily. Isabel had been crestfallen.

"Doesn't that sound good, Isabel?"

The question drew Isabel's mind back to the conversation at the table, but she hadn't heard a word of their discussion.

Emily had a sparkle in her blue-green eyes. "Well, doesn't it?"

Isabel couldn't admit she'd been miles, or rather, years, away, so she simply agreed. "Yes, Emily, great."

~*~

After breakfast, Maggie and Isabel went off to spend the rest of the morning digging around in the cute little shops and boutiques on Main Street, assuring Emily they would be back in plenty of time for their massages and mani-pedis at the spa. As a caterer and wedding planner, Camille insisted on remaining with

Emily to help Susan with any last-minute details.

As best she could, Emily had tried to send Camille off with the others, knowing how territorial and commanding both Camille and Susan could be, but her friend wouldn't hear of it, planting herself squarely in the thick of things.

When the three women entered the grand foyer of the hotel, Reverend Kinney rose from one of the chairs. Susan led them over to him and extended her hand, which he took.

"Reverend Ben Kinney," Susan introduced, "this is my sister, Emily, the bride, and her friend Camille."

He offered his hand to Emily and then to Camille. He wasn't at all what Emily was expecting. She assumed he would be older, maybe gray-haired and balding, with a round belly. But Ben Kinney was maybe mid-thirties, tall and lean, and not at all bad to look at. His brown wavy hair was a bit unkempt atop his long face, but his broad smile made up for it.

"Why don't we go out on the lawn, where the chairs will be set up?" Susan suggested. "We can talk there."

Everyone followed her out the glass atrium door that led to the expansive lawn, with yet another breathtaking view of the dazzling blue water as it reflected the color of the sunny sky. Numerous lobster boats, along with several sailboats, dotted the bay as small waves lapped at the shore.

"The white arch will go here." Susan motioned to the location as she spoke, drawing an arc with the wave of her hand. "And the white folding chairs will be set up here, with an aisle down the center. The wedding party will come out the door that we just passed through. And of course, Pastor, you'll be standing inside the arch with the groom, as usual."

He nodded his agreement.

Several large, oval-shaped flower beds, filled with colorful blossoms and shrubs, were artfully planted around the expansive lawn, adding to the natural beauty. But a constant flow of tourists were strolling by on the path that sat at the edge of the grass, cordoning it off from the shore.

"Will all these people be walking by during the wedding?" Emily asked.

"Well, actually, yes," Susan mumbled, seeming to be taken aback by the question.

Emily glanced at Camille, who was giving her the are-you-serious look.

"I don't like this, Susan." Emily shook her head. "I'm not comfortable with people traipsing by and gawking while we're saying our vows." Although, at this point, what choice did she have? It wasn't like they were going to screen off the walking path. Then, there were also the guests at the outdoor café beside the lawn to deal with, not to mention the hotel guests who might be on their balconies right behind them.

Emily continued to shake her head as she took a deep breath then exhaled firmly. Her sister hadn't explained that the wedding would be on display for any, and all, in the vicinity to watch.

"Now, Emily, people do it this way every weekend from March to October, and they pay a lot of money for the privilege. No one has ever complained about it before," Susan said. "Don't be such a drama queen. It's not going to be like when—"

"Like when what?" Emily snapped.

"Like when you married Evan in that perfect little stone chapel in Virginia."

She had to bring up Evan. Heat began to rise in Emily's cheeks. "It's just that this is not what I had envisioned when you said we could have our wedding at the inn." Emily worked to keep her voice calm and even. "I thought we'd have more privacy for the ceremony."

Tears rose in Susan's eyes and she bit at her lip. "I'm doing the best I can. I'm trying to take care of my husband, who, as you know, is laid up in the hospital, and manage three kids and all their activities, all while trying to pull together a nice wedding for you at the last minute." She wiped away a tear that had escaped down her cheek. "I'm sorry if it's not good enough."

Now Emily felt horrible.

She put an arm around Susan and hugged her, pushing a thick strand of long blond hair behind her shoulder. Emily glanced to Camille for support.

"It'll be lovely," Camille jumped in. "Really it will."

Emily paused, considering the situation. "I guess I'll just have to put the other people out of my mind and simply focus on my friends and family."

"And the groom, Emily. You'd better focus on the groom," Camille added with a little grin.

The comment elicited a small laugh from Susan as Emily released her.

"Ah, it'll all work out," the young reverend said in an off-handed way. "Just zero in on what's important, Emily, and block out all the rest. These people walking by here, they don't really amount to a hill of beans in the bigger picture, do they?"

"Uh," Emily glanced at her sister, a little surprised at his irreverent manner, "no, I guess not."

"Well said, Reverend Kinney," Camille stepped in. "I'm sure your wife appreciates your frankness."

"Oh, I'm not married." He grinned. "And you can call me Pastor Ben. That's what most of the folks around here call me."

"We won't keep you any longer, Pastor Ben," Susan said. "I just wanted you and Emily to meet. Sorry the groom hasn't arrived yet."

"I'm sure I'll meet him before the ceremony," he remarked. "It was very nice to meet you, Emily." He took her hand and cupped it in both of his. "I'm sure everything will work out…the way it's supposed to." He looked her in the eye, held her gaze uncomfortably long, then took a step back. "Nice to meet you too, Camille. Susan." Then he turned and walked back to the inn.

The way it's supposed to? What did he mean by that? And what was with the long double handshake?

CHAPTER FIVE
The Spa Treatment

AFTER GOING OER THE DETAILS of the wedding ceremony with Susan, Emily and Camille said their good-byes and hurried to the spa on the edge of the hotel grounds to meet up with Isabel and Maggie. Like giddy school girls, the four excitedly entered the spa for their pampering treatments and some much-needed girl time.

Following their individual massages, they met back in the salon for their manicures and pedicures. The lively chatter reminded Emily of chickens clucking in a henhouse, everyone having something to say about what the others were talking about, sometimes animatedly talking over each other.

Eventually, the conversation died down to a din and Emily dove in with a new subject. "Do you guys believe in ghosts?"

The replies were varied.

"Why do you ask?" Maggie blew on her wet

fingernails.

Emily hesitated. "I could have sworn I saw Evan on Main Street yesterday."

"Oh, Emily," Maggie's eyes widened, "and you think he's come back to haunt you?"

"Emily," Isabel said in her matter-of-fact way, "like I told you before, it's probably just your subconscious playing games with your mind."

Camille waved her damp nails in the air. "So this has happened before? Not just on the street yesterday?"

Emily nodded. "In my dreams mostly."

Camille raised a brow at her. "Mostly?"

"A couple of times last week I thought I smelled his aftershave when I woke up. Then, again this morning."

"This morning?" Isabel questioned with a frown.

"Maybe you should talk to someone about this." Camille curled her fingers inward and blew on her nails.

"Like a shrink?" Maggie asked.

"That's not necessary," Isabel argued. "Once you and Colin are married, I'm sure this will all clear up. You probably just feel like you're being disloyal to Evan. After you've said *I do* to Colin, I'm sure it will all go away. Trust me."

"Perhaps." Emily wasn't so sure. "Well, ladies, after we're done here, I think I'm going to drop by the hospital and check on my brother-in-law, then maybe take a nap before we go to dinner."

"When will you see Susan's kids?" Camille questioned.

"Probably not until the wedding. They're in school and then they have sports practices and stuff."

"What about the guys? When are they coming in?"

Maggie asked.

Isabel glanced down at her watch. "Alex and Colin should be in the air by now and getting into Bangor early this evening, then they'll drive up after that."

"You girls are so lucky," Maggie moaned. "Peter and Jonathan won't be here 'til Friday." Maggie crossed her arms and gave them a fake pout.

"No! Maggie, your arms! Don't do that," Camille gasped, wagging her hand at Maggie. "You'll smudge your nail polish."

~*~

Before going back to her room to take a nap, Emily headed over to the hospital to say a quick hello to her brother-in-law, Brian. She stopped at the hospital gift shop and picked up a small, green plant with a shiny Mylar balloon attached that read *Get Well*.

A young man in blue scrubs, standing at the nurse's station, gave Emily directions to Brian's room. She found it easily and pushed the door open, seeing the first bed empty and Brian laying in the other.

He was talking to an older woman with a petite build. Her light brown hair was shortly cropped and she was dressed in a classic, tailored, navy-blue wool jacket and tan slacks.

Brian's left leg was encased and hoisted in traction and his right lay on the bed in a thick white cast. The side of his face was bandaged too, and Emily assumed it must be covering damage from the airbag exploding in his face.

His gaze pitched past the woman as he noticed

Emily enter, and his face lit up. "Emily."

The woman turned and smiled warmly.

"This is my sister-in-law," Brian introduced. "Emily, this is Mayor McCormack."

"Ella, please," the woman said in a deep alto voice as she extended her hand to Emily. Her green eyes twinkled when she smiled. "Sorry, I can't stay long. I just wanted to stop by and check on Brian." She patted his shoulder and moved toward the door.

Ella scooted past Emily. "It was nice meeting you." She paused at the door and turned back. "And, Brian, Ben told me to say hello. Get well soon, dear. That's an order." The mayor grinned as she slipped out into the hall.

"The mayor, huh?" Emily teased.

"No biggie—not in this little town anyway."

"I can relate. The mayor of my town is my friend Maggie's brother." Emily glanced around for a place to set the plant down. Many of the horizontal surfaces were full of gifts and flowers from other well-wishers, so she pushed his half-eaten lunch aside and set the pot on the portable table at the foot of his bed.

"Susan told me about the automobile accident." Emily stepped to the side of the bed. "What happened?"

"I don't really know, it was so crazy. I was leaving Rock Harbor and going home one evening—you know we live on the other side of the island, near Seal Cove, right?"

Emily nodded.

"The road gets pretty winding going around the national park, and some idiot must have been drunk or something because he ran me off the road. My car flew down into a ravine. It's a miracle I survived. Must have been the airbag."

"Susan sent me a picture of you right after it happened. Is that how you got the cuts and bruises on your face?"

"I guess so. It's all such a blur."

Emily rested a hand on Brian's shoulder. "Did the cops catch the guy who did this?"

"No. There was nothing to go on. Just headlights in my rearview mirror, then someone clipped my bumper and sent me over the edge."

"You don't think someone did this on purpose?"

"I can't imagine why. I think the driver was probably trying to pass me and just got too close."

"Perhaps."

Her cynical instincts kicked in. Could someone have done this on purpose? But who would want to hurt a computer repairman? She reeled her suspicions back. "Down a ravine, huh? How did anyone find you?"

"When I didn't come home for dinner, and Susan couldn't get me on my cell, she phoned the police and insisted they send someone out on the mountain road to look for me. You know your sister, she can be pretty convincing when she wants to be."

"That's Susan."

"The cop they sent noticed my headlights shining, down, off the road a ways."

"Good thing Susan is such a bulldog." Emily chuckled. "Just don't tell her I said that."

They chatted a little while longer, until Emily began yawning. She made her good-byes and kissed Brian on his non-injured cheek.

"It was nice to see you again, Emily. Sorry I can only attend your wedding in spirit."

~*~

With her muscles still relaxed from the massage, Emily easily fell asleep and napped for a couple of hours, snoozing longer than she had intended. When she woke and looked at the glowing digital clock, her room was dark. The sun had already set and it was almost time to meet up with the girls.

She flipped on the lamp as she climbed out of bed, then hurried to change her clothes and get ready for dinner. Rather than meet in the lobby of the inn, they had decided to meet at another recommended restaurant, Paddy's Pub & Grill, since all but Emily had gone out shopping.

Instead of leaving her room by way of the exit that led to the interior hallway, Emily decided to go out through the french doors that led out onto a small deck with a view of the sparkling pool. All of the first-floor rooms on her side of the building had decks that faced the swimming pool area, along with two Adirondack chairs flanking the doors and low, white picket fences with small gates at the edge of each deck. She stepped over the gate and turned back to admire the inviting setting, feeling a lift in her spirit as she soaked up the charm.

~*~

"Hi, I'm Emily Parker," she happily told the hostess

at the restaurant. "I'm supposed to meet three friends." Emily glanced around the place and spotted them waiting at the bar. "There they are."

Paddy's Pub and Grill was situated at the end of Main Street, near the marina. The hostess seated the women on the outdoor patio that overlooked the docks. The night air was filled with the scent from the bay and, in the distance, the melodious rush of water washing over the rocks along the shoreline gave Emily a sense of peace.

"Been waiting long?" she asked her friends as they took their seats around the table.

"Just long enough to finish a Guinness," Isabel teased.

"How's Susan's husband doin'?" Maggie asked.

"Well," Emily paused, thinking back to what Brian had said about how the accident happened, "he's got a long way to go before he can walk again."

Camille lightly grasped Emily's forearm. "The way you paused makes me think there's something more to the story."

"Probably not." Emily ran her hand nervously through her mane. "Just my PI senses tingling a little. I'm sure it's nothing—just what Brian said, an accident."

Isabel's dubious expression told Emily she didn't quite believe that, but she didn't push it.

After feasting on lobster rolls and other seafood delicacies, they strolled back to the inn, laughing and chatting. Perhaps the men had arrived by now.

Standing outside the Rock Harbor Inn, not far from the lighted swimming pool, Isabel did her best to convince the girls to join her in the inn's restaurant for a piece of their famous blueberry pie. She was able to win Maggie and Camille over, but Emily just wanted to go to her room and rest.

"Oh, come on, Emily," Camille pleaded. "We're in Maine. The blueberry pie here is supposed to be fabulous."

"I need to fit into my wedding dress in a few days."

"You can work it off on a hike tomorrow," Isabel encouraged.

Emily smiled and gave her head a shake. "No, not tonight. I'm tired."

"But the boys will be here pretty soon," Isabel said.

"I'm sure Colin will find me when he gets in." Emily waved as she walked toward the pool and the decks with the little white picket fences lined up in a neat row. As she watched the other three enter the inn, eagerly heading to the restaurant, she still couldn't shake the niggling doubts about her brother-in-law's story.

A tall lamppost illuminated the swimming pool area, but the decks seemed rather dark, only touched by the moonlight. Just as well—she didn't want bright light streaming into her room while she slept.

Swinging the small picket gate open, Emily made her way to the little deck and stepped up. She paused to pull her key out, but as she moved toward the door, she stumbled over something in the dark and fell in the direction of one of the Adirondack chairs. She expected to feel the pain of the sharp edges of the wood—but no, what she landed against felt like a big sack of potatoes.

She had pushed her hands in front of her to buffer her fall, and when she made contact with the mysterious obstruction, something warm and wet oozed between the fingers on her left hand.

That was strange. Had she fallen on a sack of rotting potatoes? One that was leaking sticky, moldy goo? That was a ridiculous notion, besides, who would play such a prank? She groped around in the dark and then froze—it could be only one thing. There was a body in the chair. A dead one.

Emily screamed and then scrambled to get up as fast as she could. She rummaged frantically for her phone and flashed the dim light from the display screen toward the chair. It was a man, his face turned away from her. He was casually dressed in jeans and a sweatshirt and she might almost assume he had gotten the wrong room and had passed out drunk—except for the blood on his chest and dripping down the side of his head.

Her first thought was to dial 911, but wondered if having an out-of-state phone number would cause it ring back home or to the local emergency call center. She wasn't sure, so she raced around to the front of the inn and sprinted to the front desk.

"Call the police! There's a bloody body on my deck!"

The young woman behind the desk gawked at Emily, her eyes wide and her mouth hanging open. Her gaze darted over her and then froze on Emily's chest.

Emily followed the woman's line of vision, realizing she had blood smeared on her cream-colored sweater—and her hand.

Her eyes flashed back to the woman's stunned face. "Did you hear me? Call nine-one-one." She looked at her hand. She had no way of knowing if this man's blood was in some way tainted. A series of squeamish chills danced down her spine. "And where is the nearest sink? I need to wash this off my hand."

"Oh, God. Oh, God." The girl blinked a couple of times.

"Listen to me—I didn't do it. I tripped on him in the dark. That is how I got this blood all over me. Now make the call and point me to the washroom or give me something to clean myself, this is creeping me out."

The woman handed Emily a bunch of hand sanitizing wipes, then picked up the phone and dialed. "Hello. We need the police. I'm calling from the Rock Harbor Inn." Her voice was shaky and ragged. "A woman just reported a body."

Emily tore open the wipes and began to scrub at her hand. The wipes were not that effective and she was just smearing it around.

The woman spoke into the phone. "I'm not sure. I think so. I'll check." Her gaze shifted nervously to Emily. "Is it dead?"

"Yes. That is, I think so." In her rush to get to the front desk, Emily had forgotten to check for a pulse. It was a rookie mistake and she knew better. "I'm sorry I didn't stop to check. But there was a lot of blood."

"What room are you in?" the young clerk asked.

"Room one forty," Emily replied, leaning on the counter.

The clerk gave the information, then hung up the phone and blew out a sigh of relief. "They're on their way."

"Send the manager to meet me." Emily straightened, hoping to avoid a curious crowd. "I'm going to wait for them by the body."

"You are?" The young woman's face twisted in disgust at the very idea.

"I'm used to dead bodies. Just send the manager."

"He said he was going home a second ago, but he's probably still around here someplace. I'll find him and send him right away." The girl was shaking like a leaf.

"Take a deep breath. You'll be fine."

Emily sprinted back to where the man's body lay slumped in the deck chair. Good. A mob hadn't started to gather yet. She dialed Isabel on her cell and explained what was happening.

"We'll be right there."

Before she'd hung up, blaring sirens were approaching the inn, lights flashing. Then an ambulance and a couple of police cars screeched to a halt near the inn's entrance. A middle-aged man in a dark gray suit, likely the manager, was standing out front, pointing in her direction.

The vehicles raced forward another hundred feet or so to the edge of the parking lot, near the wing that housed Emily's room. Leaving headlights on, a uniformed officer climbed out of the first cruiser and zipped up his jacket. He looked young, average height with a slight build and a milky complexion. His medium brown hair was neatly shorn, a little longer on top, but the night was too dark to make out the color of his eyes.

As people began to gather and move near to them, the cop stepped toward Emily, haloed in the beams emanating from the headlights. He shot a glance to the crowd then called to the other uniform. "Henry! Tape this area off and have the others keep these people back."

Turning his attention back to Emily, he shone his flashlight on her face. "Are you the one who found the body?"

"I am."

"Stay here and I'll be right back." He went over to the body and performed a cursory survey of the man and the surrounding area using wide sweeps of his flashlight.

Within a minute he was back. "Police Chief Alvin Taylor, ma'am."

"Chief?" He looked so young. How much experience could he have?

"Yes, ma'am." His eyes drifted to her chest and rested there, his brows furrowing into a frown.

She reacted to his curious stare by crossing her arms over her breasts. It annoyed her, where his gaze had landed. Then she remembered—the blood soaking into her off-white sweater. Her spine stiffened. Did he actually think she was the one who killed this man? She hadn't even gotten a good look at the dead body, it was too dark.

The girls hollered to Emily from behind the yellow tape, drawing Chief Taylor's attention. "Friends of yours?"

"We're on a trip together, staying here at the inn." Emily shouted to her friends to phone Colin and her sister.

The chief turned his back on the women and faced Emily. "I'm going to have to take you down to the station and question you in-depth."

"Chief Taylor," the man in the gray suit called as he approached.

"Malone," the chief answered.

"Is there anything I can do to help?" the man offered.

"Are you the manager?" Emily asked.

"I am. Eric Malone. This is your room—where the body was found?"

"Yes. On the back deck."

"If you'd like to move, I can check to see if I have any other rooms available."

Emily shook her head. "I'll be fine, as long as he wasn't in my room."

"Whoa now," the chief stepped in. "We'll need to search your room and make sure it isn't tied to the crime scene. That you're not tied to this crime."

"I'm not." She looked down. "The blood on my sweater is from when I fell on him in the dark."

"I'll go check on that other room and leave you two to your business." The manager marched off into the growing throng of onlookers.

"Yoo-hoo! Emily!" Maggie called from the crowd.

Emily glanced over to her, then brought her attention back to the chief. "I'm happy to tell you what I know, Chief, but I'd like to have a moment with my friends, if you don't mind."

"But I do mind. I need you to wait in the back of my police car until I can fully interrogate you. I don't want you talking to anyone until I get some answers out of you." He took her by the arm and led her to his nearby vehicle.

"Am I a suspect?" Emily jerked her arm away as he opened the door to the back seat. She glanced over at her friends, who were watching her with concerned interest.

"I won't know that until I question you thoroughly and gather some more evidence from this here crime scene. Are you planning to be uncooperative, ma'am?"

"That's not my intention, Chief. And please stop calling me ma'am."

"Well, get on in there and cool your jets. I'll be back in a bit."

"Emily!"

Her head whipped around at her name being called and Chief Taylor's gaze followed. Colin, standing taller than the others, was weaving his way through the crowd with Alex close on his heels. As Colin approached the yellow tape, and the officer standing guard, he whipped out his gold shield and flashed it at the cop.

The officer nodded and Colin ducked under the tape and stalked to where Emily and Chief Taylor stood. Alex snaked his way over to Isabel and the others.

"Friend of yours?" the chief asked.

"You might say that."

"Emily, what on earth?" Colin huffed as he came to a stop, his eyes drifting over her blood-covered chest.

"Someone's dead, Colin, and the chief here thinks I'm involved."

CHAPTER SIX
The Reverend's Demise

"ARE YOU OKAY?" Colin started to reach for Emily as she stood by the police car.

"Whoa." The chief stuck his arm out to stop him.

"Chief Taylor, this is Detective Colin Andrews...my fiancé."

"Detective, huh?" He dropped his arm. "Now, don't get any ideas about bullying your way into my investigation."

"Wouldn't dream of it, Chief," Colin responded flatly. "But I would like to know what you plan to do with Emily."

"Take her down to the station for questioning, of course—she's my only witness so far—find out if that's all she is."

"What do you mean by that?" Emily asked, not wanting to give away that she already knew full well what he meant.

"I'll need to dig around. Maybe you're the one who killed the man." Chief Taylor gave her a stern glare.

"You think I'm the murderer?" Her eyes grew round with indignation. "I don't even know who the vic is."

The young chief tilted his head and frowned. "The what, now?"

"The vic, you know, the victim. Who is he?"

Chief Taylor lowered his voice and leaned in. "Reverend Ben Kinney."

"Oh no!" Her hand flew to her mouth.

Colin's expression grew serious. "You know him?"

She nodded sadly. "I met with him this morning. He was going to marry us."

"So you admit you knew the murder victim?" the chief asked.

"Barely."

"Have you questioned anyone else?" Colin asked. "The other guests? Hotel staff?"

"Well, uh, I was just about to," the chief replied, a sheepish look on his face. He turned toward a couple of officers who were holding back the crowd. "Jenkins! Fortnoy!" He motioned for them to come to him.

"You two go round up the staff and have them wait for me in the lobby. Then, go door to door inside the inn and see if any of the guests saw or heard anything, especially these rooms that face the pool."

"Yes, sir." The two officers marched off to do as they were ordered.

"Who's going to process the crime scene?" Colin asked. "And what about the medical examiner. Is he on his way?"

"I called him on the drive over. They'll have to come from Bangor, so it'll be at least an hour before they get here."

"What about me, Chief?" Emily leaned on the top of the open car door.

"Stay right here in the car and wait for me," he replied.

She crossed her arms and pursed her lips into a pout. "Wait? How long?"

"Am I going to have to put a guard on you?" The chief arched his brow.

"She's just getting chilly." Colin slid off his jacket and handed it, with a glare, to Emily. "Isn't there anyone else that can question her, Chief? Anyone down at the station that can take her statement, like a detective maybe?"

"This isn't the big city. It's me and a handful of officers. The only one down at the station right now is the night receptionist."

"Great," Emily mumbled, slipping Colin's jacket over her shoulders.

"I could round up a couple of off-duty officers I guess, but the mayor won't like the extra overtime pay."

"We're happy to help, Chief," Colin offered, "if you'll let us. I was on the force in San Francisco and now—"

"No! You just stop right there, Detective." It seemed as if Chief Taylor's pride wouldn't let him accept any outside help. "We haven't had a murder in this town for nearly fifteen years—that's a fact—but that doesn't mean I can't handle it."

"I'm a private eye," Emily explained. "We've

been—"

"Stop!" He raised a hand to her. "I'm a little short-handed at the moment, is all. I can sort this thing out. So take a load off, lady, and I'll get to you as soon as I can." The chief began to walk away. "Henry," he shouted to the officer holding the crowd back, "watch this one here that she doesn't budge."

The officer nodded and turned a stern gaze on Emily.

"Ma'am, you'd better be here when I get back," Chief Taylor shouted over his shoulder, "or you and your boyfriend are going to be in a kettle of hot water."

Emily perched on the edge of the cruiser's back seat, facing out, with the door still open. "Now what?"

Colin bent down and kissed her softly. "Do what the man says, Babe."

She nodded reluctantly.

Colin straightened. "Are you doing okay?"

"I'm fine, as long as that Chief Taylor doesn't try to pin this thing on me." Emily stuck her hands out, palms up, as if showing her innocence. But judging by the look on Colin's face, she had done the opposite.

"Emily?"

She followed his gaze to her hands. She had removed much of the blood with the moist towelettes given to her by the girl at the front desk, but some remained around her nails and dried in the folds of her skin.

"The vic's blood?"

She nodded.

"How'd that happen?"

"It was dark. I couldn't see much and I tripped over

the body." She gestured to her sweater too. "Before I knew it I was sprawled on top of him. I think I hit my hip on the arm of the wooden chair. Feels like I bruised it."

"Why the deck to your room?"

"I haven't a clue."

"Maybe I'd better get Alex over here to go with us to the police station." Colin sounded concerned.

"You think I need a lawyer?"

"Better to be safe."

"Why would someone want to kill a minister?"

"He must have had some pretty scary skeletons in his closet," Colin guessed. "How did you meet him?"

"Susan uses him for the weddings here at the inn. She, Camille, and I met with him for about ten minutes this morning. That was it."

"Well, we have a few days before the wedding. Maybe we can solve the mystery before then and you won't have to worry about it."

"No, Colin. This is our wedding. I don't want anything distracting from that."

"I don't either, but if you get detained, or worse, arres—"

"It should be pretty clear I have no motive, so I'm not going to let myself be concerned about it, unless something changes and I have cause to be concerned."

"Yeah, a case against you would be pretty weak. It's clear, though, that the chief has no experience solving this type of crime," Colin said. "He could really use someone who knows their way around a murder investigation."

"You heard him," she argued. "He doesn't want our

help, so we need to butt out."

"At the very least, Emily, we could give him some tips, point him in the right direction. We could—"

"Ugh! It's always something, isn't it? Something trying to jump in the way of our getting married." An anger rose up in her at the constant barriers, like the universe was trying to keep them apart. Three bad things had already happened to them, so from here on out it would be smooth sailing—that's what Colin had said— but no, now there was a fourth thing and it was a doozy. "Murder or no murder, we're going to get married this Saturday, come hell or high water—even if the ceremony has to take place in a jail cell. No more delays. No more bad things happening. This wedding is moving forward."

"All right now. Calm down." Colin reached for her right hand, but then hesitated, examining it for signs of blood before he kissed it. "This Saturday, Babe, you and me, 'til death do us part."

~*~

Although the chief had ordered one of his men to keep an eye on Emily, he had mentioned nothing about Colin. So, with Chief Taylor off speaking to the staff, Colin wandered over to the body, still sprawled out on the white Adirondack chair. He slid his phone out of his pocket and took a couple of photos before anyone noticed. Then he went to find Alex in the crowd.

As Colin walked past the well-lit entrance to the inn, he peeked inside, through the french doors and the surrounding wall of small-paned windows. There were several people in dark green blazers—which he assumed were management or desk clerks—milling around, and a few women in light blue dresses who appeared to be maids, seated on the sofas.

A thirty-something man with sandy-brown hair, wearing a dark gray suit stalked up to the chief, waving his arms around. The expression on his face looked more like worry than anger, which made sense if he was the manager, afraid of losing guests.

Colin watched as Chief Taylor said something to the man and then turned to speak to a younger man that appeared to be, perhaps, a maintenance worker or groundskeeper. It didn't seem like Chief Taylor was getting anywhere with any of them.

Soon, Colin moved on to find Alex to escort him to where Emily sat waiting. By the time Chief Taylor returned, Colin and Emily had brought Alex up to speed on the situation.

"Any luck?" Colin asked as Chief Taylor approached.

"I'm not sharing information with you, Detective. This is my crime scene and my case. Besides, I don't know yet how your girlfriend figures into this."

"I don't figure into this, Chief." Emily bolted off the car seat. "The killer just happened to pick my deck to drop the body. I'm an innocent tourist."

"We'll see." The chief took a long gaze at her, then turned to Alex. "And who's this?"

"Alex Martínez, attorney-at-law," Alex said, extending his hand.

The chief shook it, eying him suspiciously.

"I'm only here to advise Ms. Parker at this time."

"I see." The chief's gaze moved to Emily. "You don't figure into this, huh? Then why the lawyer?"

Emily was saved from answering by the medical examiner and his crime scene investigation team driving up, drawing the chief's attention away from her for the moment. The police worked to disburse the crowd enough that they could get through and do their work.

After an onsite examination of the Reverend's body, the attractive female ME wandered over to where the chief was still standing talking to Emily, Colin, and Alex. She pulled off her latex gloves and tugged him aside to talk privately.

They still had a keen eye on Emily, but Colin was able to inch close enough to hear most of what they were discussing. It might not be completely ethical to eavesdrop, but this was his fiancée, and besides, that boat had sailed when he took the photos with his cellphone.

The ME said the blood pattern on the man's shirt indicated he'd been stabbed, but told the chief that there had also been blunt-force trauma to the head. And until she got the body back to her lab and went over it thoroughly, she did not want to make a definitive declaration on the cause of death.

"Based on the internal temperature, I'd say he's been dead approximately two hours," the ME said, which would have put Emily's gruesome discovery within the window of his time of death.

Although it would have been better if his death had occurred hours before she'd found him, Colin surmised, surely there was no way Chief Taylor could realistically pin this on her. She barely knew the man and had no

THE HARBOR OF LIES

motive whatsoever to kill him.

Colin noticed Emily trying to edge closer and he glared at her until she froze to her spot near the car. Then he eased his way back to her so that he wouldn't attract attention to the fact that he'd been listening in.

He explained what he had overheard from the ME.

"What was he hit in the head with?" Emily asked.

"They won't know that until she takes a closer look back at the lab."

The ME cleared her throat and walked toward them. "Are these folks the victim's next of kin? Should I have a talk with them?"

"No. Don't go telling her anything, Doc," Chief Taylor moaned. "She's a suspect."

"Oh, sorry, Chief." The shapely thirty-something medical examiner stopped walking.

The chief gave Emily a defiant stare. "In the car, Miss Parker."

Emily complied and the chief strode up and closed the car door.

"Okay, Doc, we're headed to the police station for questioning. Get those results back to me as soon as possible."

"Will do." The medical examiner spun around and headed back to the dead body.

CHAPTER SEVEN
The Interrogation of Emily

AFTER ALEX AND EMILY HAD AGREED to let someone scrape under her fingernails where the Reverend's blood was, the chief allowed her to be accompanied to the washroom to clean her hands better and bag her sweater to contain the transfer of the blood—whether or not it ended up being evidence was still to be decided.

With Emily wearing Colin's jacket zipped up after relinquishing her sweater, Chief Taylor took her and Alex into an interrogation room in the small police station, but made Colin wait outside while he questioned her.

She looked at the video camera mounted in the corner just below the ceiling and tried not to fidget or appear nervous in any way.

"Tell me again why you need an attorney, ma'am. You got something to hide?"

"Of course not. He's here for my wedding. His wife is my best friend."

"I see." Chief Taylor eyed her suspiciously, leaning back in the chair. "So, let's go over why you have the victim's blood all over you."

After receiving Alex's nod of approval, she again explained how she came upon the dead body. Chief Taylor asked more of the usual questions. Did she know the deceased? Were there any problems between the two of them? Did she kill the Reverend?

"I already answered those questions at the scene, Chief Taylor, so no, no, and heck no. What else do you want to ask?"

"Well…" He didn't seem sure what else to say. Clearly he wasn't used to questioning a murder suspect. "Give me a minute."

"How long have you been the Chief of Police here?" she questioned.

"About a month. Why do you ask?"

She glanced at Alex for a moment. No, she wouldn't answer that. It was way too easy. She even felt a bit sorry for the young man, being thrown in the middle of his first murder case with no experience in solving one. "Have your men finished searching my room? I'd like to get some sleep."

He nodded. "They're done. But I'm not done with you."

"Listen, Chief Taylor," Alex said, "Colin and Emily, and their entire wedding party, are staying at the Rock Harbor Inn. I think it's pretty obvious she's not your killer, but if you have any more questions, we're happy to come back and answer them for you."

He opened his mouth to say something, but a knock at the door drew his attention. It opened and the receptionist stuck her head in. "Susan Henderson is here to see her sister." The woman nodded in Emily's direction.

"Susan's your sister?"

"Yes, why?"

"Well, why didn't you say so? She and my wife are thick as thieves. If Susan will vouch for you, I guess I can let you go—for now."

They all walked out into the waiting area. Susan rushed to Emily and threw her arms around her. "You poor thing. How awful. I got a call from one of your friends. I came right over and Colin was just telling me what happened."

"I'm fine, Sis." Emily flashed her a little smile and proceeded to introduce her to Alex.

After the quick introduction, Susan turned to the chief. "Oh, Alvin, my sister is here to get married on Saturday and you really think she could have killed Pastor Ben?"

"Now, Susan, don't be like that," Chief Taylor replied. "She claimed to have found the body, but she was covered in his blood. I couldn't just let her go 'cause she claimed to be innocent. I had to at least make an attempt to discover if there was more to it."

"She just met the man this morning," Susan explained. "I introduced them."

The chief ran a hand over his neck. "Eyah, that's what she said."

"Are we done here, Chief?" Alex asked.

"For now."

"While I was waiting," Colin said, "I phoned one of my officers back at my station and asked him to run a background check on Ben Kinney. As you can imagine, there were a number of them across the country, so we narrowed it down to northeast Maine."

"You did what, now?" Chief Taylor asked, his voice rising. "You had no right to do that. I told you before, don't go pushing your way into my investigation."

"I had to do something while I waited."

"Now, Chief," Emily rested a friendly hand on his arm, "why don't you let the detective help you?" She knew Colin would be happy to help, and it might keep him occupied while she dealt with all the wedding details.

"And Emily's a private eye," Colin offered. "She and I could—"

Susan stepped in. "Absolutely not. Emily and I have a wedding to get planned, and now we'll have to search for someone else to perform the ceremony. Poor Pastor Ben, bless his heart. But Alvin, Colin would be a great asset to you. You'd be crazy not to let him help you."

Chief Taylor's eyes narrowed as he rubbed a hand over his square jaw, pondering Colin's offer. "What'd you find out?" As quickly as he asked, he waved a hand at him. "Nope. Never mind. I'd better check the man out for myself. You all go on and get outta here."

~*~

Standing in the parking lot of the police station, Emily thanked her sister for coming, and gave her a quick squeeze before Susan walked to her car.

"I hope you all won't regret coming to Rock Harbor for your wedding because of what's happened tonight," Susan muttered.

"Don't worry, Sis," Emily said. "This isn't our first brush with murder."

"I guess not, but I don't know how you two do it." Susan gave a wan smile, then opened her car door. "See you tomorrow." She climbed in and drove away.

"I'd better get back," Alex said. "Isabel will want to hear every detail of what's going on."

Emily chuckled. "The others will too, I'm sure."

Alex gave them a ride the few blocks back to the inn. "See you in the morning," he said as he strolled off to his room. "Try to get some sleep, you guys."

Colin walked Emily to her room, pausing as she unlocked the door.

"You want to come in?" She turned around to face him.

"I'd better not. I've been up since four this morning and I'm beat."

She slipped her hands around his neck and drew his face down to hers. "Not even for a little while?"

He closed the gap between them as he slid his hands around her waist, pulled her against him, and covered her lips with his. He reached behind her and pushed the door open, guiding her backwards into the room. "Maybe for a little while."

~*~

The next morning, after Emily, Colin, and their

friends met for breakfast, they gathered in the comfortable lobby of the inn to decide what to do with their day. Camille and Maggie said they wanted to rent bicycles to ride around town and on the bike path down along the shore. Isabel and Alex decided they would go for a hike in the nearby Acadia National Park.

Susan strolled in and joined the small crowd, clutching a thick binder against her chest, just as Colin's phone began to ring. It was Chief Taylor.

"Hello, Chief. What can I do for you?"

"I tried to search for a Ben Kinney in this area and nothing came up before he moved here six months ago," he blurted out, sounding exasperated, "which is what you probably found out last night, isn't it?"

"Yes, but you were pretty adamant that you didn't want my help."

"Eyah, about that. I was just being bullheaded and prideful, at least that's what my wife said. After sleeping on it, I have to admit that I'm in over my head." He paused for several beats and then continued. "I could use your help, if you're still willing."

"Happy to help, Chief." Colin eyed Emily as he replied. The arch of her brow told him she wasn't pleased.

"What would you do first?" Chief Taylor asked. "Fingerprints?"

"Yes, run his prints, see who he really was. Such a short history screams *alias* to me."

Susan's eyes widened. "Alias?"

Colin held up a finger, hoping the shocking news would be held at bay by those listening to his side of the conversation.

Chief Taylor continued. "Eyah, I can get those from the ME. What else?"

"Check his phone records and his financials." Colin moved a few steps away from Emily and the chatty group, since they'd all seemed to ignore his gesture for quiet. "I'll come down there and we can talk it through."

"I'd appreciate that, Detective."

"Oh, and, Chief, see if you can get any security video from the inn." Colin hung up and rejoined the group.

"So," Emily said, "he wants your help now?"

Susan stepped closer. "What was that about an alias?"

"Sorry, I'm not at liberty to discuss it at this point," he replied.

"No big deal," Susan shrugged. "I'm just glad you agreed to help. Without it, poor Alvin wouldn't have a prayer of solving this case. And it's important to this whole community because Pastor Ben was becoming one of us. We all need you to find his killer." She put a hand to her face and shook her head. "So scary to think it might be one of our own folk."

He didn't dare tell her Pastor Ben was probably not who the town thought he was or that all those marriages where he had officiated wouldn't be legal now.

"You heard your sister, Emily." Colin put an arm around her. "I don't want to leave the chief hanging. Let's help him button up this case, and then all's clear to get married on Saturday."

"You think you can wrap this case up in two days?" Emily asked.

"I'll do my best." He kissed her on the side of her

head. "That's all I can give."

She lifted her eyes to him. "Maybe I should go with you. We can solve this thing faster with more people on the case."

Susan waved her hand at Emily. "Not a chance, Sis. We have wedding details to nail down." She patted her fat binder. "Now, we've got to arrange the rehearsal dinner and find someone else to perform the ceremony."

"What about the senior pastor at the Community Church?" Emily asked.

"Nope, he's doing a memorial service in Bangor that day, an old friend, but I know a ship's captain I can ask."

Colin and Emily glanced at each other. "No, Susan," she said, "we want a minister."

Not wanting to get in the middle of the two sisters, Colin excused himself. "I'd better head over to the police station and leave you ladies to the planning." He cupped Emily's face in his hands and kissed her, her lips warm and soft on his. "I'll call you later and we'll reconnect."

"Don't forget, Colin, we need to apply for our marriage license today."

"This afternoon." He began backing toward the door. "I promise."

~*~

"What'd you find?" Colin asked as he walked into Chief Taylor's office.

"Dr. McHenry told me she'd get the prints and have them run in Bangor. She'll phone me with the results."

THE HARBOR OF LIES

"If he's not, in fact, Reverend Ben Kinney, that could open up a ton of possibilities for who might have wanted him dead." Colin took a chair across the desk from the chief.

"Why would that be?" he asked. "You think he's hiding from someone?" His eyes grew round at the thought. "You mean, like maybe he was in witness protection?"

"That's one scenario," Colin said. "Or he was working undercover on a case."

The chief stood and moved to the window, looking out over Main Street. "Or he was pretending to be a minister but he was taking advantage of the good people of our town in some way."

"You stated you don't have much crime around here, so that's not likely, right?"

"Well…"

Colin's interest piqued. "You have something going on around here that you're trying to deal with?"

The chief turned away from the window and nodded. "We've had a rash of break-ins."

"What do you think is causing a spike in that sort of thing?"

"We don't want it widely known, so it needs to be kept quiet," the chief closed the door to his office, "'cause it would hamper the tourist industry we have around here."

"So, you're saying this quaint little fishing village has a seedy underbelly?"

"I wouldn't exactly call it a seedy underbelly, Detective, but we have been experiencing a problem with," he paused and cleared his throat, "with heroin."

"Heroin? Here?" Colin would never have guessed. The place was so picturesque.

"Every town has a bit of a bad element." The chief took a seat again. "I figure the drug addicts are burglarizing homes to sell the stuff to pay for their habit."

The phone on his desk buzzed and his receptionist's voice came over the speaker. "Call on line two, Chief. It's the medical examiner."

He grabbed up the receiver and punched the button to answer it. "This is Chief Taylor." He listened while the person on the other end of the line spoke. "I see. All right. So what is his name?"

The chief scribbled something on a small notepad. "Thanks, Doc." He hung up the phone then, with two fingers, spun the notepad to face Colin.

"Benjamin Kingston," Colin read aloud. "Now we're getting somewhere."

Chief Taylor entered the name into the computer, and it spit out all kinds of information—criminal history, last known address, known associates, and the like. He then did a search for Benjamin Kingston's financial history, but it didn't garner much information. A checking account in New York that hadn't had much traffic in the last six months, which was about the time the man had come to Rock Harbor.

"Any family, so you can notify them of his death?" Colin asked.

"Nothing listed."

"Google him, see what comes up." Colin moved around the desk to see the computer screen.

Chief Taylor punched his name into the search box

and hit enter. After a number of links to news stories popped up, he clicked on one of them and scanned the article. "Looks like he was a witness in some RICO case in New York. He was set to testify against some big muckety-muck, but then he disappeared."

Colin leaned in and glanced over the article. "Maybe that's who he was hiding from."

"And the kingpin's hired gun may have found where Ben was hiding out."

"I have a friend in the New York City Police Department."

"Of course you do," Chief Taylor mumbled.

"Why don't I give him a call and see what he can tell us?" Colin pulled out his phone and made the call.

The chief stared at the computer screen, listening to Colin's side of the conversation until he hung up. "Any luck?"

"Not right off." Colin slipped the phone back in his pocket. "He'll check into it and get back to me."

"I wonder how Ben got Pastor Jansen to hire him if he wasn't a minister." The chief rubbed a hand over his chin.

"Why don't we go pay him a visit and find out?" Colin suggested.

"I'll get my coat."

CHAPTER EIGHT
The Curious Sighting

AN OLDER WOMAN ESCORTED Chief Taylor and Colin into Pastor Jansen's office.

"Good to see you, Chief."

"This is Detective Colin Andrews. He's assisting me on a case."

"Detective." Pastor Jansen shook Colin's hand. "Have a seat, gentlemen." He motioned to the two chairs opposite his desk.

He was a tall, thin man, in his forties, with thick, wavy dark hair, graying at the temples. "What can I do for you?" he asked, pushing his glasses up on his nose.

"From the way your young secretary was crying out there, I'm assuming you've probably heard by now that Pastor Ben was killed last night," the chief said as he and Colin took their seats.

"We've heard." The pastor nodded as he sat down in a large leather chair behind his desk. "Poor Whitley.

She worked closely with Pastor Ben. She's taking it hard—we all are. Do you have any idea who could have done this?"

"Not yet. That's why we're here," Chief Taylor said.

Colin leaned forward in his chair. "What can you tell us about him?"

"Like what?"

"Does he have any family in the area? Did you know of anyone he might have had a beef with?"

"No family around here that I know of. He might have had some in New Hampshire, I think that's where he was from, before moving here—at least that's what it said on his resume. As far as anyone he might have had a problem with? No. As far as I know, everyone liked him. His methods were a bit unorthodox, but he was charming and friendly, and the townspeople seemed to really take to him."

"A bit unorthodox?" Colin asked.

"Irreverent sometimes."

"So why did you hire him?"

"He came highly recommended by Mayor McCormack."

"Ella?" Chief Taylor wore a quizzical expression. "She recommended him?"

The chief glanced at Colin, as if he seemed to be thinking the same thing Colin was. Why would the mayor recommend someone who was clearly not who he was pretending to be?

"There were other candidates," the pastor said, "but Ella applied considerable pressure, practically pleading with me to hire him. With her being the mayor and all, I told her I'd give him a trial period. We needed the extra help with all the growth the church has had, and like I said, the whole town seemed to warm to him. Ben was staying at her bed and breakfast, you know. Perhaps you should go talk to her."

Colin and Chief Taylor stood. "Thanks for your time," the chief said. "I think we'll just go on over and pay a visit to Miss Ella."

"By the way," Colin said, "where were you between six and eight o'clock last night?"

The pastor breathed a laugh. "You think I murdered someone? I'm a pastor."

"I don't mean to sound disrespectful, sir, but anyone is capable under the right circumstances," Colin said.

"Last night I was home with my wife and kids. They'll verify."

The chief appeared a bit embarrassed at Colin's questioning the minister. "Sorry, but we have to ask everyone. Not that we would ever think…well, you know."

"I understand." The pastor rose and shook the men's hands before ushering them out to the reception area. As Colin walked past the secretary's desk, he paused. "Miss—"

"Whitley. Whitley Donovan." Her pale green eyes were moist and rimmed with red.

"We're investigating Pastor Ben's murder," Colin said.

The young woman looked up into Colin's face, tears began to flood her eyes. She turned away and pulled a handful of tissue from the box sitting on the corner of her desk. She dabbed the tears that rolled down her cheeks.

"Is there anything you can tell us about Pastor Ben that would help us solve his murder? Anyone who might want him dead?"

Continuing to avert her eyes, she shook her head, her shoulders quaking as she wept into the tissue.

The chief pulled another tissue from the box and handed it to her. "Whitley," his voice was soft, "if you think of anything, you know where to find me."

She nodded her agreement, still not looking at them.

The chief motioned to Colin to keep moving out the door.

"Sorry, Miss Donovan, but I have to ask," Colin said, ignoring the chief's suggestion. "Where were you between six and eight o'clock last night?"

With her eyes lowered, tears trickled down her cheeks. "I was at home."

"Is there anyone that can verify that?" Colin asked.

"Just my cat." Her voice trembled with sadness, her eyes continuing to avoid his. "You can't think I had anything to do with Ben's death."

The chief laid a hand briefly on her shoulder. "Sorry, Whit, we had to ask."

Once they were outside, Colin stopped and turned to the chief. "What did you make of that?"

"Sounded to me like neither of them knew anything. Why do you ask?"

"I think there's something she's not telling us." Colin only had a feeling about her, but when someone wouldn't look him in the eye, there was usually a reason.

"How do you figure?"

"She wouldn't make eye contact. There's something fishy about that."

~*~

"Simple, Susan," Emily repeated. "I don't want anything fancy."

The two women stood on the grassy area where the ceremony would take place.

"But, Emily," Susan argued, "flowers are one of the only decorations we can have out on the lawn to make it festive. Otherwise it'll be so boring. And the photos won't look that great either."

"Photos? You mean you lined up a photographer?" She hadn't thought of that in the last-minute rush of details to get the wedding party, and guests, to Maine.

"Of course, Sis. This is what I do—I'm the wedding coordinator, remember?"

"Sorry," Emily apologized, rubbing a couple of fingers against her right temple. "I appreciate that. My mind is kind of a blur. This wedding is happening so fast, and my body is trying to catch up with all the time zones. Then, falling on a dead body and getting his blood all over me didn't help. And with Evan—"

She hadn't meant to actually say that last part to her sister, it just slipped out. Susan had never been fond of Emily marrying Evan, believing he was too old and worldly for her young naïve sister. If Susan knew he was weighing on Emily's mind as she was about to say *I do* to Colin, well, she didn't want to hear what Susan would have to say about that.

"Evan?" Susan's eyebrows wrinkled as her

expression turned perplexed. "Don't you mean Colin? Because you certainly don't want your husband-to-be to think you're confusing him with your first husband."

"Yeah, that could be bad." Emily gave a little laugh. That wasn't what she meant, but it was probably better to let Susan think it was.

Emily's phone jangled in her purse and she rummaged around inside of it, tugging the cell out. She smiled when she saw it was Colin, glad for the diversion from her sister's prying questions. "Hello. How's the investigation going?"

"Haven't turned up anything yet." Colin filled her in on how things went at the church. "I think the secretary is hiding something, but she seems pretty closed off."

"Maybe she'd open up to another woman," Emily proposed. "What's her name?"

"Whitley. You want to give it a try?"

"Can't right now. I'm still with Susan, talking about the flowers and things."

"We're heading over to the boarding house where our victim was staying to see what we can dig up there. Then I'll be back to the inn. Alex and Isabel should have returned from their hike by then. Maybe we'll get in a round of golf before dark."

"That would be wonderful. As much as I like the thought of catching this bad guy, I want you to have fun while you're here. You know what they say, all work and no play makes Jack a very dull boy."

"Who's Jack?" Colin laughed. "All right, Babe, I get it. I'll check in with you before we head out."

Emily and Susan stepped back inside the inn and

continued talking. Loud voices drew Emily's attention to the check-in desk where the manager stood, dressed in a stylish black suit and tie, arguing with a stocky man with dark wavy hair and a mustache, wearing jeans and a plaid shirt. Susan's head whipped around as well.

Soon after, the burly man stomped off. The manager came around from behind the desk, straightening his tie and glancing around the lobby, as if checking if anyone witnessed their exchange.

"I wonder what that was about," Susan mused, dragging her gaze away from the manager, bringing it back to Emily.

A young woman with long, auburn hair entered through the front doors and headed toward the desk. Susan prattled on, but Emily watched as the young woman leaned her elbows on the counter and appeared to be quarreling with the manager as well, although, they were doing a better job of keeping their voices down.

"Who's that?" Emily asked in a low voice.

"That's Pastor Ben's secretary, Whitley," Susan replied. "Or, at least, she was."

"Whitley?" That was the name Colin had given her. Emily watched as the young woman whirled away and hurried back out the doors.

"Can you excuse me for a minute?" Emily asked her sister, backing toward the french doors. "I'll be right back."

"Emily."

Susan called after her, but Emily had to try to talk to the girl and pushed through the doors. Once outside, she glanced around for Whitley and spotted her walking briskly down the driveway toward Main Street. Emily rushed after her. "Whitley!"

The woman stopped and turned toward the sound of her name.

Emily pulled to an abrupt stop, huffing a little from the run.

"I'm sorry, do I know you?" Whitley asked.

"No, you don't." Emily drew a deep breath. "I'm helping Chief Taylor figure out who murdered Pastor Ben."

Whitley's eyes moistened at the mention of it.

"I was hoping to ask you a few questions."

"Questions?" Whitley's gaze flew around the area, as if she wanted to make sure no one was watching. "I don't know anything."

"You were pretty close to him, weren't you? You and Pastor Ben, I mean."

"What are you inferring?" Her eyes rounded. "Ben was a gentleman and he—"

"You worked for the man, right?"

"Yes, but I thought you meant…uh…no, I don't know anything of importance. I've got to get back to work, I'm only on a break." Whitley turned and began walking away again, but Emily stayed with her.

"Was there anyone you can think of that would have wanted to harm him?"

Whitley stopped and faced Emily. "He was kind and thoughtful. He listened to your problems and didn't judge. Everybody loved him. Everybody." Tears came to her eyes and she blinked hard a few times.

Had she been in love with him? It almost seemed that way.

"I'd like to hear more about him. It might help find

his killer."

Whitley shook her head. "I don't know anything else."

"I couldn't help but notice you arguing with the manager back at the inn. Did that have anything to do with Ben Kinney?"

"No. I work there part-time and I told him I couldn't work for him anymore. He was irritated I was giving him such short notice because I'm on the schedule for tonight."

"I see." Interesting timing. Did her decision have anything to do with the murder? Probably not, but then again…

Whitley checked her watch. "I really need to get back." She rushed down the street and disappeared around the first corner.

Emily stood alone on the sidewalk, torn between returning to her sister and following the young woman. Colin was right—she was hiding something. Knowing Susan would be fuming if she didn't return soon, Emily hurried back to the inn.

~*~

Colin and Chief Taylor climbed the few steps to the front porch of the Bayside Bed and Breakfast. It was a large, stately old home with lots of southern charm. Three-stories high with a wide, wrap-around porch, it was painted a cheery shade of yellow with white trim and black shutters on the windows. Colin wished Emily could have been there too. She would love seeing this grand historical home.

The chief knocked on the front door, carefully avoiding the floral wreath hanging on it. A small woman opened the door, appearing to be in her late fifties, with shortly cropped brown hair.

"Hello, Chief," the woman greeted with a warm smile.

"Afternoon, Ella. Or should I say, Mayor McCormack?" He tipped his head toward her.

"Oh, Ella is just fine there, Alvin. And who is this young man?"

"This is Detective Colin Andrews. He's helping me on a case."

"A case? Ooh, that sounds official."

"We'd like to ask you a few questions, if you don't mind."

She flashed a broad grin at the men. "Where are my manners?" She stepped back and swung the door open wide. "Please, come in."

The formal entry was wide with dark, polished hardwood floors and a staircase on the right. Framed pictures hung on the walls—weathered black-and-white photos that looked like they were possibly of ancestors, or people who had originally owned the grand old house.

Ella led the men into the sitting room, which was decorated with pastel floral wallpaper and matching chintz draperies.

"Have a seat, won't you?" She motioned toward the overstuffed striped chairs that sat opposite the tufted sage-green sofa, replete with embroidered pillows.

As the men took their seats, she went to the marble-topped antique sideboard in the corner of the room, against a half-wall that abutted the dining room, which had been laid out with a fine china teapot and several matching cups and saucers.

"Can I get you some tea, gentlemen? I have freshly baked blueberry muffins to go with it."

"None for me, thanks," Colin responded.

"No, Ella, we should get right to the point," Chief Taylor said.

"Then you won't mind if I have a cup. Go on with your questions while I pour."

"We're here about the murder last night at the Rock Harbor Inn," the chief stated. "Have you heard about it?"

"I did hear that some unfortunate man was found bludgeoned to death, or some such. Our town doesn't need a scandal like that. It might hurt our tourist trade, as you can imagine." Ella moved toward the sofa with her cup and saucer.

Colin turned to the chief. "You didn't have his room checked out last night?" he muttered.

The chief leaned toward Colin, partially covered his mouth, and lowered his voice. "I didn't know I needed to. Sorry."

"So, Alvin," Ella said, drawing his attention back to her, "why do you want to talk to me about it?"

"We were told that the man lived here, Ella. One of your boarders."

She perched on the edge of the sofa with a bewildered furrow to her brow. "Oh? Which one?" She took a sip of tea as she waited for the answer.

"Pastor Ben Kinney," the chief said.

She gasped and began to cough, her cup and saucer falling from her hands, crashing down onto the coffee table. "Oh my God!" Tears filled her eyes.

CHAPTER NINE
Madam Mayor

"SORRY, I DIDN'T MEAN TO SHOCK YOU like that, Ella. We were all surprised it was Pastor Ben." Chief Taylor bent down and picked up the larger pieces of broken china.

"Please excuse me for a minute." She dashed to the kitchen and returned with a fluffy white kitchen towel and began cleaning up the spilled tea. "Oh dear." She pressed it into the carpet a few times, tears still trickling down her cheeks. With her fingers, she wiped under her eyes and then took a deep breath, settling back onto the sofa. "I wondered why he hadn't come down for breakfast. I just thought he'd left early for work. He does that sometimes, you know, meets folks for breakfast and the like."

"How well did you know Pastor Ben?" Chief Taylor asked.

"Well, I just...oh, I don't know, it

was...hmm...why do you ask?"

Why was she hesitating?

"Just trying to get the facts," the chief replied.

She sniffled loudly. "I don't understand why you think I know anything."

Colin scooted to the edge of his chair. "The senior pastor at the Community Church told us you pressured him to hire Ben. That tells us you knew him before he moved here."

Her gaze flew to Chief Taylor. There seemed to be pleading in her eyes, as if she was hoping he'd let it go.

"You need to answer the question," the chief pressed.

She used a dry corner of the kitchen towel and dabbed at her eyes. "Yes, I knew him before he came here, for quite some time actually. When I heard that the church was looking to hire someone, I thought he would be perfect for it. He needed to get out of the situation he was in and the church needed an associate pastor. So I recommended him. That's all."

"What kind of situation?" Colin asked.

"I'm not sure. I hadn't seen him for years. Then one day he contacted me and asked if I knew of any job opportunities around here. When the opening at the church came up, I put him in contact with Pastor Jansen."

"Good timing." Colin didn't hesitate to flavor his words with a bit of sarcasm.

"No, Detective, providence," she replied emphatically.

"Ella, I need to ask where you were last night between six and eight o'clock," Chief Taylor asked, knowing that Colin would if he didn't.

"Me? You think I had something to do with this murder?"

"I have to ask everyone so I can eliminate those with a solid alibi," the chief retorted.

"Well, I was here of course, cleaning up after dinner. I set out some oatmeal raisin cookies on the sideboard, then went to my room and watched a little television before I went to bed."

"We're only concerned with the time between six and eight o'clock," Colin said. "Can anyone verify that, Mrs. McCormack?"

She pursed her lips and her gaze rose toward the ceiling. "Those that were here for dinner."

"But they would have finished dinner by then, wouldn't they?" the chief asked. "By the time you were in the kitchen cleaning up, right?"

"I served dinner at six, then cleaned up. Someone might have seen me in the kitchen, I can't really say. But you know me, Alvin, I wouldn't hurt a fly, especially not Ben."

"Hmm." Colin studied her face and her demeanor, trying to determine if she was telling the truth. "We'd like to see his room, if you don't mind?" he said, hoping no evidence had been removed since last night.

"Ben's room?" Her eyes flashed wide for a moment, then narrowed. "I do mind, young man."

Something didn't feel right.

The petite woman stood and planted her hands on her hips, her gaze going to the chief. "It's bad for business, Alvin. I can't have the police traipsing around my house, scaring off my guests. They won't want to stay if they see you two tearing up his room and talking about his—" her lips trembled and her eyes filled with tears again, "his murder."

Colin stood too. "I'm sorry this is upsetting for you, ma'am, but—"

The chief shot up out of his seat, a frown wrinkling his forehead. "You know this has to be done. Are you telling me I have to get a warrant, Madam Mayor?"

She wiped her fingers over her damp cheeks and stared at the men defiantly.

What was she afraid of? Was there something that would incriminate her, or was she worried they would find out Pastor Ben was not who he claimed to be and she had known?

"What's going on here, Ella?" Chief Taylor asked. "I'd think you'd want to do all you could to help find your friend's killer."

"Not to mention how it'll look having the mayor of this tourist town impeding a murder investigation," Colin added. "I can't see how that would be good for your re-election—or your Bed and Breakfast business."

The mayor eyed Colin for a prolonged moment, as if letting his words sink in, or hoping he would back down.

Finally, she sighed. "Oh, all right, just please try to be quiet about it. I can't afford to have guests checking out. Upstairs, room six."

The men followed her up the steps and down the hall, where she unlocked the door for them.

Her eyes narrowed and she gave the men a sharp look. "Remember, quiet." She pushed the door open and let them in.

Colin followed the chief in, then turned back to Mrs. McCormack. "Thank you."

Standing in the doorway, she nodded at him. "You're welcome." Her sad gaze floated from the bed, to the chair, then the dresser, before she left them alone and went back down the stairs.

The chief and Colin both glanced around the room as they slipped on their gloves and began carefully going through Ben's things, looking in the dresser drawers, his closet, under the bed, and in the small desk tucked into one of the corners.

"Look at this." Colin pulled a small manila envelope out of the lap drawer of the desk. He unfastened the brad that held it closed and slid the contents out on the desk.

The chief joined him. "Huh. Looks like his driver's license and passport." He picked up the license and read the name. "Benjamin Kingston."

Colin leaned in for a closer look at the license. "The photo looks like the dead body I saw. Is it Ben Kinney?"

"Eyah, that's Ben Kinney all right."

Colin flipped open the passport. "The name is the same, and so is the guy in the picture."

"Let's go downstairs and see what Miss Ella really knows about this man," the chief said as he moved toward the door.

"Hold up," Colin called out. "It's probably best we don't mention it to her just yet."

"Why not?"

"What if she knows more than she's telling? At this point, we can't rule anyone out."

"You think the mayor could be our murderer?" the

chief asked, looking perplexed at the thought.

"In a murder investigation, everyone is a suspect until you can rule them out. Let's head back to the police station and do a background check on this Benjamin Kingston and find out who we're really dealing with."

"Oh, I gotcha." The chief nodded slowly. "Maybe she knew who he really was."

"You're catching on, Chief." Colin grinned. "I guess it's possible she doesn't know his true identity, but let's have some real ammunition before we question her again."

~*~

Susan took Emily to meet with the photographer, and then they stopped in at the florist shop on Main Street. As Susan pulled the shop's door open, a boisterous laugh caught Emily's attention. She glanced down the street at the throng of people crowding the sidewalks. For an instant she thought she saw Evan again, ducking into a café half a block away.

"I'll be right back," she told her sister. "You go on in and start looking at the flowers."

"But, Emily!"

She hurried toward the café, squeezing through the crowd like a salmon swimming upstream. When she reached the glass door, she paused there for a moment, peering inside. Was she losing her mind? She had to find out. Emily opened the door and stepped in, frantically gazing around the place.

"Can I help you?" the young man at the counter asked.

The little café was full of customers, with a few crowded just inside the door, waiting for a table.

"I'm looking for someone, a man," she replied, not looking at the young man, continuing to glance around the busy restaurant. Evan wasn't there.

Of course he wasn't there. He's dead. Emily shook her head.

"Do you see him?" the man asked over the clanking silverware and noisy conversations.

"No, sorry to bother you. He's not here." She felt foolish. Why was she dashing about hunting for ghosts?

"Do you want to wait for him?"

She shook her head. "It would be an awfully long wait." With that, she turned and left.

What was she going to tell Susan? She didn't want her sister to think she was going crazy too—thinking she kept seeing Evan, how he had been haunting her thoughts. She'd already told the girls, and they hadn't believed her, dismissing it as subconscious guilt rearing its ugly head. Even if they were right, she didn't want her sister putting in her two-cents about it.

Emily reached the flower shop and went in. A string of little brass bells tied on a red ribbon jangled as she came in. Susan was at the back of the shop, standing beside a middle-aged woman in a green smock with a head of frizzy blond hair. They were looking at flowers in five-gallon buckets congregated on the floor. They both turned at the sound of the bells.

"Emily, there you are. Where did you run off to?" Susan asked.

"Sorry, I thought I saw someone I used to know, but I was wrong." Emily slipped her jacket off and folded it over her arm.

Susan accepted Emily's excuse and made the introductions, then the three women set about choosing flowers for the wedding.

~*~

As soon as they were finished with the florist, Susan told Emily they were done for the day and she was off to see Brian at the hospital before heading home to meet her children as they got off the school bus.

"I can't wait to see the kids," Emily said.

"They'll be here for the wedding. This afternoon will be homework and football practice before supper, and heading to bed early for school tomorrow."

"Give them a hug for me and tell them I'm anxious to see them."

Susan happily agreed. "Tomorrow we'll need to finalize last-minute details." They'd need to nail down a minister to officiate the ceremony on Saturday, and the rest of the guests should be arriving in time for the rehearsal dinner.

"I don't think we really need a rehearsal dinner, Susan."

"It's tradition. There's a lovely room upstairs in the inn, with stunning views of the bay."

"Can't we all just go to dinner at a restaurant? Nothing fancy." That's the way Emily liked it. "Besides, what's there to rehearse? The music starts and then I walk down the aisle to Colin."

Her sister's mouth turned down. "You're taking the fun out of it."

"I just don't want a big fuss."

Susan shaded her eyes against the sun as she glanced up at the sky, which for the most part was clear and blue with a few wispy clouds and a handful of noisy seagulls flying over. Then her gaze moved to the edge of the bay, and Emily's followed. There, gray clouds were gathering on the horizon. "I hope the weather holds until after the wedding."

Emily studied the distant clouds. "Are you expecting bad weather?"

"No, not this early. I checked weather-dot-com this morning and a storm is moving up the eastern coast, but they expect it to turn and go out to sea long before it reaches Maine."

"That's good." Emily gave her sister a grateful smile. The good weather had better hold—storm or no storm, there was going to be a wedding this Saturday in Rock Harbor.

"Now, don't forget to apply for the marriage license this afternoon. They'll turn it around in a day."

"I won't forget." Emily pulled her cell out of her coat pocket. "As a matter of fact, I'll phone Colin as soon as you're off."

Emily hugged Susan good-bye and watched as her sister walked down Main Street toward the inn. She took a seat on a wrought-iron bench facing the street and dialed Colin's number.

"All done with your sister?" he asked.

"For today. Are you free to go with me and apply for our marriage license?"

"Not quite, Babe."

"Where are you?"

"I'm at the police station with the chief, doing a background check on our vic."

"Oh, I thought you already did that."

"I did, but a lot has changed. How fast can you get over here?"

"Within minutes. You're just down the block and around the corner."

Isabel plopped down on the bench beside Emily. "Hey, Em. What are you doing?"

"Isabel!" Emily put an arm around her friend and gave her a quick hug. "Where's Alex?"

"Taking a nap. That hike this morning wore him out."

"Isabel's there with you?" Colin asked.

Emily covered the phone with her hand. "I'm talking to Colin," she whispered.

"Emily?" Colin questioned, drawing her attention back.

"I'm here," she said. "Isabel just popped by."

"Why don't you bring her with you? We might need her help."

"That sounds serious. What's going on?" Emily glanced sideways at her friend.

"I'll tell you when you get here."

CHAPTER TEN
Whitley's Heartbreak

NOT LONG AFTER EMILY'S PHONE conversation with Colin, she and Isabel reached the police station and were escorted into the chief's office, where he and Colin were huddled around the computer monitor on the desk.

"Somebody call for the dynamic duo?" Emily chuckled, attempting to lighten the mood.

"The FBI, at your service," Isabel played along.

"Hey, there's my bride." Colin smiled at the women.

Emily wanted to rush over to him and kiss him full on the mouth. Her mind had been busy with all things wedding for the last few hours, not on the murder case. She reined herself in, though, moved close to him, and settled for giving him a quick peck on the cheek.

"Do you know the chief, Isabel?" Colin asked.

"No, we haven't met yet," she replied.

"Chief Taylor, this is FBI Agent Isabel Martínez,"

Colin introduced.

The chief stood as Isabel leaned over the desk and they shook hands. "How can I help?" she asked, taking a seat in one of the chairs.

Colin relayed what had happened so far, including the visit they had paid to Mayor Ella McCormack.

"The mayor?" Emily asked. "I met her at the hospital yesterday."

"The hospital?" Colin questioned with a tilt of his head.

"She was visiting Brian, Susan's husband. Nice lady."

"Huh. Okay, now let's get back to what we found." Colin spread the items out on the desk. "These are the driver's license and passport we discovered in the victim's room. It appears our Ben Kinney was, in fact, Benjamin Kingston, as we suspected."

"Maybe the good mayor can shed some light on who this guy is," Emily said. "What have you turned up in your background search?"

Colin perched on the corner of the desk. "It appears Mr. Kingston was from New York City. Besides a few parking tickets, there's not much on his record, until about nine months ago. It looks like he was arrested as part of a RICO sting. He was working as an accountant for an investment firm that the Feds had their eye on for laundering money and other illegal activities."

"Was he indicted?" Isabel sat up straighter and leaned forward. This was the type of thing she routinely investigated back home.

"There's nothing on him after the arrest," Colin replied. "You think maybe he made a deal with the Feds to turn State's evidence?"

"Could be," Isabel said. "Maybe they promised him something in return for his testimony. Has the case gone to trial?"

"I thought about that, but Alvin and I couldn't find anywhere that it had."

"Alvin?" Emily asked.

"Chief Taylor," Colin muttered. "Sorry, slip of the tongue."

The young chief rocked back in his squeaky wooden chair. "No worries there, Detective."

"So, Isabel," Colin continued, "could you check with the FBI and see what they know about our murder victim?"

"Sure, I'll make a few calls, but if he was here posing as a minister, he wouldn't have been in witness protection. That's not the kind of job they would have set up for him. I wonder how he would have gotten a gig like that."

Colin huffed. "Apparently he was old friends with the mayor. According to the senior pastor at the church, Mrs. McCormack put considerable pressure on him to hire Ben, an accusation she denies, of course."

"Let's see…who should we believe? A minister or a politician?" Isabel breathed a laugh.

"Maybe you should run a check on her too," Emily suggested. "Isn't it possible she knows what he was hiding from?"

"Sure," Isabel replied, "she might have some skeletons in her closet too."

"Our thought exactly," Colin said. "We were just about to do that when you girls walked in. After that we'll head back over to question her again."

"And I'll go pay another visit to Whitley over at the church," Emily said. "I think your instincts were right about her, Colin. That girl definitely knows something she's not saying."

"Protecting someone?" Colin asked.

Emily thought for a moment. "More like afraid of someone."

"Sounds like we all have our assignments." Isabel stood, preparing to leave. "Anyone else hungry, besides me?"

"I am." Emily raised her hand. "I can't concentrate when I'm hungry. Why don't we take a short break and grab a quick lunch?"

The men enthusiastically agreed.

"How about a lobster roll at the Boiling Pot?" The chief grabbed his jacket off the coat rack. "The best in town."

~*~

After a delicious lunch, Emily left the others to their assignments and headed to the Community Church. When she breezed through the church office doors, Whitley greeted her from behind her desk in the reception area.

"Hello, again." Whitley twirled a strand of long, auburn hair around her finger. Perhaps a nervous tell. "What can I do for you?"

"When we were talking earlier, I got the feeling there was more you wanted to say about Pastor Ben. So, I thought I'd give you another opportunity"

Whitley relocated the stapler on her desk, stuck a couple of paper clips in the drawer, stacked a few pages together. "Uh, no, I don't think so." She avoided making eye contact with Emily.

Emily leaned down and put her hands flat on the desk, keeping a soft, even tone to her voice. "Is there some reason *why* you don't want to help us find Pastor Ben's killer?"

Whitley's eyes rounded and glistened with tears, her lips trembling slightly. "Of course not." She glanced around, then lowered her voice. "I can't talk about it *heyah*."

"Heyah?" Emily repeated. Then she recalled what the clerk at the inn had told them about not saying their Rs. "Oh. You mean here?"

"That's what I said. *Heyah*." Whitley gave her an odd look, then shook it off. "I am due for an afternoon break. Let me just tell the book*keepah* she needs to catch the phone and we can step outside."

Before long, they were seated together on a park bench in a garden-like area along the flagstone walkway to the front of the church.

"Ben's death is all my fault," Whitley cried. "I don't know how I can live with myself."

"Your fault?"

"If I hadn't…"

Whitley looked away, toward the old cemetery beside the church, again twisting a strand of hair around her forefinger.

"Hadn't what?" Apparently Emily was going to have to coax the information out of the young woman.

Whitley didn't answer right away. She wiped a tear

away with her hand, her eyes still gazing off toward the graves in the distance.

"Whitley?"

She slowly turned toward Emily. "I loved him, you know."

"I had my suspicions. Did he return your feelings?"

She shrugged. "I knew he felt something." Her cheeks flushed deep pink. Was it the crisp autumn breeze or was she embarrassed to expose their relationship? "He'd flirt with me a little when no one else was around, tell me I was tempting him, that I had to be careful or he would forget he was a minister and…well, let's just say I could get him in a lot of trouble."

"What kind of trouble?" Emily suspected what she meant, but she didn't want to just assume.

"He never told me straight out, but I got the message. He was a man with needs and urges. That's how God made all men, you know. It's not good for man to be alone. That's why God made Eve."

"I see." Disappointment colored her response. Emily had come for more information than the fact he was a man who needed to have his sexual needs met.

"What Ben needed was a wife," Whitley continued, "and I would have been a good one. But it never went too far beyond the flirtation. Maybe if we'd had more time—"

But did it go *somewhere* beyond the flirting?

Emily rested a comforting hand on Whitley's shoulder. "So, why do you think his death was your fault?"

Whitley ran her fingers nervously through her hair

and exhaled loudly. Her gaze bounced around the garden before she went on. She dropped her voice to little more than a whisper. "I'm afraid to tell you."

"Sometimes we have to do the thing we're most afraid of. You want to help us find who did this to Ben, don't you?"

Whitley nodded. "But I could be next to die if I do."

"No one will know where I got the information, I promise, but you've got to tell me."

"If I tell you, then you could become a target too."

"Don't worry about me, Whitley. Just tell me what's going on."

"All right, but I warned you."

Emily nodded. She could take care of herself.

"One night, a few weeks ago, I was working at the inn," her voice remained low, "and I overheard Eric Malone, the manager, in the room behind the front desk. He was talking on the phone to someone. The door was almost shut, and I'm sure he didn't think I could *heyah* him."

"Why is that?"

"Well, he wouldn't have said what he said, of course."

"And what was it he said?"

"Well, I don't know who he was talking to," Whitley continued, "but I heard him say something about *heroin*, and he mentioned something about using his boat and that he'd be making another run soon."

"He has a boat?"

"A big white trawler that he operates as a side business. He uses it to take clients on short ocean cruises between Rock Harbor and Boston. Sometimes they take people out on fishing excursions for a few hours too. It's not really a fishing boat, but people seem to like to sit in cushy chairs on the rear deck and throw their lines in the water."

Heroin? From Boston? Chief Taylor would definitely be interested in that.

"What's the name of his boat?" Emily asked.

"Hoosier Daddy."

"Clever. Is Eric from Indiana?"

"I think he is. Why do you ask?"

"The Hoosiers…Indiana…" Emily raised her eyebrows in question.

"I don't get it."

"It's not important." Emily blinked and moved on. "Have you ever been on the Hoosier Daddy?"

"Once. He took me out to dinner, then we went down to the docks and he showed me around the boat."

"You dated him?"

"Only once." Whitley shook her head. "He wasn't the guy for me. I guess he thought he could get to second base with me on his boat, maybe third. He started putting his hands on me and I slapped his face. Good thing my brother showed up, or who knows what that man might have tried."

"Your brother? Why would he just show up on Eric's boat?"

"He works for Eric. He and another guy run the boat for him. My brother said he noticed lights on from up at the inn, and that there were people on the boat when no one should have been *theyah*."

"He was at the inn? Does he work there too?" Emily asked.

"Part-time."

"What's your brother's name?"

"Caleb. Why?"

"Just wondering." Hopefully Whitley's brother wasn't involved in running drugs. Probably not, if he was anything like her. "Who's the other guy?"

"Rosco." Whitley grimaced. "Caleb calls him The Sicilian. Doesn't like him much, but a job's a job, my brother says."

Was Rosco the man Emily saw quarreling with the manager before Whitley came in?

"Is Rosco a burly man with olive skin, brooding eyes, and unruly black hair?"

"Good description, but you left out the sour disposition. How did you know?"

"I saw him arguing with Eric Malone at the inn yesterday." Now that character looked more like someone she'd expect to be involved in something illegal. "Do you know his last name?"

"Ciminella, I think—or something like that. Why? Is that important?"

"Don't worry. It's just routine to run a background check on any potential suspects."

"You consider him a suspect?"

"Everyone is a suspect until we eliminate them. Even you."

"Me? I would never hurt a hair on Ben's head. I loved him." Whitley sucked in a quick shuddering breath. "There was never a harsh word between us."

"I believe you," Emily said, hoping to relax the young woman, "but you still haven't told me why you think Ben's death was your fault."

"Because I told him about what I'd overheard. I had to tell somebody." Whitley lowered her eyes to her hands, fidgeting in her lap. "Now he's dead."

"Look at me, Whitley."

Her moist gaze slowly rose to meet Emily's.

"Did you mention it to anyone else?"

CHAPTER ELEVEN
Uncovering Ben Kinney

WHITLEY SHOOK HER HEAD SADLY AS she pulled a tissue from her pocket. "I didn't tell anyone else what I'd heard."

"And you're positive Eric doesn't know you overheard his conversation?"

Her head bobbed slightly. "I'm sure. I only listened for a minute. I'd heard enough. Then I hurried out to the lobby and fluffed pillows on the sofas—and anything else I could find to look busy when he came out of the back office." Whitley paused, wiping her nose with the tissue. "When Ben was killed, I knew I couldn't work there anymore."

Could Ben have been murdered because he was investigating Whitley's story? If Eric Malone really was running drugs with his boat, and Ben went sniffing around, that would be a pretty strong motive for murder. Mr. Malone was worth checking out.

On the other hand, Colin and Chief Taylor had reason to believe Ben was hiding from some very bad people who would do anything to stop him from testifying against them. Could they have found him? The way he was killed didn't scream professional hit, but it did get the job done.

Colin and the chief had better nail that possibility down so they weren't spending precious time accusing townspeople of this murder.

"Like I told you," Whitley moaned, "it's all my fault. Poor Ben." The tears began to flow.

Though Whitley was taking the blame on herself, maybe she simply misunderstood what she had overheard. Just because Eric used the word *heroin* while he was on the phone didn't mean he was the one bringing it in to Rock Harbor. She'd admitted she hadn't caught the entire conversation, only a few snippets through an almost-closed door. He could have merely been commenting on the drug problem to a friend, then going on to talk about his boat business.

What a tragedy if assumptions and misunderstandings had somehow gotten Ben killed?

Emily put a comforting arm around Whitley. Here was this sweet, young woman, grieving for the man she loved, believing it may have been her fault he was killed. A heavy sadness settled over Emily, an empathy of sorts. She had been in Whitley's shoes, experienced what she was feeling, only ten times over, when Evan had died. Even now, marrying a police detective, Emily couldn't help but wonder if she might one day know that grief again.

She patted Whitley's shoulder. "Don't worry, we'll

figure this thing out."

Emily probably shouldn't have promised that—time was running out before the wedding and then they'd be off on their honeymoon—but the words tumbled out, along with the desire to help lift the young woman's burden. If they could find the truth, and discover who murdered Ben, maybe Whitley could forgive herself and move on with her life.

"I'd better get back to work before someone comes looking for me."

"Call me if you want to talk again," Emily said, handing her a business card.

Whitley took it and hurried back into the church.

~*~

"Thanks for the info, Isabel." Colin hung up the phone and turned to Chief Taylor, who was eagerly waiting to hear what Isabel had found out.

"Well...what'd she say?"

"Her contacts at the FBI confirmed Ben Kingston was an accountant for Dominick & Pelosi Investments."

"Never heard of them. Big outfit?"

Colin nodded. "The Feds had been after his boss for money laundering, among other things, and they scooped Ben up in the mass arrest. They're convinced he knew what his boss was up to, and that he participated, whether willingly or unwillingly. Ben claimed he didn't know anything about the illegal activities, said he just kept the books, but word was he had a CD with a second set of books on it, for his own protection."

The chief rubbed his chin. "Which proves he did

know."

"Exactly what I thought." Colin claimed one of the chairs across the desk from Chief Taylor. "The Feds offered to stick him in witness protection, like we suspected, in exchange for his testimony and turning over the file."

"Did he take them up on it?"

"According to Isabel's source, Ben did, but then he slipped away."

"I expect they got the CD from him first."

"Not according to Isabel. He was supposed to hand it over, but he shook his escorts before that happened."

"You think he brought it with him to Rock Harbor?"

"We didn't find anything when we searched his room, but he could have hidden it somewhere else," Colin said. "But where?"

"You think maybe somewhere else in Ella's house?"

"It would make sense. We should get a few of your men and go search the entire house. When we were there last, we had no idea we should be looking for a CD." Colin rose to his feet and slid his jacket on. "But I'm afraid we'll need to get a search warrant this time."

"Knowing her, she will probably demand it."

Colin had to agree. Even with the short time he'd spent with the woman, he would say that even with her charming ways, she was a tough old bird. "How hard will that be?"

"Well, the Hancock County seat is over in Ellsworth," the chief said. "I have a cousin who works in the courthouse over there. I'll give her a call and see if she can rush this thing through with Judge Wilcox."

"In Ellsworth? You don't have a courthouse here on the island?"

That would certainly delay things, and with the wedding coming up soon, every minute counted.

"Nope. We don't have much crime here, so everything gets handled over in Ellsworth. Don't worry. It's only about a half hour away."

"Man, I thought Paradise Valley was small," Colin huffed.

"Paradise Valley?"

"Yeah, in Idaho, just outside of Boise. That's where Emily and I work."

"I thought you were some big-time detective from the mean streets of San Francisco." Chief Taylor quirked one side of his mouth.

"I was, at one time. I could tell you stories that would make your hair stand on end."

"Huh. Small town cop now, just like me." Chief Taylor raised a curious eyebrow. It seemed as though Colin had lost some street cred in the chief's eyes.

Colin crossed his arms defiantly. "True. Except I'm the one with years of experience solving murder cases. But, if you don't need my help…"

The chief's attitude rankled Colin. If his help wasn't appreciated, this young and inexperienced Chief of Police could go right ahead and try to work this case alone. He didn't need that condescending attitude. He could be out golfing right now with Alex, instead of assisting with this case.

Colin had been an aggressive homicide detective, in one of the largest cities in the world, and had successfully closed most of his cases. This pipsqueak had never even worked one single murder investigation.

The chief waved a dismissive hand. "Now, don't get all riled up. I was just taken aback a might. I appreciate your help. I was just thinking you were this hard-boiled detective, is all."

"I am. I was. I saw a lot of horrific crimes in my time on the force there. Eventually, I just needed a change of scenery." Colin didn't see the need to go into the story about why he really left, that his previous fiancée had been brutally killed in the line of duty in San Francisco.

"Now that we got that out of the way, what's our next step, Detective—besides getting a search warrant for the bed and breakfast?" Chief Taylor pushed back from his desk and went to the coat rack.

Colin followed him toward the door. "With the new information we have, we should go and pay another call on Madam Mayor and see what we can shake out of her," he said, making a motion with his hands as if he was actually shaking her.

Chief Taylor's eyes widened. "Hey, you can't be putting your hands on the mayor."

Colin chuckled. "Figure of speech, Alvin."

"Oh." He blushed a little then grabbed his coat off the rack. "I just, well, you know." He cleared his throat. "We ought to head on over there if we're going to."

~*~

After Chief Taylor called his cousin at the courthouse, and put the paperwork in motion to get the search warrant, he and Colin drove to the bed and breakfast again.

"Back so soon?" Mrs. McCormack asked, standing in the doorway. "I hope this means you have a suspect under arrest for Ben's murder."

"We have some leads we're following, Ella. Mind if we come in?" the chief asked.

"Oh, sure, sure." She stepped back to let them in. "I see you still have your friend helping you."

The word *friend* was a stretch, but Colin didn't argue.

The men stepped past her into the grand entry then paused, waiting for her to lead them into the living room.

Ella gestured toward the overstuffed chairs and the men took a seat. "So what's this about?" She sat on the sofa facing them.

"Just some further questions as we're digging into this case. You told us that you knew Ben Kinney for quite a few years," Chief Taylor said.

"That's right, but I hadn't seen him for, I don't know how long. Why do you ask?"

Colin leaned toward her, perching on the edge of his chair. "We find it odd that you pushed so hard to get him hired at the church, if you hadn't seen him for a long time. How exactly did you know him?"

Her eyes flashed panic, then she regained her composure.

"Well, I had known him since he was a boy. You know how it is, Alvin. They grow up and go off to have their own lives and you hardly hear from them again." There was something sad in her voice and her gaze fell to the hands folded in her lap. "Then one day, out of the blue…"

Years of interrogations gave Colin a sense about these things—there was something more to the story—so he pushed. "Mrs. McCormack, what are you not telling us?"

"What do you mean? I answered your question."

"There's more to it than that. I can tell."

"Where are my manners?" She rose to her feet and went to the sideboard. "Can I get anyone else a cup of tea?"

"Now, Ella," Chief Taylor said, "you know we didn't come *heyah* for tea. If you know something that could help us solve this murder, now's the time to tell us. We're going to find out sooner or later. Ben Kinney is dead, Ella. Whatever you tell us can't hurt him now."

She spun away from the tea service, tears welling in her eyes. "Of course I know he's dead," she cried, almost shouting. "No need to remind me of that, Alvin." She returned to the sofa, without her cup of tea, and sank down onto the cushions.

"We need to search Ben's room again," the chief said.

"Why?" Her eyes were brimming and a tiny line formed between her brows.

Colin glanced around the living room, seeing stacks of CDs lined up on one shelf of a cherry-wood bookcase. "And if we don't find what we're looking for there, we'll need to search the whole house." Maybe Ben had hidden his incriminating CD in one of those cases.

She drew a deep breath before replying. "I don't mind you searching Ben's room again, but you'll need a warrant before I let you search everywhere else. You'll shoo my guests away for sure, tearing up my whole house."

"Last time we were here we found Ben's driver's license and passport," Chief Taylor paused and looked Ella in the eye, "so we know his name wasn't really Ben Kinney. If you knew him since he was a boy, we're pretty sure you also knew that wasn't his real name. Am I right?"

She nodded reluctantly, not saying a word.

"We know he wasn't really a minister either," Colin said, "but yet you somehow wrangled him a job at the church. Why?"

She pinched her lips tightly together.

"Come on, Miss Ella. Spill."

Ella set her gaze on Chief Taylor. A few tears trickled down her cheeks and she wiped them away with her hands. "I can't."

Why was she holding back? Did she have something to do with his murder?

"Or won't." Colin shot out of his chair. "Mayor or not, you can't withhold information. Did you have something to do with his death?"

Why else would she be so cagey with her answers?

"Come on, Detective." The chief motioned for him to sit down.

Colin did as he was asked. "Answer the question."

"Now, calm down," the chief continued. "I'm sure Ella wants us to find Ben's killer. Don't you?"

"Of course, I do. He was the son of a very dear old friend."

"Holy cow, Ella. Why didn't you say so?" the chief asked.

Her old friend's son? Now it made sense. She had known him since he was a boy. He had grown up and gone off to find his own life. But why wouldn't she want to help them find his killer?

"I know this looks bad, but he was like a son to me. You have to understand, I didn't want to say anything because I'm the mayor and I was…harboring a fugitive from the FBI." She buried her face in her hands, her shoulders quaking as she cried. "He was in trouble—bad trouble—how could I not help him?"

"We understand, Ella," the chief said sympathetically, "but still…"

"Oh, Alvin, I had to help him." She turned her attention to Colin. "Wouldn't you do just about anything to protect someone you love?"

Thinking of Emily and his folks, Colin could relate. He nodded as he sat back down in the chair. "I'm curious though, how did Ben pull off being a minister all these months?"

Ella gave him a weak smile. "He was raised in church. He had years of Sunday school, memorizing scripture verses and hearing Bible stories when he was a kid. He was such a sweet boy. Too bad he changed when he went out on his own, when he moved to the big city. But he's always been good with people, so it wasn't hard for him to fake it."

"Didn't Pastor Jansen ask for references or anything?" Colin asked.

"He did," Ella answered with a small nod. "But I insisted he hire Ben, give him a chance at least, and if it didn't work out after a few of months, he could look for someone else."

"He hired him on your word alone?" Chief Taylor asked.

"Well, that and..." she bit her bottom lip, "the fact that I told him I would block his request for a building permit to add on to the church if he didn't do it. I know that was wrong, but I had to do whatever I could. You understand, don't you, Alvin?"

CHAPTER TWELVE
Searching the B & B

HAD MISS ELLA, AND HER DEAR FRIEND, known what crimes Ben had been involved in? That the FBI had offered him witness protection in exchange for his testimony? Had Ben shared with her that he was hiding out from people who wanted him dead?

"What exactly did Ben tell you?" Colin asked.

"That he had gotten himself into a bit of trouble down in New York and he needed to lay low for a while. He didn't want anyone from his past life knowing where he was or they might put him in jail."

"Not that someone would kill him if they knew where he was?" Chief Taylor asked.

"Oh, dear God, no," Ella gasped. "Nothing like that. Why? How much trouble was he in?"

"A lot," the chief replied. "It's hard to believe he didn't tell you all about it."

"I guess he didn't want to worry me." Sadness filled

her eyes as she lifted her gaze to the chief. "Do you think that's what happened, that they found him and killed him?"

"Maybe."

Colin took another look at the CDs on the bookshelf. "We really need to search your place for any evidence that could help us find whoever might have killed him." The CD had to be here or at Ben's office. If someone from New York tracked him to this town, it wouldn't be long before they figured out where Ben had been living and came looking for it, which could put Ella and her guests in danger too.

"Like I said before," Ella went on, "I can't afford to have you scaring away my guests, but if you're careful and quiet, I guess it couldn't hurt. Are you looking for something in particular? Maybe I could help."

"Well, there is a—" the chief began.

Colin cut the chief a sideways glance, interrupting him before he gave everything away. "Yes, there is a chance he might have made some notes. You know, something that could give us some clues."

"Oh yes." Chief Taylor cleared his throat. "Notes and stuff. We'll comb through the main living areas on this floor, and then Ben's bedroom again, before we disturb any of the guest rooms."

Ella stood. "I'll stick around to make sure you don't drive away any of my folks."

Colin eyed the stack of CDs again. "I'll start with this bookcase, if that's okay with you, Chief."

He nodded his approval. "If you'll stand outside of the room, Ella, that'd be a big help."

She planted herself back on the sofa and crossed her

arms. "How about I just wait right here? Then I'll follow you up to Ben's bedroom."

Chief Taylor glared at her as he considered it. "All right, but you stay put." He moved to the sideboard and went through it, then rummaged through drawers in the side tables, and anywhere else that made sense to look, while Colin opened every one of the CD cases, which could easily have been fifty or sixty.

Colin glanced over his shoulder, finding Ella watching with interest as they rifled through her things.

The whistle of a teakettle sounded from the kitchen. "I almost forgot," she said, "I put a fresh pot on the stove to boil right before you arrived. Anyone else like a cup of tea?"

Both men shook their heads.

She rose and hurried to the kitchen.

As soon as she was away from the sofa, Colin pulled up the cushions and poked around in the crevices, hoping to find that Ben had hidden the missing CD there and she was covering for him, but there was nothing but crumbs. "Why don't we search his bedroom?"

Chief Taylor pushed a cabinet drawer shut. "We'll need to get the key from Ella."

She appeared in the doorway to the dining room, a steaming cup of tea with matching saucer in her hands. "Someone call my name?"

"We're headed up to Ben's room. Can you let us in, please?" Chief Taylor offered a polite smile.

She crossed the room with her tea and headed for the foyer. The men followed her up the stairs and down the hall, anxiously waiting as she unlocked the door and pushed it open.

After they had entered, Ella settled on the edge of the bed, her cup nervously rattling against the saucer. She took a sip and watched as they searched through all of Ben's belongings again.

"Ella, we need you to stand outside the doorway, please." Chief Taylor motioned with his hand toward the door. "We have to tear this bed apart."

"Oh, Alvin, why on earth?" She slowly ran her free hand over the quilted bedspread that looked like a family heirloom.

"Sorry, Ella."

She stood and set her cup and saucer on the nightstand. "At least let me fold the quilt. I made it myself years ago, and I don't want to find it in a heap on the floor."

After she removed it, the men pulled the rest of the bedding off, shook the pillow out of its case, raised the mattress off the box spring and checked between them. Colin got down on the floor and checked under the bed with a small flashlight. Something glinted off the underside of the box spring.

"Help me lift this off, Chief." Colin pushed the mattress to the side and they raised the box spring again.

Once it was upright, it was clear that there was a slit in the bottom of it. Colin reached inside and felt around, but nothing except a copy of a men's magazine was in there. If Ben had previously hidden the CD there, it was gone now.

"Are we done *heyah*, Detective?" the chief asked.

Colin nodded, disappointed they hadn't found what they'd come for. Then, his gaze moved to Ella as she stood in the doorway. "Sorry, ma'am."

"Let's put this bed back together," Chief Taylor ordered.

Colin raised his eyebrows at the chief. "What about the other rooms?"

The chief glanced over at Ella with questioning eyes, as if hoping for her approval without the search warrant.

"Oh, I guess it would be all right, once you're finished putting that bed back together. My guests are all out of their rooms at the moment, so make it quick before they return. And you can't leave anything disturbed, or I swear they'll check out in a New York minute and it'll be your fault, Alvin."

Colin and the chief restacked the mattress and box spring, then moved through the other guest rooms quickly but thoroughly, doing as the mayor had asked. They saved her room for last, but their search turned up nothing.

Then Colin had an idea. "Are there any computers in the house?" Maybe Ben left it hidden in the D drive.

"Yes, down in my little office off the kitchen, but what on earth would you want—"

Colin skidded past her and down the stairs, with Chief Taylor not far behind. When he reached the desktop computer, he popped the drive open expectantly. It was empty.

He slammed a fist on the desk. "Damn!" He was so sure he was right.

"Watch your language, young man," Ella chastised as she stood in the doorway. "If I knew what you were looking for, maybe I could help."

"Sorry, but we can't discuss an ongoing

investigation." The chief pitched Colin a look and tilted his head toward the door. "I guess we should be shoving off now."

They said their good-byes and marched to the police car.

"Let's hope Emily had better luck with Ben's secretary," the chief muttered as they climbed in.

Whitley. "Shoot!" Colin slammed the palm of his hand on the dashboard.

A wide-eyed Chief Taylor jumped in his seat. "What the heck?"

"The church. Why didn't I think of it sooner? Maybe it's in Ben's computer at the church."

"All right, all right. Calm down now. That's easy enough to check into. Sheesh, you big-city types can get so worked up."

As they drove away from the bed and breakfast, Colin phoned Emily, anxious to know how her meeting went with Whitley. She told him she would be waiting for him at the police station and she'd tell him everything then.

~*~

Emily sat waiting in the small reception area and stood when Colin and the chief arrived.

"Let's head on back to my office." Chief Taylor led the way, and they followed him through the secure door, down the hall and into his office, taking seats around the chief's desk.

"Whitley was pretty closed off at first," Emily began, "but eventually I got her to open up." There was no need to tell them how she had left the poor girl in tears. "She said she had overheard Eric Malone, the manager at the inn, on the phone one night."

Colin's brow twisted in confusion. "How did she happen to overhear him at the inn?"

"She had been working part-time as a night clerk," Emily explained. "He said something that sounded like *heroin,* and he mentioned his boat business."

"Boat business?" Colin asked.

The chief leaned back in his squeaky chair and linked his hands behind his head. "He has himself a beauty of a trawler—you should see it. He runs short cruises between Rock Harbor and Boston. And then there's the fishing trips he offers the boat for, too, taking tourists out on the bay."

Colin leaned forward in his seat, resting an elbow on his knee. "Heroin? Boats?"

The chief bolted upright, his hands flying down hard to his desk. "You think he's the one bringing the drugs into town?"

"Now, Chief," Emily cautioned, raising a hand toward him, "Whitley said she overheard him through a mostly closed door, so she may have been mistaken. We can't jump to conclusions because he could have just been talking to a friend about his boat business, couldn't he?"

"Perhaps," the chief replied, mulling over the possibility, "but it sounds pretty fishy." He snorted. "No pun intended."

Colin glowered at him before turning his attention back to Emily. "What else did she say?"

"She said she had told Ben what she'd overheard.

139

That was a day or two before he turned up dead. The poor thing is blaming herself for confiding in him. She thinks she got him killed."

"Maybe she did," the chief mused. "Sounds like she may have stumbled onto our drug source, and if that's the case, she could be in danger too."

"That's why she begged me not to tell anyone she told me," Emily said. "So you can't bring her name into this, in any way." She glanced from the chief to Colin, seeking their consent.

Chief Taylor nodded, but Colin was another story. "If you find the killer, Chief, she'll likely be called on to testify at the trial."

Emily straightened in her seat. "Not if we can gather enough evidence to prove his guilt without her testimony."

"True enough." Colin seemed to agree, gazing at Emily before turning to the chief. "So you'd better use us while you can, to help you get that evidence."

The chief cocked his head quizzically. "While I can?"

"You've only got us for one more day," Emily reminded him. "We're getting married on Saturday."

Colin reached over and took Emily's hand. "That's right, and then we're off on our honeymoon." He raised his eyebrows to her with a roguish grin.

Her heart skipped a beat at the thought of it.

"Oh, gotcha," Chief Taylor replied with a nod.

"Wait. I almost forgot." Emily pulled a small notepad out of her pocket. She glanced down at her notes. "Eric Malone has two men working on his boat, Whitley said."

"Her brother's one of them, right?" the chief asked.

"Yes, Caleb Donovan. But I saw the other guy he has working for him, a man named Rosco. He was arguing with Malone at the inn, and he looked like a pretty shady character. Do you know him, Chief?"

"Oh, I've seen him around. I only know him by his first name, like you said, Rosco. If we can get a last name, I'll do a background check."

"Already on it." Emily peered down at her notes again. "Try Ciminella. That's what Whitley gave me."

"If this is about drug runners," Colin reasoned, "then it's entirely possible it had nothing to do with thugs from New York hunting for Ben Kingston."

"But we can't be sure of that. We need more proof," Emily said. "Chief, you'd better ask for a search warrant for that boat. Then test it for any traces of drugs. Do you have a drug-sniffing dog around here?"

"No, but I'm sure I could have one brought over from Bangor. But if I'm to get another search warrant, I'll need more justification than what you've given me. And even if I could get one, it'll take a while. Remember," his gaze went to Colin, "the judges are over in Ellsworth, and it's getting late."

"Ellsworth? Where the heck is that?" Emily asked.

"Half an hour away," Colin responded.

"I've got an idea." The chief's face lit up and he jumped out of his chair. "Maybe we can get Whitley to cozy up to Eric Malone and see what she can find out for us."

"Absolutely not." Emily shook her head vehemently, considering what Whitley had told her about their date. "You can't ask her to put herself in danger. She's a civilian with no experience at this kind of thing."

The chief cast her a questioning frown. "You got a better idea?"

Emily looked over at Colin, quirking an eyebrow at him. "Maggie?"

"Who's Maggie?" the chief asked. "Code name for a secret weapon?"

"No," Colin replied with a shake of his head, ignoring the chief's question, "that's not a good idea. She's a civilian too."

"Yes, but she can handle herself. You know she's helped me on a number of cases, and I wouldn't be asking her to do anything dangerous, just smile, swivel her hips, and get chummy with Mr. Malone."

"Who's Maggie?" Chief Taylor asked again.

Emily turned back to the chief. "One of my friends that came for the wedding. The stunning blonde."

"Ahhh." The chief's eyes lit up with understanding, and an impish grin spread across his face as he sat back down.

"So you've seen her?" Emily asked.

"Eyah, at the inn, the night of the murder."

"Then you know what I'm talking about."

"Eyah." His eyebrows rose at the thought of her.

"Now, you wouldn't happen to have a GPS beacon of some kind around here, would you, Chief?" Emily asked. "Something we could slip onto the boat to see where it goes?"

"Without a search warrant, I can't authorize planting a tracker. I could get in a heap of trouble. You're a PI, don't you have one?"

"I don't carry them around with me all the time. It's not like I knew I'd stumble over a dead body and we'd be working a case while we were in Maine for our wedding," she paused and shot Colin a steamy glare, "or I might have packed a couple."

Colin leaned on the desk, quickly shifting his gaze away from Emily, and eyed the chief. "Come on, Alvin, work with us here. We're trying to help you out, the least you could do is—"

"All right, all right. But you can't say where you got this." Chief Taylor opened his side desk drawer. He pulled out a small black disc, about the size of a gambling token, with what looked like a tiny computer chip on one side, and he laid it on his desktop. "There's a hunting tracker. We stick one of these in our pockets when we go up into the mountains, in case we get lost and need to be rescued."

Emily happily snatched it up and dropped it in her purse. "Thanks. That's perfect. Now, do you happen to have a wire?"

"Eyah, somewhere in my desk—but we can't record anything without a warrant," the chief replied, as if it rarely got any use.

"I don't want to record the conversation, just listen in, in case Maggie does happen to get in over her head."

The chief threw her a worried look before bending down to rummage around in the deep bottom drawer of his desk.

"So, of course, I'll need a listening device to go with that wire."

"Of course." The chief rolled his eyes like an irritated teenager and dug back into the drawer.

"What's your plan, Emily?" Colin asked.

She explained what she had come up with and Colin snickered. "Good thing Peter isn't coming 'til tomorrow night."

The chief laid a dark gray plastic box, which housed the equipment, on his desk. "Who's Peter?"

CHAPTER THIRTEEN
Was Emily Nuts?

"WE SHOULD BE GOING, CHIEF." Emily shrugged her coat on. "We're meeting friends for dinner."

Colin's phone rang and he tugged it out of his pocket. "Hey, it's Marconi from NYPD." He pushed the answer button. "Hello, this is Detective Andrews."

He paused and listened briefly. "I'm here with Emily and the Chief of Police in Rock Harbor. I'm going to put you on speaker so we can all hear what you've got to say." Colin clicked the speaker icon and held his phone out. "Go ahead."

"Well, your guy Ben Kingston is a popular fella."

Colin looked over at the chief. "What do you mean?"

"Word on the street is that he's got a two-hundred-thousand-dollar bounty on his head. I'd say the people he's supposed to testify against really don't want him showing up at the courthouse."

"Which means they've put the word out, and probably his picture." Colin cast a glance at Emily. "Hey, what do you have on a Rosco Ciminella?"

"I've heard the name Ciminella before, but I don't think it was connected to someone named Rosco. Maybe he's a relative. I'll check it out. I can't promise you anything, but I'll get back to you when I know something more."

"Thanks, buddy." Colin shoved the phone back in his pocket.

"You two better get going," the chief said. "I'll see if I can find something out about Rosco on my own. And if anything turns up, I'll give you a jingle."

~*~

By the time Colin and Emily left the police station, night had fallen and the temperature was beginning to drop. The inn was only a few blocks away, a short pleasant walk down Main Street. The old-fashioned streetlamps illuminated both sides of the narrow street that was crowded with cars and an abundance of tourists who bustled in and out of the warmly lit shops and cafés.

Colin zipped up his coat and circled an arm snugly around Emily's shoulders as they walked.

On a clear night, stars twinkled across the sky in a heavenly show, but on this night the thick layer of clouds were blocking their light.

They stopped and admired a display of unique Christmas ornaments in the window of one of the local shops. Bright autumn-colored leaves, encased in a sparkling resin, had been strategically hung by narrow silk ribbons on an expansive, bare, white birch branch.

In the reflection of the glass, for just an instant, Emily could have sworn she saw Evan passing behind her. She whirled around, almost knocking into a couple of teenagers walking by.

"Sorry," she gasped, thrusting out her hands to steady them.

"What's the matter, Babe?" Colin asked, concern coloring his voice.

How could she answer that? There was no way she was going to tell him that visions of her dead husband were haunting her, that she was seeing him everywhere, especially with their wedding right around the corner. "See the shop across the street? I saw its reflection in the glass. Come on, let's go check it out and pick up some souvenirs." She grabbed Colin by the hand and dragged him across the street, dodging moving vehicles.

"What are you, nuts?" He laughed as they reached the sidewalk on the other side.

Maybe a little, she was beginning to think, but she didn't dare say it out loud.

After buying a stack of postcards with photos of the area, they headed back to the inn to meet up with their friends for dinner. In the privacy of the long, dimly-lit driveway that led from Main Street to the charming inn, they paused and took in the stunning view of the bay.

A few of the boats docked in the marina were lit, casting a faint glow over the dark water. The large boats—the whale watchers and touring sailboats—were moored in relative darkness behind the restaurants that perched along the shoreline. The silvery moonlight that had shown on the water the night before was now diffused behind the brooding clouds.

The cool night air was laced with the smells of the sea, mingled with the delicious scent of food being prepared at various restaurants nearby.

"I love you, Emily." Colin drew her into his arms and she felt the warmth of his body pressed against hers.

It was an intimate and romantic moment, just the two of them. There hadn't been many of them lately—thanks to the unfortunate turn of events—but standing alone, enveloped in each other's arms, they were shrouded in near darkness as they looked out over the twinkling lights on the water. It was almost as if they were shut away in a world all their own.

She raised her face to him and he kissed her. His mouth was warm and moist on hers, sending a tingling heat flooding through every part of her body.

"I can't wait to marry you, Babe." His voice was low and deep, little more than a whisper. He rested his cheek against her temple as he held her close.

"Only two more days." She tipped her head back a little to gaze up into his eyes, then she snuggled once more against his strong chest, surrounded by the safety of his arms. "Then we're off to the bright lights of New York City. Think of all the exciting things we'll do."

"If we ever leave our hotel room."

The romantic comment drew her gaze up to meet his. He raised his brows to her and a playfully naughty grin curled on his lips. "That can be pretty exciting too," he said.

He pulled her tight against him and kissed her thoroughly. She began to melt from the heat of it.

Honeymooning in New York City was her idea.

Colin had wanted to go somewhere warm, preferably Hawaii. But she had spent her honeymoon with Evan in Hawaii, and this time around, she wanted to go somewhere totally different. Although she didn't tell Colin that was why. How could she?

Instead, she had sold him on the idea of seeing the Statue of Liberty, taking in a show or two on Broadway, enjoying a romantic horse-drawn carriage ride through Central Park, and a whole host of other fun and exciting things to do. Of course, he let her have her way. That's how Colin was—strong, chivalrous, and loving, not to mention honest to a fault—the one thing Evan was not.

Evan had lied to her the entire time they had dated, and all the years they were married. It wasn't until after he was killed that she had begun to learn the truth of who he actually was, and what he really did for a living.

With a crisp breeze swirling around them, Colin and Emily clung to each other, staring out over the dazzling marina and shoreline, listening to the water lap against them. However, as much as she enjoyed nestling in Colin's warm embrace, it hadn't been sufficient to keep her mind from floating back to thoughts of Evan, and all the lies he'd harbored.

That's enough! Emily gave her mind a mental shake. She had spent far too much time on this trip thinking about that man. She tightened her hold around Colin's torso, enjoying his well-defined muscles and the strength of his body. She could only imagine the feeling of him against her soft curves.

Her heart belonged to this solid man, and there was nowhere else she would rather be than here with him. *Simply close your eyes and enjoy snuggling in his arms.*

That was a nice thought, but she knew it wasn't possible, for, soon, their friends would be phoning them to find out where they were.

At least they were able to steal a few nuggets of time together, here and there, to enjoy these days in Rock Harbor. Before long, they would find themselves standing under the wedding arch, reciting their marriage vows, surrounded by the people they cared about the most, trying not to notice the passersby watching them as they wandered about.

The thought of their impending wedding warmed her heart and she gave Colin a little extra squeeze, laying her head against his chest, hearing his heart beat rhythmically, strong and steady, just like him.

She relaxed and her mind drifted back to the case. As much as she tried to block it out and enjoy the few precious moments with Colin, it kept floating back into her head.

Sure, the investigation was getting in the way of their enjoying all the area had to offer, but they couldn't lose sight of the fact that it wasn't *their* case, it belonged to Chief Taylor and the town of Rock Harbor. They would do what they could to assist him, but when it came time for their wedding and the ensuing honeymoon, if the case wasn't solved, then the chief was on his own.

With any luck, they could get the investigation far enough toward a conclusion that he and his staff could finish it when they were gone, but Colin and Emily couldn't let themselves get so involved that they couldn't walk away.

However, Emily had not expected to feel such a

kinship to Whitley—a young woman grieving the loss of the man she loved, who'd turned out not to be the person she thought he was. It seemed to keep Emily emotionally tied to this case, pushing her to continue digging for the truth.

And then there was Colin, with his strong ex-Marine sense of justice and honor. Once he began pursuing a murderer, he would have a hard time dropping the case before it was solved. But what choice did they have? They were quickly running out of time.

Wrapped in Colin's embrace, Emily silently renewed her resolve—case or no case, come hell or high water, they were getting married this Saturday.

~*~

Colin held the door for Emily as they entered the inn. Maggie and Camille were seated on one of the cushy sofas, chatting away. The girls turned when they saw their friends come in.

"There y'all are!" Maggie called out from across the room, jumping up off the sofa. "Oh my gosh, Emily! We were about to send out a search party for y'all."

"No need to shout, Maggie." Emily was a little embarrassed by her boisterous display.

The hotel manager strode over to them from the check-in desk. "Is everything all right?"

"Yes, fine." Camille said, shooting Maggie a sideways glance. "Just a little excessive exuberance, I'm afraid."

Maggie blushed. "Sorry."

"I hope you're enjoying your stay." The manager's

gaze bounced around to each of them, a polite smile spread on his face. "If there's anything you need, just let us know."

He sounded sincere, and his expression seemed to match his voice. Was he as on-the-level as he appeared? Wearing a handsomely tailored black suit with a rich, burgundy tie, and his wavy brown hair neatly combed, he didn't look like any drug runner Emily had seen before. Could Whitley have misunderstood?

"Oh, we sure will." Maggie returned his smile. Her eyes followed him as he walked back to the counter.

"Now, who wants to go for dinner?" Camille asked, tugging on Maggie's arm to draw her attention back in.

"Me." Emily waved her hand around. "I'm starved."

Colin chuckled. "We just need to round up Alex and Isabel."

"I'll call them," Maggie offered, pulling out her cellphone.

"Okay," Colin agreed. "Then why don't you girls ask the manager for a recommendation. Emily and I need to go and change our clothes." He checked his watched. "We'll meet back here in about ten minutes."

Camille and Maggie made a beeline to the front desk and Colin and Emily wandered off down the hallway toward their rooms.

Susan had made reservations for Colin to have a room down the hall from Emily's. "No hanky-panky until the wedding night," she had jokingly warned him.

"I don't really need to change," Colin said as they stopped at Emily's door. "I just figured you'd like to."

She unlocked the door and turned back to him.

Slowly, she slid a hand around his neck and pulled him down to her. "That was thoughtful of you." She kissed him, enjoying the feel of his lips against hers.

Colin snaked a hand around her waist, pushing the door open with his other one. His lips were still on hers as he backed her into her room.

"I would like to change out of this sweater," she told him between kisses.

"Need help taking it off?" He grinned down at her.

A couple of loud knocks sounded from the door and they froze momentarily. Emily's surprised gaze was reflected in Colin's eyes.

"Emily, it's Isabel," came the slightly muffled voice through the door. "Are you ready for dinner?"

She shrugged at Colin. "Coming."

His mischievous expression fell to resignation.

Emily hurried to the door and pulled it open. "Almost ready." There stood Isabel, with Alex waiting behind her.

Colin peeked playfully over Emily's shoulder and grinned. "I'm ready."

"She meant for dinner," Emily whispered over her shoulder.

"Sorry," Isabel said, her brows raising a bit, "did we interrupt something?" A rosiness bloomed in her cheeks.

"Oh, Isabel," Alex murmured, "they're about to be married. I remember when we ran off and got married, we could hardly keep our—"

Isabel jabbed her elbow into her husband's gut.

After an uncomfortable moment of silence, Colin spoke up. "Why don't I let you change, Babe, and I'll wait for you in the lobby." He squeezed past her, toward the open door. "I need to talk to Alex about the fishing trip tomorrow anyway."

"Wait." Emily longed to be with Colin as much as he desired her, and she didn't want him to walk away without knowing it. She grabbed him by the front of his shirt while he was still within her reach. She ran her hands up his firm chest and laced them behind his neck. Pushing up on her tiptoes, she planted a long, wet kiss on him. She didn't care who was watching, she needed to show him that he was all she wanted.

Alex cleared his throat. "We'll wait for you in the lobby, Colin."

When Isabel and Alex were gone, having left the door hanging wide open, Emily and Colin broke into laughter.

"You showed them." Colin gave her a wink and a satisfied grin, and left her to change.

After a quick wardrobe transformation, a fluff of her hair, and a dab of lip gloss, Emily joined him and their friends in the lobby.

They were seated on the various plump chairs and sofas, strategically placed to face the roaring fire blazing in the ornate fireplace. A pleasant warmth swirled in her chest as she watched them chatting and laughing with each other as she approached, happy to be part of this close-knit crowd.

"I thought you guys were hungry." Emily skirted Colin's chair and relaxed into his lap.

"Ravenous," Isabel responded, rising to her feet. "The restaurant is only about a block or so away. Let's roll."

~*~

The group decided to walk, since it was such a short distance to the eatery. The hotel manager had suggested The Lobster Shack, perched on pilings down on the water. "The best lobster in town," Eric Malone had said.

Emily zipped up her jacket as a chilly breeze whipped by them. She linked her hand through Colin's elbow and strolled with him, alongside their friends, down the long driveway.

Maggie sidled up to her on the other side. "I meant to ask, how are the final weddin' plans comin'?"

"Great, according to Susan." Emily smiled. "The rest of the guests should be arriving by tomorrow night, and then we have the wedding rehearsal—although, I don't know what there is to rehearse. The music starts, I walk down the aisle, then meet Colin and the minister under the arch. We exchange our vows and, *voila*, we're married. I have nothing to worry about—my sister keeps telling me—she has everything under control."

Maggie grinned and her blue eyes twinkled as they approached the glow of the streetlamp marking the roadway. "It'll be so nice to have Peter here, finally."

"And my folks too," Colin added.

Emily nodded. "Now, if only Susan has found someone else to marry us, since the murder victim turned out to be the minister."

"Speakin' of murder victims, how's the case goin'?" Maggie asked.

"Slowly," Emily replied. "Too many possible suspects."

"We've got to focus on narrowing the field

155

tomorrow," Colin said, "because it's the last day we can assist the chief with working this case."

"Anythin' I can do to help?" Maggie offered.

Emily linked her other arm through Maggie's. "As a matter of fact…"

As they walked to the restaurant, Emily explained her plan to Maggie. "The point is to get the tracker on the boat without anyone seeing you do it. Can you accomplish that?"

Maggie gave her a nod and a smile.

Emily dug the tiny tracker out of her pocket and handed it to her friend, who promptly stuck it in her handbag.

"No problem, Em, you've given me much harder assignments than this before. Flirtin' with a man is like a piece of good ol' southern peach pie." Maggie winked at Emily and tossed her long blond waves over one shoulder for emphasis. "God didn't give me these baby blues for nothin'."

CHAPTER FOURTEEN
No Hanky-Panky

EMILY AND HER ENTOURAGE arrived at The Lobster Shack, and music and chatter drifted out as Alex opened the main door, allowing the women to enter first. The place was teeming with customers—talking as they ate and drank—clustered around small wooden tables with a glossy resin finish. The place vibrated with a fun feeling of merriment.

"Something smells good," Isabel declared over the din as they crowded around the hostess stand. The air was heavy with the scent of fish and freshly baked bread.

The walls were covered with lacquered, knotty-pine paneling and casually dotted with framed photos of celebrities that had visited the popular establishment over the years. Above the bar were colorful license plates from all over the country, set end-to-end in neat rows, nailed to the wall over an interesting array of liquor bottles in all shapes and sizes.

"How many?" a reed-thin young woman asked over the noise as she took her place behind the hostess station, her long, dark hair pulled up into a high ponytail.

"Six," Alex answered her loudly.

"Name?"

"Alex."

She wrote his name on her list. "It'll be about twenty minutes."

Alex looked to Colin with a questioning expression, as if wondering if they wanted to wait that long.

"No problem," Colin called out above the noise. With arms spread out, he corralled the girls, who were trying to chat over the din, and herded them to a corner where a few wooden chairs were lined up. "Come on, ladies, have a seat."

"You don't have to be so pushy." Camille shook her glossy, manicured fingers through her spikey red hair as she sank down onto a chair with a slight huff.

"Please?" Colin said politely, a slight edge of sarcasm coloring the word.

"Like herding cats," Alex muttered to his friend.

"I heard that," Isabel quipped, leaning against the wall.

"Y'all know what today is, don't you?" Maggie took a seat beside Emily.

"Thursday?" Emily answered.

"That's right, and you know what that means?" Maggie smiled at Camille, who was seated on the other side of her.

Camille's eyes lit up with recognition. "Girls night. I'd almost forgotten with the trip and all."

For the past six years, the four girlfriends had met

every Thursday night for a girls-only potluck dinner. Each one took turns hosting it in their homes, with a dinner theme for each night. These get-togethers had become a sacred ritual for the girls, something they looked forward to each week, a time to catch up and stay connected. No one ever missed it, except for something extremely important.

"I'm guessing the theme for tonight is seafood?" Camille joked.

"Give the lady a prize," Alex teased.

"In case any of you girls forget," Emily jumped in, "I won't be able to come for the next two Thursdays." She playfully batted her eyes at Colin as he stood across from her. "I'll be on my honeymoon."

"Well, as long as it's something important, we'll forgive you." Camille grinned with a hint of mischief curling on her lips.

"We're not in Paradise Valley tonight," Emily's gaze drifted to each of the women, "so I suppose there's no harm in letting the boys have dinner with us—just this one time."

The men looked at each other and chuckled.

Maggie giggled too. "Well, if we have to."

~*~

After dinner, the gang poured out of the busy bar and grill and strolled back toward the inn, chatting about their delicious meals. Alex and Isabel peeled off from the bunch to do some window shopping in the quaint downtown area, while Maggie and Camille stuck with Emily and Colin.

"Evening, folks," the doorman greeted, as they strolled through the entrance.

Across the grand foyer, Emily spotted Eric Malone. "There he is," she whispered to Maggie, tilting her head slightly in his direction.

"I'm calling it a night." Camille hugged Emily and Maggie and headed down the hall to her room.

"Goodnight, Camille," Emily called after her.

"I'll go and see if I can talk to our subject." Maggie slowly moved toward the check-in desk, swaying her hips as she approached. She cast a quick glance back over her shoulder at her friends.

Emily and Colin went and stood by the warm fire and surreptitiously watched while Maggie engaged the manager in conversation. It seemed to be going well, a nice give and take. Then Maggie threw her head back slightly and laughed at something Eric said.

Colin leaned his cheek gently against Emily's temple. "That woman is dangerous," he whispered. "The poor guy doesn't have a chance."

"I'm just glad Peter hasn't arrived yet, or she wouldn't be able to work her magic."

A small crowd of new guests blew through the doors, along with a chilly gust of wind, rustling a few colorful leaves in with them. Chatting among themselves, they made their way to the check-in counter and bunched around it, jostling Maggie out of the way.

"I'd better leave you to your work. Maybe we'll talk again later," Maggie said above the chatter of the guests. Then she backed away from the front desk and headed toward her room.

Emily and Colin hurried across the lobby to catch

up with her.

"What happened?" Emily asked, a little irritated by the crowd of rude guests.

"Oh, he was pleasant enough, maybe even interested," Maggie replied, "but he had to take care of checkin' in all those noisy people. I'll try again tomorrow."

"You've got to get him to show you around his boat if this is going to work," Emily said. If she couldn't, then what? Would it be on Emily to plant the device somehow? She could put on a show as well as Maggie could, but would Colin let her?

"I know the plan," Maggie assured her, "but I can't make him do it. Give me one more day."

"One more day is all we have," Emily huffed.

"It's just as well, Maggie," Colin said. "If you come on too strong all at once, he'll know something's up."

"You're right, and we can't have that," Emily added. Although, it would have been better to know the tracker had been planted. One less thing weighing on her mind.

"Well, I'm headin' to my room. I'll leave you two lovebirds to enjoy the rest of your evenin'." Maggie gave Emily a quick hug. "'Night."

Emily returned the embrace, hoping Maggie would have more success with Eric tomorrow. "Thanks for your help," Emily called as Maggie strolled down the hallway to her room.

Maggie waved a casual hand in the air. "You're welcome."

"Now for some alone time with the love of my life." Colin took Emily's hand and kissed it. "Sorry we haven't had much of it since we got here."

"No need to apologize." Emily smiled. "There will be plenty of time for us to be alone as soon as we're married and off on our honeymoon."

"Yeah, the honeymoon," he echoed with yearning in his eyes.

They walked a few doors down to her room. Emily paused and rested her back against the door. Leaning in, Colin slid a hand around her waist and she raised her chin, looking deeply into his adoring eyes. He lowered his lips to hers and kissed her slowly, softly.

"Best not to give the other guests a show," Emily quietly gasped when she came up for air, her body responding to the pleasure of his kisses. With her gaze not leaving his, she tugged her key card out of her pocket. "Want to come in for a little while?"

"I would, but," Colin gave her a roguish smile, "what would your sister say?"

"Well…why don't you ask her?" another female voice inquired with a tinge of sarcasm.

Colin pulled up quick and Emily's eyes grew wide.

"Oh, Susan," she gasped.

"Sorry to interrupt," Susan said, "but I really need to speak to my sister. You don't mind, do you?"

Emily looked at Colin and shrugged her displeasure.

"Besides, the wedding is day after tomorrow, Colin. I think you can keep your hands off her for a little while longer. Remember what I said about no hanky-panky?" Susan joked, adding a playful smile. "Now skedaddle," she made a shooing motion with her hands, "and let me talk to my sister."

"Well, I, uh…" Colin's puzzled gaze darted between Emily and Susan. "I guess I'll see you in the morning then, Babe." He kissed her lightly on the lips before wandering off down the hall, muttering to himself.

Following him with her eyes, Emily swore she heard him repeat the words *hanky-panky* in there somewhere. A bit annoyed at the intrusion, she unlocked the door and pushed it open.

Susan followed her inside.

"What was so important that it couldn't wait until morning?" Emily shrugged out of her jacket and laid it on the bed, still feeling the taste of Colin's kiss on her lips.

"Your wedding gown. It probably got wrinkled on the trip, so I have a dry cleaner standing by to press it first thing in the morning." Susan opened the closet door and pulled the dress out.

Emily spun back toward her sister, her hands angrily fisting on her hips. "That's it?"

Susan's expression softened and her gaze fell to the dress she'd draped over her arm. "Well…no."

"What then?" Emily's voice rose with irritation.

Susan slowly raised her head and looked Emily in the eye. "It's Dad."

Emily's hands relaxed as her frustration quickly turned to concern. "What's happened?"

Quite a few years earlier, their father had been placed in a health care facility when his Alzheimer's disease had progressed and it was clear he needed help. Eventually, he began having a harder and harder time recognizing any of his children, or grandchildren. When he no longer knew who any of them were, it was too much for them, and both sisters stopped visiting him.

"I got an upsetting call late this afternoon from the facility he's in," Susan explained.

"A call? Why?"

"The woman who phoned, a Doctor Patel, claims Dad is getting worse, that he's sometimes belligerent. He needs more constant care and that means more money. They're raising his monthly charge by five hundred dollars to cover the extra nursing costs."

"Starting when?"

"The first of the year. They wanted to start next month, but I told her about Brian's accident and all the expenses, and she agreed to delay it until January. Although, I don't know what good putting it off a couple of months will do."

Emily dropped onto the edge of the bed, absorbing the news. Her mind began thinking through her options as to how she was going to come up with her share of the increase.

Susan settled beside her. "I know this isn't exactly the best way to start your new married life, Emily, but I thought you should know. With the mountain of bills piling up for Brian's medical care, I don't see how we can squeeze another five hundred dollars out of our budget. You know, the whole can't-get-blood-from-turnips thing."

"Yeah," Emily muttered as she nodded mindlessly, her thoughts drifting to the small balance in her checking account. There was no way she could expect anything more from her sister, especially not at this time. "I've always paid my share of the costs for Dad's expenses, you know that. I would never shirk my responsibility."

Susan brushed a strand of curls off Emily's face. "I know, hon."

An image of the wads of cash that Evan had hidden away in a safe deposit box before he died popped into her mind. She had discovered it, long after his death, but she hadn't wanted to spend a dime of it, not knowing where it may have come from.

Was it stolen? Or payment for a contract hit? Or was it ill-gotten gain from some other dangerous and nefarious undertaking he may have been involved in?

From what she had learned about Evan after his murder, any, or all, of those things could have been real possibilities.

"With you and Colin consolidating your household expenses, I was hoping..." Susan looked at her with uncertainty in her eyes.

"Don't you worry about the extra money." Emily draped a comforting arm around her sister and hugged her. "Colin and I can handle it."

~*~

After discussing their father's situation awhile longer, Susan left, taking Emily's wedding dress with her.

As Emily changed into her pajamas, thoughts of the cash in the safe deposit box floated in and out of her mind. Though she had avoided spending the money on herself, she had loaned some of it to a friend once, to help him out of a serious bind. He had since repaid her and she had put the money back into the safe deposit box, but she had never told Colin about it. Was that going to come back to bite her?

She went into the bathroom and brushed her teeth, imagining Evan's face in the mirror. *Where did all that money come from, Evan?* It wasn't as if she expected to get an answer, but she couldn't help but wonder about it.

After his death, Emily had slowly begun to discover clue after painful clue that her wonderful husband wasn't the man he'd made her believe he was. Yes, he had showered her with love and passion that most women only dreamed of, and he had fiercely protected her like she was a precious jewel. She felt nothing but safe and loved for the five years they were married, but that façade began to crumble as she'd uncovered the truth.

Why hadn't she ever told Colin about the money? She had told him about the other things she'd found in Evan's hidden safe deposit box—the mysterious old photograph, the various passports, the suspicious gun—but never the money. She stared at her own image in the mirror, directly into her own eyes. Was she being as secretive and deceptive with Colin as Evan had been with her?

"No!" The word rushed out with a painful rasp, escaping from her heart, through her lips.

She could never be like Evan, the way he had lied to her at every turn to keep his false persona intact. The questionable cash was the only thing she had ever hidden from Colin. But now, blood money or not, she was probably going to have to finally start dipping into it to pay for her father's care.

A shiver danced down her back as she continued to peer intently into the mirror, into her own eyes. She could no longer keep the money secret from Colin. Why had she wanted to? It wasn't that he would care she had the money, but now he would certainly want to know why she'd felt the need to hide it from him. She wanted to know the answer to that too.

Was it because it had been Evan's money? Because it represented his deceptions?

Or was it because Colin would see how totally in love with Evan she had been, so in love that she had swallowed whatever story he fed her—hook, line, and sinker? How Evan had held her in his spell and at his very touch her panties would melt?

Just the thought of them together, even now, made her body vibrate with desire.

She splashed cold water on her face, then buried it in a towel. Tomorrow she would look for the right opportunity to tell Colin about the money before he somehow found out on his own. Waiting until after the wedding wouldn't be fair to him—he had a right to know before they said I do.

But what if he told her he couldn't marry a liar?

CHAPTER FIFTEEN
Had Emily Lied?

IT WAS A LITTLE AFTER NINE o'clock on Thursday night. Isabel and Alex had just returned from their jaunt downtown, lugging a couple of bags full of souvenirs into their room. So much for window shopping.

"I think I'll take a shower before bed." Alex set the bags of treasures down on the dresser. "You won't get too lonely out here without me, will you?" He tossed her a mischievous look that told her he had something romantic on his mind.

"I think I'll manage," she replied with a teasing smile. "Don't be long."

Alex grinned and shut the bathroom door, just as Isabel's phone began to ring.

"Hello."

"Hey, this is Emily. I didn't interrupt anything, did I?"

"No, Alex is in the shower. Although, if you had

called a little later…"

"I get it," Emily said. "So, now's a good time to talk?"

What did she want to talk about? Maybe she'd been seeing visions of Evan again. "Everything okay, Em?"

"I've done a horrible thing and I have to come clean with Colin."

"How horrible?" Isabel sat down on the corner of the bed.

"What's that supposed to mean? Horrible is horrible."

Isabel was quite sure that Emily couldn't do something horrible if her life depended on it. "Tell me what you did and I'll tell you if you should worry about it."

"I lied to Colin."

That wasn't like Emily at all. "About what?"

"Well, not exactly lied."

Didn't think so.

"More like an omission. I didn't tell him something I should have."

"Like what?" Isabel asked.

"Something that I found."

"Stop beating around the bush, Emily, and come out with it." The small hairs on the back of Isabel's neck raised in anticipation. "What exactly happened?"

There was a long pause on the line.

"Emily?"

"Okay, here it is." Emily cleared her throat. "Evan left me some money in the safe deposit box he had hidden away and I never told Colin about it. I told him about all the other things I found in the box, but not

170

about the money."

"I see." Isabel's shoulders relaxed and the hairs on her neck laid back down. The way Emily had led up to it, she thought it would be something worse. Isabel already knew about all of what Emily had found in the box, including the money. Evan had told her about it before his death…but she couldn't tell Emily that.

Isabel's relationship with Evan had been different than Emily's relationship with him had been. Although, there was a time when Isabel had wanted what they had. She had grown fond of Evan when they'd worked together in DC, and she had begun to develop feelings for him—romantic feelings—but once Evan married Emily, Isabel moved on. After she'd relocated to Paradise Valley, Isabel fell head-over-heels in love with Alex and she found her own version of happiness in that department.

Long after his funeral, Emily discovered that Isabel had been Evan's handler, and she'd had to fight her way back into Emily's good graces for keeping that from her. It would serve no good purpose now to tell Emily that she knew all about the money, so she kept her mouth shut.

"That's all you have to say? I see?" Emily's voice was laced with a distinct level of irritation.

"I'm not sure what else you want me to say. Do you really think Colin would care that Evan left you some money?"

"No, but I think he will care that I didn't disclose it when I was telling him about all the other items, especially since some of those things helped us find Evan's killer. What if this is blood money?"

"Oh, Emily. I think you're getting yourself all worked up over nothing. The money was probably just a nest egg for you. Evan's line of work was very dangerous and he probably wanted to make sure you were taken care of. I'm sure that's all it was."

Isabel wasn't really sure, but it seemed to be what Emily needed to hear.

"Either way, I've got some explaining to do," Emily said.

"All you have to say is that Evan left you some money and you wanted him to know that. You don't have to go into the details about where you found it and when."

"You want me to hide the truth from him?" Emily's voice wavered, as if she was near tears.

"I want you to be happy. You love Colin and he loves you. Don't screw it up."

The sound of sniffles came across the phone line. "But I—"

"No buts! Colin is offering you something Evan never could."

"What's that?"

"A normal life. Take it and be happy."

~*~

Emily waited up for a while after her conversation with Isabel. She thought Colin might call, but he never did. He did eventually text her a sweet love message, wishing her a good night.

It was just as well. He would have heard the upset in her voice and pressed her to find out what was the matter. After talking with Isabel, she could see her friend's point—giving Colin all the details about the cash now would only open up something that was better left alone.

With so much on her mind, Emily tossed and turned for a few hours, until she finally drifted off to a deep sleep.

At a little after eight in the morning, her phone rang. She lazily reached for it on the nightstand. "Hello," she answered in a groggy voice, pushing her curls off her face.

"Wake up, sleepy head," Colin said cheerfully.

"Good morning to you too, sweetheart." Emily's response carried a touch of sarcasm. He wouldn't sound so chipper if he'd had the night she'd had.

"Everything okay with your sister, Babe? She sounded pretty serious last night."

"Yeah, it was just something about my dad. I'll tell you later." Emily yawned and pushed up on one elbow. "Come by in about an hour and we can go to breakfast."

"I'll let the others know to meet us in the lobby."

As soon as Emily hung up, she slung her legs over the side of the bed and rested on the edge of it for a moment, trying to get her eyes to focus before wandering into the bathroom. Sitting there, she thought she smelled a familiar scent. She sniffed the air. Couldn't be. But yet, she swore she caught a faint whiff of the same aftershave Evan used to wear.

"Am I going nuts?" She rubbed her eyes, then scrubbed her fingers back and forth through her tousled hair, trying to come fully awake. "Oh, God, this has got to stop."

Forcing herself to her feet, she tugged her nightgown over her head and threw it on the bed. "I need a shower and a strong cup of coffee."

~*~

As the friends filed out of the small café, appropriately named The Breakfast Place, Colin received a phone call from Chief Taylor. With the girls excitedly chatting about the wedding, he stepped away from them to answer it. "Morning, Chief. What's up?"

"I heard from the medical examiner this morning. She gave me the official cause of death. It appears that while our victim did suffer blunt-force trauma to the side of his head—which we saw the night he was found—his death was due to the stab wound in his chest."

"That makes sense," Colin replied. "If Ben had been stabbed first, the head wound wouldn't have bled like it did. His heart would have stopped pumping blood."

"Eyah, makes sense."

"I know he didn't die from the blunt-force trauma," Colin said, "but could the ME identify what Ben was hit with?"

"No, but she emailed me a picture of the wound. Looks like the killer used something flat, and—not really sure how to describe it—I guess kind of T-shaped or something. Anyway, why does it matter now? The stab wound is what killed him."

"It might not mean anything, but I'm hoping it could help us narrow down who our perp might be."

"Oh, I get it."

Emily came up behind Colin. "Did the ME say anything else?"

Colin relayed her question to the chief.

"She said the stab wound was deep but narrow, like a knife with a long skinny blade—like a fish fileting knife, maybe—right in the heart."

"Man, in an area like this, there must be hundreds of people who have those," Colin surmised.

"Have what?" Emily asked in the background.

Colin held a finger up to Emily and continued speaking to the chief. "Am I right?"

"Eyah," the chief responded.

"I'd like to get a look at the picture the ME sent over."

"I want to come too," Emily said, tugging on Colin's sleeve.

Colin nodded to her. "Maybe together we can figure out what it was, Chief."

~*~

Alex and Isabel had talked Camille and Maggie into going with them over to Seal Cove to the antique car museum. They invited Emily and Colin too, but they declined because of the case.

Leaving the door open, Alex climbed into the rental car and turned back to Colin as he pulled his seatbelt on. "Don't forget you promised to go fishing with me this afternoon. One o'clock, on the dock." Alex grinned at his own rhyming.

"One o'clock. I won't forget." Colin closed the car door for him.

As Maggie climbed into the back seat with Camille, Emily bent down to whisper to her friend. "And don't forget what you need to do this afternoon."

Maggie nodded. "Don't worry, we'll be back in a couple of hours."

"You guys have fun!" Emily called out, waving at her friends as they drove away.

Casually dressed for the cool weather, Emily and Colin headed on foot to the police station, just a few blocks away. As they approached the entrance, someone called her name and they both turned.

Whitley Donovan came rushing toward them, her floral dress billowing in the wind. Furiously waving one hand, with the other she held her deep green cardigan snuggly wrapped around her body. In the breeze, her auburn tresses floated around her shoulders.

When she reached Colin and Emily, she was nearly out of breath. "I'm glad I caught you, Emily."

"Calm down," she urged the young woman, whose cheeks were flushed from exertion. "Take a minute and breathe."

Whitley pulled in a few gasps of air and dug a small yellow note out of her dress pocket. She handed Emily the handwritten message that read, simply, *this Friday night*.

"I tried your cellphone and left you a voicemail." Whitley pressed a hand to her chest and sucked in another deep breath.

Emily looked at her phone and saw the voicemail icon. "It must have been so noisy in the restaurant I didn't hear it. Sorry."

Colin peered over Emily's shoulder and read the

note. "What does that mean?"

"It means they're taking the boat out tonight," Whitley replied. "Caleb said he had to leave this evening to pick up a couple in Boston first thing in the morning. He asked me to check on Momma while he was gone."

"Is your mom sick?" Emily asked. It wasn't like the poor girl didn't have enough on her mind.

"Not exactly. She's in the nursing home. Caleb always goes on Friday nights and spends a little time with her, but not tonight because he has to work."

Whitley's comment reminded Emily of her own father, and a sliver of guilt pricked her. She used to go to visit him whenever she could, but once he didn't know who she was anymore, what was the point?

"That can be expensive," Emily said, speaking from experience.

"I do what I can, but my brother pays the lion's share of her staying in that place. That's why he works the two jobs."

"The fishing boat and doing maintenance at the inn, right?" Emily confirmed.

Colin crossed his arms and his interest seemed to pique. "He's the maintenance man at the inn?"

"Oh, didn't I tell you that?" Emily asked ruefully. "Sorry."

"Is that important?" Whitley asked, her green eyes widening.

"We can't say at this point." Colin glanced at Emily and met her gaze. She could see his wheels turning.

She turned back to Whitley. "Isn't Caleb afraid he'll get caught in the storm tonight?"

Colin's eyes rounded at the prospect. "What

storm?"

"Reports are saying there's a storm down south, off the coast of Massachusetts," Whitley reported, "but the weatherman says it's turning and going east out into the Atlantic Ocean, so it's nothing for us to be concerned about. They had been getting hammered down around Boston, but it's supposed to be calm by mid—Mister, you look worried."

Colin rubbed his jaw and drew in a quick breath. "It's just that my friend and I are going fishing this afternoon." He cast Emily a wary glance. "The guide said he had a cancellation and cut the price in half if we wanted to go. No wonder we got such a good deal."

"Who are you going with?" Whitley asked.

"Harvey McKenna."

"I know Harv, he's an experienced fisherman. Don't worry, he wouldn't take you out if it wasn't safe. As long as you stay pretty close to the bay, you should be fine."

A pendant hanging around Whitley's neck, on a long silver chain, caught Emily's attention. It was rectangular with rounded corners and deep blue rhinestones covering the face of it. "That's a pretty necklace, Whitley. Very unusual."

She lifted the pendant and looked down at it with a sad smile. "Ben gave it to me for my birthday."

"That was sweet of him," Emily said.

Whitley nodded slightly, still holding it. "That was how Ben was." She paused and stared down at it as she rubbed her finger over the stones. She sighed and then looked up at Emily and Colin. "I've got to get back to work." She began backing away. "Good luck out on the boat!" Casually she waved a hand in the air as she turned and hurried toward the church.

"Let's get inside and see what the chief is up to," Colin glanced up at the cloudy gray sky, hesitation pooling in his eyes, "before it starts raining."

CHAPTER SIXTEEN
The Security Video

"HEY, CHIEF. ANYTHING NEW we should know about?" Colin asked as he and Emily strolled into the chief's office.

Seated at his desk, Chief Taylor was concentrating intently on his computer screen, but he looked up when they came through the door and his expression lightened. "As a matter of fact, there is. I finally got the security footage from the Rock Harbor Inn. Here, take a look-see."

Colin and Emily hooked their jackets on the coat rack and came around behind the desk for a good look. The chief clicked on the little arrow icon and the black-and-white images began to play. The video was grainy and dark. Poor lighting and thick tree branches in the way made it difficult to clearly make out what was happening.

"All I see are two shadowy figures standing there."

Colin squinted and cocked his head. "I assume they're talking...at least that's what it kind of looks like between the leaves."

"Wait for it," the chief sang. "There! Did you see that?" He hit the pause button.

"See what?" Emily quirked one side of her mouth.

Colin leaned down toward the monitor and rested a hand on the desk. "Did one guy just swing something?"

"Looks like he clobbered the other guy, maybe?" Emily added.

"Could be." The chief wrinkled his nose at the screen. "Let me play it again." He rewound the video and ran it once more. "Look there," the chief pointed at the image on the screen, "this guy fell to the ground and the other one ran off."

"How can you tell?" Emily asked, but got no reply.

"What do you think he hit him with?" Colin asked.

The chief shrugged. "Can't tell."

"Then what happened?" Emily asked.

"That's as far as I got before you two showed up."

"Could he have already been stabbed by this point?" Emily questioned. "And then the slam to his head finished him off?"

"No, I don't think so. Look at him," Colin said, "he's just lying there. If that were the case, how did his body wind up in the chair on your deck?"

"Why don't we watch and see," Chief Taylor suggested. "That is, if we can make it out."

In silence, the three huddled around the computer screen, straining to decipher the images and watching to see what happened next. Several minutes passed and nothing did.

"Come on," Colin groaned impatiently, hunched over the desk.

"This is fun," Emily commented sardonically as she crossed her arms and waited.

Colin straightened. "There has to be something coming, because that's not where his body was discovered."

After almost five minutes, the video showed the man on the ground stirring. He appeared to be trying to get to his feet a couple of times, but staggered back down.

"That must've been some crack on the head." The chief pointed to the screen. "Knocked him out for a while."

"Too bad someone didn't find him while he was on the ground." Emily shot a knowing glance at Colin and he held her gaze for a moment.

He knew what she was thinking. It had only been a few days ago that she had suffered a similar trauma when he discovered her out cold on the side of the house. If she'd been hit any harder, it could have been possible they wouldn't have made it to Rock Harbor, planning to get married on Saturday. "Yeah, too bad."

"The inn really needs to get a better security set up," Colin said, turning his attention back to the case at hand. "This video is ridiculously bad."

"Eyah, they've got the camera mounted in a bad place, looks like."

Finally, after a few tries, the victim, presumably Ben, struggled to his feet as another dark figure approached him. From their aggressive body language, pitching back and forth, they appeared to argue a bit when the second person thrust forward with what looked like the left arm, seeming to make contact with Ben's body. Something glinted in the low light. A knife maybe?

The man fell to the ground again and lay motionless. The other person, who seemed to be male too, based on the muscular build, squatted down and pulled Ben to a sitting position.

Was he grabbing Ben by his upper torso? They watched as it looked like he was dragging Ben away, in the direction of the rear decks that faced the pool side of the inn.

"So there were two people who attacked Ben," Emily gasped. "I never would have guessed."

"Certainly looks that way," the chief said.

Colin rubbed a few fingers over his jaw. "I wonder if the first one knew about the second one." Two people wanting to murder Ben on the same night? What were the chances?

"No way to tell," Emily softly replied. "Not yet anyway."

Colin turned to the chief. "Any luck finding the CD at Ben's office?"

"I went over to the church and had Whitley check Ben's computer, but nope, not there."

"What about the other computers they have?" Colin reclaimed a chair. "Seemed like there was one on each desk when we paid the pastor a visit."

"I'm way ahead of you, Detective. I had her check them all, but still nothing."

"Where could he have hidden it?" Colin muttered under his breath. Not at the bed and breakfast, not at his office. "You think maybe he had it on him when he was killed?"

"Oh, I see where you're going with that." Chief Taylor's eyes lit up with understanding as he rocked back in his chair. "If he was killed by someone working for the kingpin, they probably checked his body for that CD. Maybe he had it on him and now it's in his old boss's hands."

"Only if Mr. Dominick knew Ben had burned a copy for himself," Emily piped in, taking the seat next to Colin.

"Which we don't really know," Colin remarked.

"Well here's another thought for you, fellas." Emily cast them a mischievous grin, leaning back in the chair. "As I was listening to you guys go back and forth about the CD, it occurred to me that we all should take a big step into the twenty-first century."

"Huh?" The chief scratched his head. "What do you mean by that?"

"We've saved computer data on CDs for what, the last twenty years? But think about it—what is a more current way of saving that information nowadays?" she asked. "A smaller, more portable way…"

As if the light bulb came on in Colin's mind, he sat up straight in his seat. "A thumb drive."

"A what, now?" the chief asked.

"A thumb drive, Chief," Emily repeated. "A tiny device you plug into one of the USB ports on your computer."

The chief studied his computer, his head bobbing from side to side as he checked it out. "A USB port?"

"So, instead of looking for a CD," Colin reasoned

aloud, "maybe Ben actually stored his boss's financial data on a thumb drive, and we should be looking for that."

"Or heaven forbid, a cloud drive," Emily mused. "But let's not go there yet."

"A cloud drive?" the chief questioned with a frown. He got no reply.

"If he hid it in a cloud drive, we're SOL," Colin said.

"It would be easy enough for him to save it to a portable thumb drive," Emily continued, "and they come in all kinds of fun shapes and sizes now. Sometimes they don't even look like a thumb drive."

"That's right," Colin agreed. "I've seen them look like different bobbles you'd hang on a key ring or a lanyard."

New information should make the search easier, but this only made it more difficult. The drive could be disguised as any number of other items.

"The thumb drive could have been on Ben's key ring," Emily offered.

"We didn't find a set of keys in his room," Colin said, "so he may have had them with him when he died."

The chief leaned back in his chair. "I'll give the ME a call. She would still have Ben's personal effects."

"Assuming whoever killed him didn't get their hands on it," Colin said.

"Or perhaps he may have given it to someone else for safekeeping," Emily suggested.

"But who?" the chief asked. "Ella? Pastor Jansen? His secretary?"

"Whitley?" Emily's eyes lit up and she scooted to

the edge of her chair. "Listen, guys, what if it looks like a sparkly pendant dangling on a chain and it's hanging around a certain young redhead's pretty little neck?"

~*~

Emily's phone jangled in her pocket. She didn't recognize the number, so she answered it with some curiosity. "Hello?"

"Emily, I'm glad I caught you. This is Whitley."

"Oh. Hello, Whitley." *Speak of the devil.* Emily glanced at Colin and then the chief before speaking into the phone. "Is everything okay?"

"You had asked yesterday if I knew of anyone else that Ben was close to, or someone who may have had a problem with him. I don't know why I didn't think of it sooner, but there were a few times I knew of that he had met with Brian Henderson."

Emily's brother-in-law? How could he be connected with this? Susan and the children would be devastated if he had something to do with Ben's demise.

"Brian Henderson?" She eyed Colin. His face twisted into a puzzled expression at the name. "And they argued?"

"It's probably nothing," Whitley continued, "but I did see them quarreling once in the parking lot a couple of weeks or so ago. Brian looked pretty angry. So did Ben."

"But, Whitley, Brian was in a car accident about that long ago. Are you sure it was him?"

The chief was looking a bit curious now too.

"I'm positive. As a matter of fact, I think it may

have been the day of the accident, now that you mention it." Whitley paused. "Sorry, I'd forgotten about it until after I saw you this afternoon and something jogged my memory about Brian. He's related to you, right?"

"Yes, he's my brother-in-law. Do you know Brian and Susan?"

"No, not really, but I know the chief's wife and she's good friends with your sister. You know small towns, everyone knows everyone else's business whether you want them to or not."

"How very true." Emily thought fondly of her own small town for a moment, then brought her focus back to the case. "Anything else you can remember?"

"No, that's about it. I'll call you if anything else comes to mind."

"Hey, Whitley, before you go," Emily exchanged a glance with Colin, "I can't stop thinking about that beautiful pendant you're wearing. I'd love to get one for myself before we leave Rock Harbor. Do you happen to know where Ben got that one?"

"No, he never said. He did say it was valuable, though, and that I should be very careful with it. You might try some of the nicer jewelry shops on the island."

"I'll do that. Thanks." After she hung up, Emily filled Colin and the chief in on her conversation.

"We need to get a closer look at that pendant." Colin stood. "With the Feds' star witness gone, it might be just what they're looking for to put Mr. Dominick away."

"Don't get your hopes up until we know," Emily warned. "It might be nothing more than a necklace, but you're right, until we can get our hands on it, we really won't know." She had better figure out a way to get a closer look at it, because Colin could never leave a detail like that hanging.

"She swears she saw Ben arguing with Susan's husband the day of the car accident?" Colin asked.

"Yes, but she didn't know what it was about." Emily retrieved her jacket from the coat hooks and slid it on.

Colin checked his watch. "We've got some time before I have to meet Alex down at the dock. Why don't we go pay your brother-in-law a visit, Emily?"

She handed him his coat. "While you're out fishing, I'll see if I can get a better look at Whitley's necklace."

The chief's chair creaked as he rose from it. "You'll let me know if either of you learn anything, won't you?"

"Sure." Colin nodded, shrugging his coat on.

"I'll stay in front of the computer and take a gander at the video a few more times," the chief said. "Maybe something will pop up—who knows?"

~*~

Brian and Colin had never met, so Emily happily made the introductions around the hospital bed. They chatted casually for a few minutes, talking about the last-minute wedding Susan had organized and how Brian wished he could be at the ceremony.

Keenly aware of the time, Emily steered the conversation to the fact that she and Colin were helping the Chief of Police with Ben Kinney's murder investigation. "Brian, someone told me today that they saw you arguing with Ben a couple of weeks ago and it looked pretty heated."

"Really, Emily? I've been laying in this hospital bed for the past two weeks. Are you saying you think maybe I killed him?"

"No, it's not that," she was quick to say. "I was just hoping you could tell us what the argument was about, then maybe it would shed some light on his state of mind and the events leading up to the murder."

"It was a personal matter." Brian's lips grew tight. "It couldn't have had anything to do with why he was killed."

"That's probably true, but you never know," Colin said. "Sometimes what seems totally unconnected could provide a missing clue. What have we got to lose?"

Brian answered Colin with a slight nod of his head.

"So..." Emily said, rolling her hand as a gesture urging him to let the story out.

Brian looked out the window, to the sky of gray clouds, the expression in his eyes appearing strained as he thought about what he was going to say.

"Brian?" she softly urged.

He brought his gaze back in and settled it on Emily. "Like I told you, it was personal."

"I'd never want to pry, but this is important." Was it something embarrassing? Something about Susan?

Brian pulled in a deep breath and blew it out. "Okay, but promise me you'll keep this under your hat."

Tiny hairs bristled on the back of her neck. Had he been stepping out on her sister, or something equally as shameful, and that's why he seemed so reluctant to admit it?

"Sure," Colin quickly responded. "Mums the

word."

Colin's hasty agreement irritated Emily—what did he have at stake? Of course he could jump right in and make that promise, it wasn't his sister Brian might be talking about. Emily held her breath.

"Ben is my cousin." He paused and a shadow of sadness passed over his face. "Or, at least, he was."

Emily exhaled, grateful it was not something worse. "Why do you want to keep *that* a secret?"

"Because he's a criminal, of course. I knew he was lying to the whole town, not telling anyone who he really was, but I couldn't turn him in. He's family, you know?"

"How does Mayor McCormack know him?" Colin asked.

"How? That's easy. She's his mother."

"His mother? She told us she was..." Colin cast a glance at Emily. "Well, it doesn't matter now. So that makes Mayor McCormack your aunt."

"Sort of."

Emily tilted her head as a frown formed on her brow. "I don't understand. What do you mean *sort of*?"

"Ben's father and my mother were brother and sister. Uncle Charles died when Ben was about four. Ella raised him by herself in New Hampshire. We were close when we were growing up, but then they moved away when he was about twelve. We lost track of each other."

"So you didn't keep in contact with Mrs. McCormack either?" Emily asked.

"No, and she wasn't McCormack then, she was Kingston. It wasn't until Susan and I moved to the island that I found out she lived here with her second husband.

We're cordial with each other, but it's not like we're really family anymore."

"So what about Ben?" Colin inquired.

"I'd seen his picture on Internet news sites, you know, about the arrest and the trial and stuff. And I remember all the press coverage when he disappeared, and how the FBI was hunting for him. So, when he showed up in Rock Harbor, I knew right away who he was. He looked pretty much the same as when we were kids, only taller, darker hair, with a five o'clock shadow."

"Wouldn't anyone else in town recognize him from the news?" Emily asked.

"The news photos showed him with short, neat hair and dressed in a business suit. By the time he came to Rock Harbor, his hair had grown out a bit and hung down on his forehead, kind of loose and shaggy."

Emily recalled thinking his wavy brown hair was a bit unkempt when they first met.

"And sometimes he wore glasses, which I think were just plain glass, to change his appearance," Brian added.

"Okay, so you recognized him and nobody else did, that you know of," Colin said, showing a little impatience at the pace of the story. "But what was the fight about?"

"I was trying to get him to turn himself in. I figured if the Feds wanted him to testify against a big dog, there could be someone looking to kill him. Not only was he putting himself in danger, but his mother and maybe other people in town."

"Like you and your family?" Colin questioned.

"That's right. I have Susan and the kids to think about, but he wouldn't do it."

"When's the last time you saw him?" Emily asked.

"I stopped by the bed and breakfast that evening after work to try again to talk some sense into him, get him to see he needed to turn himself in before someone got hurt, but no, he wouldn't budge." Brian ran a hand through his hair, sadness pooling in his eyes—or was it something else? His gaze drifted out the window again, his bottom lip quivering. "Why wouldn't he listen to me?"

Emily gently took hold of one of Brian's hands, hoping to calm him enough to get him to continue opening up. "Then what happened?"

Brian closed his eyes briefly, his features twisting as if he was reliving the moment in his mind, then his face relaxed and he opened his eyes. His serious gaze moved back to Emily. "I drove home. Or, at least, I tried to. That's the night someone ran me off the road."

CHAPTER SEVENTEEN
The Boys Cast Off

BRIAN LAID IN THE HOSPITAL BED recounting the accident to Colin, as he had to Emily when she'd come to visit him a couple of days before.

"You honestly think it was just a drunk driver trying to pass you?" Colin questioned.

"At the time I did, but now..." He looked down at his hands folded across his abdomen and shook his head slowly.

"But why you?" Emily asked.

Colin gave her a slight nod. "That's what I was wondering too, Brian. Why you?"

"I have no idea." Brian rubbed a couple of fingers over his forehead, closing his eyes, as if his head was aching. "I've been laying here for days wracking my brain, trying to figure that out."

"Maybe..." Emily lifted Brian's chin and slowly moved his face to the side to study his profile. Then she gently pulled it back to look at him straight on. "Same face shape, same wavy brown hair, same build. You know," she crossed her arms and took a step back to study him further, "you and Ben look enough alike that you could pass for brothers."

"Brothers?" Colin's eyes lit up. He must have figured out where she was going. "You said you left the bed and breakfast and were heading home when the accident happened?"

"That's right."

"And it was already dark?" she questioned.

"Yeah."

"What do you drive, Brian?" Emily asked.

"A dark green Subaru Forester. Why?"

"And Ben?" Colin asked.

"Ella loaned him her car, a Forester too, a little older than mine but still in good shape."

"What color?"

"Dark blue."

Emily's and Colin's eyes met. That had to be it.

"What?" Brian groaned.

"In the dark," Emily explained, "maybe whoever ran your car into the ravine thought you were Ben. You were coming from the B and B, after all. And with all the other similarities…"

~*~

"Hmm, so this is the boat you're going ocean fishing in?" Emily stood on the edge of the dock and admired the sleek vessel while her three girlfriends milled around, oohing and aahing over the different boats.

"Yes, ma'am," the captain said from the boat. "She's a Sea Ray 370 Express Cruiser with plenty of elbow room and a steady glide."

"And you're not concerned about the storm some people are saying is coming in?" Emily quirked an eyebrow at Colin, though her question was for the captain.

"I check the weather regularly, ma'am, and they say the storm's headed out to sea. We're not going that far out, so no worries." The captain started up the engine.

"Besides," Colin puffed out his chest, "what's a little wind and rain among men?" He added a few manly grunts for effect.

Alex grunted too, then they had a good laugh.

"Hmm." Emily wasn't convinced, but she wasn't going to play the nagging wife when they weren't even married yet.

"We'll be fine, Emily," Alex added. "Don't worry so much."

Isabel didn't look convinced either. "For landlubbers, you guys are taking this pretty well."

"Give me a kiss for good luck, Isabel, and we'll be back before you know it."

She did as her husband requested and added a hug for good measure.

"Don't I get a kiss too?" Colin asked.

"Heck no," Alex snapped. "Get your own woman."

Colin tucked a free hand around Emily's waist and grinned. "I was referring to my woman."

Emily cupped his face between her hands and kissed him softly. "Make sure you come back to me,

Colin."

"Get aboard, fellas, if you're still planning on going," the captain called out as he began to untie the boat from the dock.

Colin and Alex stepped over the gangway and took their seats, decked out for a cold, damp afternoon of fishing.

The girls stood on the dock and waved as the men sped away on the choppy gray waters, a flock of seagulls squawking overhead.

"Now," Maggie said in a low voice, leaning close to Emily, "which one is the inn manager's boat?"

Emily's gaze drifted around as she surveyed the boats along the dock, spotting the surly Rosco Ciminella moving about on the Hoosier Daddy. "Three slips down, but don't look now," she said, keeping her voice down. "One of the workers is on the boat."

"Okay," Maggie whispered.

"Just glance at it as we pass by. With a little luck, you can get Eric to bring you down here later, like we planned."

"I'll do my best."

~*~

Susan phoned Emily to let her know that she hadn't yet located a minister to marry them, but not to worry, she would find one. Her wedding dress was being pressed at the cleaners, and Susan would pick it up in the morning and bring it by the inn.

"That man of yours is behaving himself, isn't he?"

"Behaving himself?" What did she mean by that?

The hanky-panky speech again?

"He's a sexy guy, that Colin Andrews," Susan said. "Testosterone oozing out all over, just waiting to have his way with you."

"Do you actually hear yourself when you talk?" Emily asked, not at all trying to couch the sarcasm.

"You know what I mean."

"Well, I can't argue, he is a sexy hunk of a man." Emily let out a little giggle as she thought of his smoky hazel eyes, his handsome face, that rock-hard body. The thought of it was beginning to get her excited. She took a deep breath to calm herself. "But he's a whole lot more than that, Susan. He's the best man I know."

"Hey!" Susan chided. "My Brian isn't exactly chopped liver."

"No, he's not, of course. He's wonderful—for you."

"I have to agree with you, Emily, your Colin is a fine man and I believe you two will be very happy. You deserve it after all you've been through."

Emily sensed her sister had stopped the sentence just short of saying after all she'd been through with Evan.

"Now, about the rehearsal dinner—"

"Do you mind if we skip the rehearsal dinner, Sis?" Emily asked.

"What? Why?"

"The girls want to take me out for some fun, a little bachelorette party, they said, before I become an old married lady. Oh, and, of course, you're invited too."

Susan grew quiet. That wasn't a good sign.

"Susan?"

"I'm here." Her voice was high and thin.

"I hope you don't mind. Camille's daughter is here from college, and Colin's mom should be here by then too. We plan to take them with us. Won't you come too? We'll make a party of it."

"I might join you later." Susan gave a soft sigh. "I'll text you when I'm free and you can let me know where you all are."

When she's free? She was planning to be available for the rehearsal dinner she had planned, which was nothing more than all of them having dinner together in a reserved back room of some restaurant. It sounded more like Emily had hurt her sister's feelings. "Look, Susan, I know you made plans, and I hate to change things at the last minute, but—"

"No, no. I'll simply cancel our reservations and you can do what you want." Susan's words were cool and quick. "Like I said, text me."

"Okay." She hadn't meant to throw a wet blanket on Susan's plans, but the bachelorette party sounded like so much more fun. Maybe Susan would change her mind and join them.

~*~

Camille and Maggie decided to head over to Southwest Harbor to do a little shopping. Some of the locals had told them it was the best shopping on the island and they were both eager to check it out.

Emily and Isabel chose to stop in at the West Street Café for a quick bite of lunch and something warm to drink. The nippy breeze and drizzly gray day made a cup of hot coffee and some clam chowder sound absolutely perfect.

The interior of the café was done in a cheery yellow, with white paint trimming the large windows that ran across the front and all along one side. The hostess sat them in one of the red vinyl booths by a window, giving them a view of the street and part of the wharf. The place was fairly empty and quiet, it being early afternoon, and the delicious scent of bacon and cinnamon rolls hung in the air.

"With the wedding tomorrow, time is running out for you to help solve this case," Isabel said, once they were served their orders. "While the guys are off fishing, I wondered if there was anything I could help you work on."

Emily stirred sugar into her coffee. "That's hard to say, not knowing if Ben was murdered to keep him from testifying in New York, or if he was digging around in this heroin trafficking mess."

She shared with Isabel all that she and Colin had discovered so far. "Ben's secretary thinks it's her fault he's dead because she's the one who told him about the heroin."

"What does the police chief have to say about all this?"

"Alvin? Not much. He's pretty green when it comes to murder investigations. He's never been part of one and he's soaking up what we tell him like a sponge."

"So you and Colin are doing most of the work?"

"Well, trying to keep it in an advisory capacity. We don't want to overstep. Chief Nelson, back home, said he doesn't mind us helping Chief Taylor, but in the end, the investigation has to be his responsibility—not ours.

Colin is trying to get Alvin to think things through with us."

"That young chief will appreciate that when you guys are gone."

"So, now that I've brought you up to speed on where we are, Isabel, what do you think? Murdered by a hired assassin for the kingpin in New York or killed by the drug runners?"

Isabel gave her a pensive look before answering. "I always like to say that forensic evidence doesn't lie, but the problem is, you don't have any. No blood, no hairs, no clear video."

"What did cops do fifty years ago, before we had a fingerprint database and DNA testing?" Emily gave her head a light shake and took a sip of her coffee.

"Fifty years ago? Heck, even twenty years ago. The technology keeps getting better all the time. But years ago, before all that, they had to go primarily on eyewitness testimony, motive, and opportunity to commit the crime."

"Well, for us, eyewitness testimony is out—we've got none of that so far. That video tape was so grainy and obscured, it could have been Big Foot and we couldn't tell."

Isabel chuckled.

"And motive?" Emily continued. "Again, it's a toss-up—to stop Ben from testifying against some powerful people, or to keep him from exposing the heroin business in this area—take your pick."

"That only leaves opportunity." Isabel set her cup down. "Who had opportunity that night, between six and eight pm?"

"Whitley, his secretary, for one, but she was in love with the man."

"That doesn't mean she couldn't have done it," Isabel said. "Love is one of the top motives for murder. Now, who else can we add to the list?"

"If Whitley was right about the drugs, then I'd say Eric Malone or his men, Rosco or Caleb. But if it was about the trial, then it could be anyone wanting to collect the bounty."

"Do we know why Ben was outside of the inn?"

"To meet someone maybe?"

"Do you know if the chief checked Ben's phone records?"

"They tried. Colin mentioned that they couldn't find that he had phone service, at least not one in any of his names. Maybe the chief can have some of his men check calls made to and from the bed and breakfast."

"And the church," Isabel added. "He could have made calls from his office. Each extension should have its own number. But he'll probably need a warrant."

"But if it was someone who came to town specifically to kill Ben for the reward, how will we ever figure out who it was? They could have slipped into town, done the job, and left before anyone even knew they were here. It's not like they have security cameras on the roads around here. Hmmm…" Emily tapped a quick beat on the table. "Isabel, did I tell you about Susan's husband?"

"The guy with two broken legs?"

"Yes, Brian."

Emily explained to Isabel that Brian had confessed that Ben was his cousin, and that he had confirmed what

Whitley had told them about the two men arguing earlier in the day before he was forced off the road and into the ravine. She also mentioned her own conclusion that Brian and Ben had a distinct family resemblance and drove similar vehicles.

"And you think a hit man mixed Brian up with Ben?"

"It is possible, don't you think?" Emily took a spoonful of her chowder.

"Well..." Isabel pursed her lips as she thought about it. "Similar cars, similar-looking men, in the dark, leaving the bed and breakfast where Ben lived...anything's possible."

"See our quandary? There's nothing clear cut pointing to a specific suspect. Only wild fingers pointing in all different directions." Emily ran a frustrated hand through her hair. "Maybe the same person who ran Brian off the road came back later and finished the job."

"All right, you're looking stressed over this. Let's talk about something else for a while," Isabel suggested. "I find that getting my mind on other things, and then coming back to the case, helps me look at it with fresh eyes."

"That's my wish for Colin." Emily gazed out the window, toward the bay as a small flock of seagulls flew overhead. "It'll do him good to be out fishing for a few hours, clear his head, you know?"

"And how about you, Emily? Getting nervous about the wedding tomorrow?"

Emily turned back to Isabel and smiled. "Excited more than nervous, but..."

Isabel took a sip and set her coffee cup down. "But

what?"

"But I can't seem to get away from these visions of Evan. They had better go away once we're married."

"He's still bothering you?"

Emily glanced out the window again, watching a cuddling young couple stroll by. "Yeah. This morning, I swear I got a whiff of his aftershave again."

"I wish he would leave you alone—his ghost, I mean, you know? I wish his ghost would quit haunting you."

Emily nodded, bringing her gaze back inside. "Me too, but I don't believe in ghosts."

"Then what?"

"Imagination is a powerful thing, Isabel. With the wedding planning and everything, I think I'm manifesting images from the last time I got married. That time, I never entertained the idea of something going wrong, and then Evan almost stood me up, so this time I think I am preparing myself for anything. I think it is simply old memories being stirred up."

Isabel flashed her an I-told-you-so look.

"Go ahead, say it."

"Say what? That I said that from the beginning?"

"Yes, Isabel. You told me so, and I think you were right."

"You'll be fine once you and Colin finally say *I do*. Evan's ghost will have no choice but to quit bothering you then." Isabel smiled and patted Emily's hand across the table. "Now, finish your chowder before we get back to the case."

~*~

After lunch, Emily had finished telling Isabel about her suspicions, including that she thought Whitley's pendant may, in fact, be a thumb drive with the missing information the Feds were after. So, they left the café and headed to the church, to visit Whitley at her office. Maybe they could get a closer look at it.

"Sorry, Whitley is gone for the day," Pastor Jansen told them. "Is there something I can help you with?"

"We'd like her home address, if you don't mind," Emily replied.

"Well, I don't normally give out that information, but these are extenuating circumstances, and I know she's fond of you, Emily. Let me call the bookkeeper and get it for you." The pastor went to the phone on the reception desk and made the call.

"What if she's not there?" Isabel asked in a low voice.

Emily shrugged. "I'm not sure."

"There you go." Pastor Jansen pulled a page off a small notepad and handed it to Emily. "It's just a few blocks from here. Anything else?"

"That should do it." Emily smiled. "If you see her, tell her I have some more questions about that pendant I liked so much."

"Will do."

The girls left and beat it over to the address on the note. They knocked and waited, then knocked again, but there was no answer.

"Where could she be?" Emily closed her eyes and thought for a moment. "The nursing home."

"What nursing home?"

"Whitley's mother is in a nursing home. She told

me earlier she was going over there today to check in on her."

"Do you have any idea where it is?" Isabel asked.

Emily pulled out her phone. "No, but the chief will." She called him and got the name of the home, its address, and directions how to get there.

They walked a short four blocks and caught Whitley coming out the front door of the home as they approached. "Whitley!"

The young woman smiled as she saw them coming her way. "Emily, what a surprise."

"Whitley, this is my friend, Isabel."

The two shook hands and smiled politely.

Whitley was not wearing the pendant, which made Emily a little suspicious. "I don't see that lovely necklace you had on earlier."

"No, I gave it to my mother, temporarily. She was asking me all sorts of questions about it—how much it cost me, where I got it, who gave it to me? You know, like that. I thought it'd be best to avoid the whole unpleasant scene and I offered to let her wear it. She seemed happy with that."

"Yes," Isabel said, "my mother is exactly the same way."

Emily recognized Isabel was attempting to identify with Whitley, to get her to relax and open up. She followed suit. "Yes, my mom, too."

"I'll be back tonight and figure out a way to get it back from her. Maybe she won't even remember having it, dementia, you know."

"Oh, I'm sorry to hear that." Emily really was sorry, knowing from experience what Whitley had to look forward to with her mother.

"Say, did you have any luck finding a necklace like it?" Whitley asked Emily.

"No, not yet. I was hoping to get a closer look at yours."

"You're welcome to take another look at it," Whitley said, "but with my mom having it...it won't be today."

"How about tonight?" Isabel suggested. "We'll be out on the town. You could give Emily a call when you've gotten it back and we can stop by."

"Do you mind?" Emily asked. "It's just that Colin and I are leaving on Sunday and—"

"Oh sure. No problem. That is, if I can get it back from her any time soon."

~*~

Later that afternoon, while the men were still out fishing, Emily met Maggie in the lobby of the inn. She was dressed in tight jeans and a winter-white ski jacket over a snug-fitting turquoise sweater.

"Ready to go?" Emily pitched her head in the direction of the front desk, where Eric Malone stood, checking in a middle-aged couple.

Maggie nonchalantly glanced over as well, then brought her attention back to Emily. "Ready as I'll ever be."

"Did you manage to fit the wire under that sweater?"

Maggie appraised herself then leaned in close enough to whisper to Emily. "I did. But why do I need to wear a wire? You think this is goin' to get rough?"

"No, nothing to worry about." Emily waved her hand casually at her friend. "But just to be safe, I've got the other end of it in my purse, with these little headphones." She stuck one of them in her ear. "Let's do a sound check. Say something."

"What would you like me to say?"

"That was perfect. Loud and clear. Now, Maggie, I'll be listening the whole time. If you need my help, just say the word *cinnamon*."

A slight frown formed on Maggie's brow. "Why would I say that?"

"Like a code word for *I need help*."

"But that's crazy. How would I use the word cinnamon?"

"You could say something like *it smells like cinnamon in here*, or something like that."

"Okay, cinnamon."

"Got the tracker?" Emily asked.

Maggie patted the front pocket of her form-fitting jeans.

"No, it'd be better if you stuck it in one of your jacket pockets," Emily said, taking a quick peak at the front desk, "easier to get to it without our Mr. Malone noticing."

Maggie complied. "There. Happy?"

Emily took another glance toward the manager. "Okay, you're up." She walked away and sat on one of the plush chairs in the lobby, watching Maggie sashay over to the front desk as the couple wandered off down the hall toward their room.

CHAPTER EIGHTEEN
Maggie's Ploy

EMILY LISTENED IN AS MAGGIE made small talk with Eric Malone at the front desk, asking about recommendations for restaurants and things to do around town. She asked him how long he had been the manager of the lovely Rock Harbor Inn and did he enjoy running such a magnificent place.

Eric appeared pleased that Maggie had stopped by. As the conversation went back and forth, Maggie got Eric to open up about his side business and how, in a year or two, he expected to be able to leave the inn and operate a small fleet of boats full-time.

Emily watched as Maggie leaned her ample breasts on the high counter as she oohed and aahed over his grand plans.

"Cruising from here to Boston? Oh my, that would be fabulous, Mr. Malone," Maggie gushed.

"Oh, please, call me Eric."

"Okay, Eric."

Emily envisioned Maggie batting her big blue eyes at him.

"I'd love to see your big ol' boat sometime," Maggie went on. "I've never been on one before and yours just sounds so wonderful. Does it have a comfy cabin below?"

Emily couldn't see Maggie's face, but from the position of her body and the various expressions of interest on the manager's face, she could tell Maggie was having quite an effect on the man.

"Yes, it has a spacious cabin below, with all the amenities—a kitchen, a nice bathroom, and a comfortable queen stateroom."

"A big ol' bed on a boat? Oh, I'd just *love* to see it," Maggie said, drawing out the word love with her sexy Texas drawl.

Don't push too hard, Maggie.

"You would?"

Even from across the lobby, Emily saw the man's eyes light up.

"That is, if you have the time. I know you're a big important man around this place."

A broad smile spread across Eric's face. "For you, I'll make the time."

"Of course, I'm only here for a short while though…"

Eric Malone peered down at his watch. "You know, I have a break coming, right about now." His face spread into a wide grin. "Just let me get someone to watch the front desk here and I'll take you down to see my boat."

Before long, the manager brought a young woman

up front to take over for him. Emily recognized her as the clerk who was there when she ran in to report the dead body on her deck.

"Shall we?" Eric made a sweeping gesture with his hand toward the front door.

Maggie giggled. "Absolutely."

The two walked out the door, heading for the driveway. Emily gave them a little space before she got up and followed them, at a safe distance, down to the docks.

~*~

"This is my boat," Eric stated proudly, motioning toward the large forty-foot white trawler.

"Oh, Hoosier Daddy. That's clever," Maggie said, referring to the name of the boat.

"I like it." He took her hand and helped her over the gangway and onto the boat.

"It's so pretty, all white and sparkly." Maggie stuck her hands in her jacket pockets as she took a seat on the luxurious white cushions around the stern of the boat.

"We offer deluxe fishing excursions, in addition to the day cruises to and from Boston."

"That sounds excitin'. Maybe I'll take one of those cruises someday."

"I think you'd find that it's a comfortable long-distance cruiser, designed with seakeeping abilities in the open waters. The fantail stern here," he made a sweeping gesture with his hand, "provides good buoyancy in a following sea."

Even listening through the earphones, it was

obvious Eric was trying to impress Maggie.

"Seakeepin' abilities? A followin' sea?" Maggie questioned. "You lost me."

"Seakeeping waters means the open ocean and a following sea is, well, when the sea is coming from astern, over the back of the boat—following."

"Oh m'gosh, that sounds dangerous. Like that movie *The Perfect Storm*. Did you see that movie? Scared me to death. Have you taken this boat out in dangerous waters like that?"

He sat down beside her. "Well, no. I've never actually had to test it out in an angry storm, but that's what the man who sold it to me said."

From where Emily had stopped and hidden herself near the dock, she watched the interaction between Maggie and Eric. She felt her coat pocket, where she had tucked her gun, in case she had to rescue her friend.

"What kind of boat is that really big one over there?" Maggie asked, pointing toward a vessel a good five times the size of the Hoosier Daddy.

Emily assumed Maggie was taking the opportunity of making Eric look away to pull the tracker out of her pocket and stuff it down between two cushions—at least, she hoped so.

Eric stood and looked to where Maggie had pointed. "That's a whale watcher," he replied, turning back to Maggie and taking a seat again. "If you're going to be here long enough, that would be a fun thing for you and your friends to do."

"It's getting kind of chilly out here." Maggie pulled her jacket tighter around her chest. "How about a tour of the cabin?"

"Sure. Right this way." Eric opened the door that led below and held it for her.

Maggie descended the few steps. "Oh!" she gasped loudly.

Emily had moved down to the dock, waiting about thirty feet away, pretending to be looking at the boats. At Maggie's gasp, her senses perked up, detecting possible danger.

"Hello there," Maggie went on. "I wasn't expectin' anyone down here."

Who was there?

Eric stepped down right behind Maggie. "Hey, Rosco. I didn't know you'd be here. He's one of my employees who runs the boat for me. He didn't scare you, did he?"

Emily inched closer to Hoosier Daddy, her hand on the weapon in her pocket.

"A little startled, is all."

"Just cleaning up, boss, getting ready for the next trip." Rosco grunted. There was a gruffness to his voice that sounded like trouble. "I'll come back later." He came up out of the cabin and stepped off the boat, onto the dock.

Thank goodness.

But what if he recognized Emily? She struck up a quick conversation with an older couple lounging on their boat nearby, asking them about the area, while keeping her back to Rosco, until he stomped off past her.

That was close.

"Eric," Maggie's voice drew Emily back to her friend on the boat, "your man didn't seem to like me bein' here."

"Don't mind him. He doesn't like anyone."

"Then why do you keep him around? I'd think he would offend your customers."

"He pretty much keeps to himself. He maintains the boat and keeps it clean when he's not behind the controls, piloting her. Now, my other guy, Caleb, he's the one who caters to the guests. He's more the people person. You'd like him."

As she listened to Eric talk about Caleb, Emily thought about him and his sister, Whitley. She prayed he wasn't involved in trafficking heroin—for Whitley's sake. But only time would tell, as this operation played out. If he was, regardless of their mother depending on him to cover the cost of her care, he would have to pay for his part in the crime.

"Let me give you a quick tour. This here is one of the two staterooms. Pretty sweet, huh?"

"Ooh, big bed for a boat," Maggie gushed.

"And very comfortable," he cleared his throat, "or so I've heard."

Did he say *bed*? Whitley had told Emily that Eric had tried to come on to her, here on his boat. Emily was getting nervous. "Come on," she murmured under her breath. "The tracker is planted, now get out of there, Maggie."

"It's a beautiful boat, Eric. You could fit a lot of folks down here."

"That's how you make money with this thing. The more you can carry, the better," he said. "Go ahead. Sit on the bed and see how you like it? Lay down, if you want."

Oh no. "Be smart, Maggie."

Emily heard a *ping*.

"That's my phone," Eric said. "Text message. I better check it." He paused a moment. "Well, I've got to get back to the inn. Someone's asking for me."

"Yes, I have to get back too. My friends will be expectin' me."

Emily scooted up the dock, toward the inn, when she heard them talk about leaving. Partially hidden by the rock wall, she watched as Eric helped Maggie over the gangway and onto the dock. "Thank you so much, Eric," Emily heard Maggie say.

The air was getting chilly now, so Emily scurried back to the inn, making sure to stay as far as possible ahead of them.

Maggie and Eric hurried back to the inn at a brisk clip as well, reaching the place within a few minutes, not far behind Emily.

From a seat near the toasty fireplace, Emily watched Eric open the door for Maggie, who slid past him and into the warm lobby.

She paused as they neared the front desk. "Thank you so much for showin' me your lovely boat. That was so fun."

"Happy to do it. If you're not busy tonight, I get off in a couple of hours and I'd love to take you to dinner," Eric offered.

"Oh, that's so sweet," Maggie replied, "but my boyfriend is due in from Seattle shortly." She rolled her wrist to look at her watch. "He should be arrivin' anytime."

Eric's expression fell, appearing crushed by her response.

Maggie began backing away with a smile plastered on her pretty face. "But I do appreciate the kind offer." She turned away from him, covertly glancing across the lobby at Emily. Then with a grin, she headed off down the hallway to her room, apparently proud of pulling off her assignment.

Emily followed after her. When she caught up, Maggie filled in the blanks on how things went. "Wait 'til I tell Peter I helped you on another case. He'll get such a kick out of it."

"No. You can't." Emily shook her head. "Planting that tracker could get the chief in hot water, so, please, don't tell anyone."

"Oh, all right. My lips are sealed." Maggie gave a pout.

"Thanks, my friend." Emily gave her a hug. "Good job."

"Are you ever goin' to tell me what that little stunt was about?"

"Later, I promise. Deal?"

"Deal." Maggie checked her watch again. "I'd better get a move on. I've got some primpin' to do before Peter gets here."

~*~

It was almost five o'clock when Colin and Alex returned from their fishing excursion. Emily and Isabel were seated on a flowered sofa in the lobby, chatting, when the boys came lumbering into the inn, bundled in heavy jackets and hats.

"Hey, guys." Emily and Isabel rushed over to greet

them.

"Where are the fish?" Emily asked.

"Like we'd have any place to store them, or cook them," Colin replied with slight sarcastic tone. It didn't appear they had much fun.

"Must have been catch and release." Isabel laughed a little.

"Ha ha," Colin said glumly.

Alex grimaced. "Very funny," he added before letting out a big sneeze.

"Didn't catch anything?" Isabel asked.

"Just a cold," Alex replied.

"And a case of motion sickness," Colin moaned. "The water wasn't too bad on the way out, but then it turned pretty rough coming back."

Alex sneezed again. "The captain said we must have caught the outer edge of that storm."

Isabel put a hand on her husband's forehead. "You feel a little feverish. Are you going to be okay to go out with the guys tonight?"

"Of course he is." Colin gave him a couple of hard pats on the back. "It's my bachelor party."

"Yeah, I'll be fine," Alex muttered. "You don't need to be fussing over me, Isabel."

"Let's go back to our room." Isabel tugged on his arm. She sniffed the air around him and wrinkled her nose. "I think a hot bath and a nap will do you good."

Alex shrugged and raised his eyebrows to Colin before turning back to his wife. "Yes, dear." He let her lead him toward their room.

"Now that they're gone," Colin said, keeping his voice down, "I was wondering if Maggie was able to plant the tracker."

"That's what you were thinking about out on the open seas?"

"I want to get this case buttoned down as much as possible before the wedding tomorrow."

Emily smiled. "Well, you would have been proud of her."

"Fantastic. We'll need to check in with the chief later and make sure he's monitoring the boat's movement."

"Do you really think they'll still be going out with the water so choppy?"

"It was rocky for Alex and me, but we're not used to it." Colin shrugged his coat off. "The captain didn't seem put off by it in the least. He claims it's too early in the season for a really bad storm, and the forecast has it moving east. I'm pretty sure that if a great deal of money is involved, they'll risk running the boat down to Boston tonight."

"By the time they get back tomorrow, the chief should have the search warrant, right?" If everything went according to plan, that is.

"That's what he told me. We'll watch their progress coming back and be waiting on the dock to exercise the warrant."

"What do you mean *we*?" Emily arched a brow. "What about the wedding?"

"Well, I meant it figuratively," Colin replied. "What I meant to say was Chief Taylor and his men will be on the dock to search the boat."

"That's better." Emily peeked at her watch. "The rest of the party should be here soon, so you might want to get cleaned up."

"A nice warm shower sounds like a good idea," Colin agreed. "I must smell pretty bad."

Emily tugged his hat off and kissed him. "You smell sexy, like a man of the sea."

He slipped an arm around her back and pulled her close. "Let me get cleaned up and I'll show you sexy."

CHAPTER NINETEEN
The Boys Are Back in Town

"OH, MY, MR. ANDREWS," Emily gushed in her best southern accent, fanning herself with Colin's hat, "you take my breath away."

The sounds of talking and laughter drew Colin's and Emily's attention toward the front door of the inn. Two men and a young woman had just entered the lobby, letting in a gust of cool air.

Colin's and Emily's faces lit up. It was the very people they had been expecting—Jonathan, Peter, and Molly.

"Hey, guys!" Colin called out, smiling at them as he hurried over and gave both men a handshake and a clap on the back.

Emily rushed to hug Molly, Camille's daughter, a college student who had been able to get away from school for this special weekend. She had been like a niece to Emily over the years. She had fiery red hair like her mother, flowing down around her shoulders. "I'm so glad you could come."

"I thought Red would be here to greet us," said Camille's husband, Jonathan, scanning the lobby.

"Where's Maggie?" asked Peter, glancing around the room as well. He was Maggie's boyfriend, and also happened to be Camille's brother.

"Getting ready for you—where else?" Emily chuckled.

"Where's Mom?" Molly asked.

"In her room, I believe," Emily answered. "Why don't you all get checked in and I'll let them know you're here."

"We're still doing the bachelorette thing tonight, aren't we?" Molly asked, her deep blue eyes lighting up with eagerness.

Emily nodded with a grin. "That's the plan."

"Mr. Andrews?" Eric Malone called out as he approached the small crowd.

Colin raised his hand. "That's me."

"I have a message for you." Eric handed him a small piece of paper. "It came in a few hours ago. They said they tried your phone several times but just got voicemail, so they called here."

Colin took the note and looked it over. It read that his parents were stuck in Atlanta, Georgia. Because of the storm, their flight from San Francisco had been delayed getting in, so they missed their connecting flight to Portland, Maine. They were now scheduled to take a five am flight to Portland and expected to arrive in Rock Harbor in the late morning, intending to make it in time for the wedding.

"Are they all right?" Emily asked.

"Fine, but they won't be here until tomorrow." He handed her the note. "Their flight was delayed."

Knowing Emily wouldn't have either of her parents at the ceremony was bad enough, if his parents didn't make it for the wedding either, that would be such a disappointment. She looked concerned.

"Don't worry, Babe. They'll be here."

She nodded sadly.

"I'm going to go hop in the shower." He gave her another quick kiss. "I'll stop by your room before the girls take you out on the town."

~*~

Emily decided to get cleaned up too, turning on the water in the shower to heat up. She pulled her hair up into a clip to keep it from getting wet, then disrobed, dropping her clothes on the floor. She stepped in for a quick wash before the girls stopped by her room to fetch her.

The water felt good cascading over her body, warm and relaxing. Standing with her back to the flow, her thoughts filled with Colin—the man who made her feel like there was nothing she couldn't do, the man who appreciated her strengths and balanced her weaknesses.

Their wedding was finally taking place. Tomorrow. The thought of it made her almost giddy. After all they had been through, they would at last be husband and wife.

In her mind, she pictured Colin, dressed in his best suit, standing under the flower-and-tulle-covered arch, waiting for her to glide down the aisle to him. She couldn't help but smile at the image, which brought a school-girl giggle bubbling out of her.

Tonight would be their last night of single life. She wondered what the boys had in store for him. They had better not keep him out too late—she wanted him at his best for the wedding tomorrow.

After toweling off, she wrapped the fluffy white bathrobe around herself and tied it, then let her hair loose from the clip, running her fingers through it. Checking herself in the mirror, she found her makeup was mostly intact, while a few little droplets of water dripped from the fringes of the curls that brushed against her shoulders. There was no time to doddle. The girls would be knocking on her door before long.

She opened the bathroom door and headed for the closet, with her handsome fiancé still on her mind.

Her peripheral vision caught a reflection in the mirror, and her heart thumped as she turned toward it for a double-take. Emily screamed, her hand rushing to her chest to calm the hammering there. There was a man, standing in her room—but it couldn't be. "Oh, God! Oh, God!"

"Shhh." He put a finger to his lips, then reached out to her.

"No!" She jumped back, screaming, her hands wildly beating the air. "No. No. No. I'm just seeing things. This isn't real. *You* are not real. You are a ghost, and I don't believe in ghosts."

Emily squeezed her eyes shut. When she opened them again, he would have disappeared, just as he had before. This was not real.

She felt lightheaded, needed to lie down. Emily shot her eyes open, her heart pounded in her ears, and her chest became tight. She gasped for air as chills slithered all up and down her back. Frozen in place, her feet were unable to move. "You're. Dead. Evan. Is dead."

"Not true, love. I assure you, I'm actually very much alive. Here, touch me."

"No," Emily gasped. The room began to ebb and flow in and out of focus. Everything was spinning. She was going to be sick.

Staggering backward, she slumped against the dresser, her hands reaching behind her, grasping the surface, trying to steady her balance, but then it all went gray and woozy.

"Breathe, love. Just breathe."

Her legs turned to rubber and her vision blurred— her world was about to collapse around her, but rather than crash to the floor, he lunged forward, and she felt his arms sliding around her.

"There, there. I've got you."

She blinked her eyes repeatedly, her mind still not able to grasp the enormity of the situation. "It can't be. You can't be. You're dead. I saw you dead." She leaned against him, dizzy, her knees still weak.

Evan put a couple of fingers under her chin, lifting her face. "As you can see, I am quite alive." He leaned down and kissed her tenderly.

His lips were sensual and moist, the kiss drawing her into the dream—it was just as she remembered. Instinctively, she melted against his body, a flicker of heat stirring in her.

Then reality set in.

"No." She pulled away, forcing herself to stand on her own feet, shaking her head and staring at the husband she'd thought she had lost. It couldn't be, yet on some level she knew it was.

"How can you be alive? I saw the crime scene photos, your body on the floor, the blood…"

"Maybe you should sit down, love."

Emily settled on the edge of the bed, one hand wrapped around her stomach and the other hand to her forehead. How was this possible?

"The blood," she said again as she raised her eyes to him. "How can you be standing here, alive and well?"

"It wasn't real, Emily." He took a step closer. "*This* is real." He claimed the space beside her on the bed, reaching out, taking her hand, placing it over his heart.

"I don't understand." She recognized the words coming out of his mouth, felt the pounding of his heart beneath her hand, but none of it made sense to her foggy and confused brain.

He brought her hand down to her lap and let it rest there. "Because of the work I did before I met you, my life was in grave danger, and so was yours. I thought I could leave it behind, start over—I tried, but it followed me."

He stood and poured her a glass of water from the bottle on the nightstand.

She took it and had a sip, the fog beginning to clear. "Followed you?"

"Yes, to Paradise Valley. So I had to disappear, had to fake my death and go into hiding."

"Why didn't you take me with you?"

"It had to seem real, or we would certainly have

both wound up dead. I needed them to see you grieve, Emily. I'm sorry."

"But the blood, the funeral, the murder investigation. How could it possibly not be real?"

He paced in front of her. "Drugs are miraculous little things. When one knows what to use, and in what quantity, they can make one *appear* dead. Of course, I had help."

"Who helped you? Who?" she demanded.

"Sorry, my love, but I can't tell you that."

"Can't tell me or won't?" she snapped.

Emily felt her lips tightening and her jaw clenching as anger began to rise in her. She glared into his eyes, not sure what else to say, but feeling the need to say something. "And what about the woman sitting in prison for your murder?"

"Well, she *did* shoot at me, after all. Fortunately, she only grazed me, but I assure you, it was her intention to kill me."

"We put her away for the rest of her life, Evan. That's not right."

"Don't worry about her." He sat on the bed beside her again. "I still have friends in high places. She'll be out in a few years."

How far out did this conspiracy go? Who was helping him?

Emily scrubbed both hands through her hair as she moaned. "No, this can't be real. I really am just going crazy from stress."

"Oh, but it is real, love." He put his arm around her shoulders. "You have to know, Emily, it was for the best."

Her heart was still pounding hard in her chest as she glared at him. Maybe she wasn't crazy. She could be dreaming. That's it—maybe this was just another one of her nightmares. She slapped her cheeks a couple of times and shook her head rapidly.

"What are you doing?" A puzzled expression drifted through his eyes.

"I'm trying to wake up. If I'm not crazy then this has to be a bad dream." She pinched his leg and squeezed hard.

"Ouch!" He shot to his feet. "I'm bloody afraid it's not, Emily."

Then what? What logical explanation could there be? She glared at him, looking into those piercing blue eyes she had missed for so long, and that sexy crooked smile that melted her heart.

How could he still be alive? She had lived through the murder investigation, she had even been under suspicion herself for a time. Emily tried to fit the pieces together. Recall what she could from that terrible time.

"What about Detective Tolliver? Did he know?"

Tolliver had been Colin's predecessor. He was the Paradise Valley police detective when Evan had been killed. He had been the one to investigate the murder and had come up empty—or so he had said.

"Yes, he knew. He helped make the murder appear legitimate."

"But why?" Emily pleaded, her eyes growing moist.

"Because I paid him a tidy sum. He gladly took the money and, once the investigation was wrapped up, he retired—to sunny Florida, I believe."

The money in the safe deposit box? There must

have been more of it than what she had found—the money he had paid to Detective Toliver.

"I have so many questions, Evan. All the things you left in the safe deposit box, like the cash and the—"

"Forget about that for now," he cut in, sitting next to her again. He cupped her face in his hands. "We have plenty of time to talk about those things, love. Come away with me—tonight. We'll travel the world, like we always said we'd do. I'm still crazy for you."

Emily pushed his hands away and bolted from the bed. "I can't. I'm marrying Colin tomorrow."

"But you don't have to, not anymore." He rose and took her hand. "Steal away with me, tonight."

She recoiled her hand and sucked in a quick breath. "How can you do this to me? Why now, Evan? Why did you come back after all this time?"

"I've been keeping an eye on you since I…since I went away."

She crossed her arms over her breasts, protectively. "You've been watching me?"

"You've got it all wrong. I've been watching *over* you."

"What's the difference?"

"I wanted to let you get on with your life, so you would stay safe, but I simply couldn't. I tried, Emily— you have to believe me—but when I heard you were about to get married to that chap, I had to see you one more time. I hadn't planned to let you see me, but as the wedding drew closer, I just had to tell you…I still love you, Emily. And, hope against hope, I had to ask you to run away with me. Now. Tonight."

Emily shook her head insistently. She couldn't look

at him. "No. I can't. I won't. I'm marrying Colin tomorrow."

"Please, love." Evan put his hands on her arms. "I'll be smarter this time. I know now we can't blend into a small town, but we could live like royalty in another country."

She looked him in the eye and yanked away from his hold. "What are you talking about? Didn't you hear me? I can't go with you. Not tonight. Not ever."

"Sure you can. I've watched how you've become a stronger woman—so much more than the sweet young Emily I married. I'd say you're developing into quite a good investigator. I never dreamed you could do some of the things I've seen you do."

Seen her do?

"Don't you understand, Emily? We could be great together—in every way."

"No. That's just plain crazy." Her mind filled with the dangerous, and sometimes murderous, work she'd learned he had done. "I could never do the kinds of things you've done."

"I'm not saying you have to, love," he countered. "You could come and work at the global security firm I work for—we'd make quite a team—or you can do whatever suits your fancy. Just come away with me."

"Listen to me, Evan, it's too late."

"It's not too late. You're not married yet. I know you love me, Emily."

His pleading carried a profound emotional angst she'd never heard from him before, and it drew Emily to look deeply into Evan's pale blue eyes, to study the details of his face. This was all so surreal. She could hardly believe he was standing right in front of her, very much alive and well. She couldn't deny that she still loved him—she always would—but he was dead to her, and she had moved on.

Memories flooded her mind. Her heart had been ripped to shreds when Evan died. Inconsolable for weeks, she had mourned, painfully, grieving the loss of her husband and their life together. With time, and discovering the truth, she was eventually able to get on with her life, and it had been Colin who had helped her to find love again. Now, she had pledged herself to him, promised to love him 'til death do us part.

They had been through a lot together, saved each other's lives—trusted each other like no one else she'd ever known. Evan hadn't trusted her enough to tell her the truth, to let her into his world.

A cool draft reminded Emily she had nothing on but a bathrobe. "I've got to get dressed."

She grabbed some clothes from the closet and headed to the bathroom, hoping to put some distance between them until she could get her head clear.

"Not on my account, I hope." Evan had apparently gained control of his emotions and a mischievous look filled his eyes. As she squeezed past him, he clasped a few fingers on the belt to her robe, causing her to pause. "I always loved the beautiful curves of your body, Emily."

He would tug it off if she let him—that much she knew. Her body trembled at the thought of him caressing her, making love to her, but she knew that would be a huge mistake—probably the biggest mistake of her life.

"Do you remember when we—"

"That's enough!" Emily cinched the robe tighter as she slapped his hand away. "That was a long time ago, before you *died*. My body is no longer yours."

"But, Emily…"

"I can't believe you thought I would just fall back into your arms. I'm not that naïve, doe-eyed young girl you married, Evan." She stepped into the bathroom and shut the door.

"I know that," he snapped back, then his voice became calm again. "What I did, Emily, I did to protect you."

From the sound of his voice, Emily could tell he was right on the other side of the door. She pressed her back against it, as if that would somehow shut him out completely.

"If I hadn't left," he continued, "hadn't made everyone believe I was dead, eventually I would have been—and you—don't you see? Everything I did, I did for you."

And now he wanted her back. Maybe he was the crazy one.

She gave no reply, her body vibrating with shock and anger, her mind swirling as she tried to comprehend the reality she knew to be true. She pulled her jeans on, zipped them up, and tugged her navy-blue sweater over her head.

Gazing in the mirror, she ran her fingers through her curls, fluffed her hair in place, wondering what was coming next.

"I'm not leaving, Emily."

She reached for the doorknob, but hesitated, not ready to face Evan again. She leaned her back against the door and let out a long sigh of exasperation.

Now what?

Her emotions were a jumble and her head was spinning.

Oh, God—Colin. What was she going to tell him?

CHAPTER TWENTY
A Huge Surprise

THINKING SHE WAS READY, Emily opened the bathroom door. Evan filled the doorway, looking as ruggedly handsome as she remembered him. Her breath caught again at the sight of him. It was so surreal, her brain was still having trouble accepting it.

Her eyes locked on his. She stood there for a moment, immobilized, unable to look away. Drawn into his magnetic gaze, an uneasy feeling swirled in her chest. She could hardly believe she was actually looking into the face of the husband she thought was dead, the man she had loved, but never thought she would see again.

How could this be happening?

Evan was only inches away, the expression in his eyes speaking volumes, loving her and wanting her, every bit as much as he had the day he died—only he hadn't died. His piercing blue eyes were alive with emotion and seemed to cut through the dreamlike fog to peer deeply into her soul.

"You can't tell me you don't love me anymore." His penetrating gaze held hers. "I can see it in your eyes."

The shock was wearing off, at least a little, and her fiancé's image flooded her mind. She shook her head to break Evan's hold on her. "Don't say that."

"But, Emily…"

Standing so close to him, she caught that familiar trail of his aftershave. That scent. She had smelled it as recently as that morning, when she had awakened from sleep. "Were you in my room before?"

"Before?" His eyes flared briefly.

"Yes, before this time, before now?"

"Why do you ask?"

"Your aftershave. I swear I smelled it when I woke up this morning. I thought I was dreaming, but now…"

He looked away and stepped aside to let her pass, but said nothing in reply.

Anger rose in her. Rather than walk past, she stood toe to toe with him, searching his face, but his eyes would not meet hers. "You *have* been in my room, while I was asleep—haven't you?"

"Only a few times."

"I knew it!"

"I had to see you—make sure you were okay." His gaze locked onto hers once more. "You don't know how hard it was to stand there, watching you sleep. It took every ounce of strength I possess not to crawl in bed with you." He reached out for her, sliding his hands around her waist. "I ache for you, Emily."

At his touch and his nearness, her resolve began to wane. Her body reacted, desiring to know how it would feel to be with him again, but then her mind screamed no. She willed herself to push away from him. "It's not that easy, Evan."

She sat on the edge of the bed, demanding her heart rate to calm down. She pulled on her dark socks, trying to avoid his gaze. "I thought you were dead."

He knelt down near her. "But I'm not."

She pulled on her low-heeled black boots. "You can't ask me to undo my life since you left. I've moved on. I'm marrying Colin tomorrow. I—"

She stood, then he stood, finding herself face to face with him again, the very thing she was trying to avoid. Her body vibrated with so many different emotions that she couldn't even name them all. She drew in a deep breath to calm herself, shook her head to try to clear it. "I love him."

He touched her hair and twirled a curl loosely around his finger, leaning in to smell it. "Your hair always reminded me of silky strands of gold, especially when we made love. The way it fell around your face, like a halo."

A tingle feathered up her back and she batted his hand away. "Colin loves me as much as you do—only he's not running from anyone who's trying to kill him. And he doesn't lie to me."

Evan grabbed her by the shoulders. His voice became intense. "No, Emily, you can't—"

A sharp rap at the door cut him off. "Emily? It's Isabel."

She glared at Evan and tugged away from him.

"Let's see what she thinks about this."

Rushing to the door, Emily flung it open, shooting Evan a defiant glance over her shoulder. She expected to hear a gasp of surprise out of her friend as she turned back to the door, but all she heard was deafening silence.

There stood Isabel, speechless, her mouth gaping open, with Colin standing tall behind her, his face twisted in confusion.

Emily's heart nearly stopped. How would she explain this to Colin? She didn't understand it herself.

"Evan?" Isabel finally gasped the word as she strode across the room toward him.

"Hello, Isabel," Evan greeted with a smug grin. He crossed his arms and leaned against the dresser. "You're looking well."

"What are you doing here?" she asked, lowering her voice, but it did not escape Emily's hearing.

"I had to come," he said. "I had to see Emily and talk to her."

What?

That wasn't the exchange Emily had expected to hear between them. It sounded like Isabel was only surprised to see him in Emily's room, not shocked to see that he was alive.

"Emily?" Colin spoke slowly and deliberately. "What's going on here?"

She turned back to Colin, who was still standing, rigid, in the doorway, his attention focused on Evan. Emily had never seen quite that look on Colin's face before. It was a mixture of surprise, confusion, and disbelief.

"Did Isabel say Evan? As in Evan Parker...your

dead husband?"

"Why don't you come in?" Emily tugged on Colin's arm. "We need to talk."

Colin took a few steps into the room. "But how is that possible?"

"I don't know," she moaned. "I was as surprised as you are. All this time I thought he was dead, but here he is. He just showed up in my room a little while ago and...and...oh heck, I don't even know what."

What could she say? She wasn't about to tell Colin that Evan had asked her to leave him standing at the altar and run away to some foreign country.

"Well, let's just find out what." Colin moved past her, looking as serious as Emily had ever seen him. In a few long strides, he was face to face with Evan, standing several inches taller. He warily stuck out his hand. His voice was cool and even, his expression unwavering. "Colin Andrews."

Evan accepted it and shook firmly. "Evan Parker." His eyes seemed to assess his competition.

"This is a rather awkward situation." Colin paused and glanced at Emily, who was standing almost behind him, wanting to hide from what was sure to come.

Awkward didn't even begin to describe the atmosphere in the room. The thick uneasiness was palpable. How on earth could this possibly turn out well?

"I'm not going to mince words here, Parker. We all thought you were dead. How can you, all of a sudden, be alive again? And at such an inconvenient time?"

"Colin, is it?" Evan arched a brow, as if he hadn't heard the name clearly in the introduction. "I had to go dark for a bit, to protect Emily and myself. Things have changed and I'm here to ask Emily to come away with me, travel the world, like we'd always planned. We are still married, you know."

Still married? She hadn't considered that. With the wedding tomorrow...

Colin spun around to Emily. "Did you know about this?"

"Well, no, I…"

Her mind was stuck mulling over the possibility of still being married to Evan. "He just sprang it on me, right before you guys knocked on the door."

"And you're considering it?"

Emily saw such hurt in his eyes. "I...I…" Why wouldn't the words come? She wanted to tell Colin she wouldn't dream of considering it, and that she loved him, but instead she sounded like a blathering idiot.

"She's still my wife, old chap," Evan said, "and I've come back to claim her."

"Emily is marrying me." Colin ground out the words through clenched teeth.

"I beg to differ," Evan replied. "She's mine, and that's the end of it."

"Not if I can help it!" Colin turned on Evan, his eyes wide with anger, grabbing him by the collar, landing a punch squarely on his jaw.

Evan's head pitched to the right, but his body remained planted. He was every bit a match for Colin and he came back swinging.

~*~

"Stop it! Stop it!" Emily yelled, but neither of the

men paid her any mind, appearing intent on doing each other physical harm. "Do something, Isabel."

"I'm not getting in the middle of this. I warned Ev—I mean—"

Emily's eyes widened and her mouth dropped open. "What do you mean you warned him? You knew he was alive?"

"Well, I...that is, uh..." Isabel was lost for a response. How could she tell her best friend that she had known all along that her dead husband wasn't dead, that she had helped him stage everything so he could go into hiding? How could she make Emily understand it was for her own good?

Emily tried one more time to get the men to stop fighting. But all of her hollering did no good. "You handle it, Isabel. I've got to get out of here!" She grabbed her jacket and ran out of the room.

"Emily, wait!" she called after her, but she was gone.

Isabel spun back around and grabbed the ice bucket off the dresser. It sloshed around, full of cold water and partially melted ice. With one quick toss, she poured it over the men.

That got their attention. They froze in a jumble of arms and legs.

"What the hell, Isabel?" Evan gasped, his back on the floor.

"Emily's gone," she said. "She couldn't stand you two fighting like playground bullies."

"I'll go after her," Colin groaned, seeming to use all his might to hold Evan pinned down. He released Evan and jumped to his feet.

"No. I've got to go after her," Evan said, getting up as well.

They both started for the door, but Isabel stepped in front of them and blocked the doorway.

"Get out of my way," Colin ordered.

"No. Stop! She needs some time to cool down and think through this whole mess. This is a lot for anyone to take in. She'll come back when she's ready." Whether Emily would ever speak to her again was another story.

~*~

Emily dashed out of the inn, tugging her jacket on. The wind was picking up and the temperature was dropping as the sun had already gone down. Shivering in the damp sea air, gold and orange leaves rustled past her feet as she marched down the long driveway toward Main Street.

When she reached the street, she glanced around, not sure where to go, but anywhere other than that hotel room would do. She needed to clear her head before going back.

Still, she had a hard time wrapping her mind around the idea that Evan was really alive. She should be thrilled, jumping into his arms, showering him with kisses. But he had deceived her yet again, expected her to overlook the enormity of it, and run away with him like all was forgiven and forgotten.

And then there was Colin, the wonderful man whom she loved unreservedly and had promised to marry the very next day. What must he be thinking?

The sight of these two men punching each other,

over her, was too much—she had to get out of there, but now what? She would have to face them eventually, but for now she simply needed time to think.

Her phone rang in her pocket. She saw it was Isabel calling and sent it directly to voicemail. She wasn't ready to talk to anyone yet. She silenced her phone and stuck it back in her pocket so there would be no more distractions.

Perhaps getting her mind on something else for a while might help. She glanced down toward the boats that bobbed along the dock, thinking about the stunt Maggie had pulled off earlier that day, hoping it wasn't for nothing.

Had Colin remembered to call the chief about following the GPS transponder? After all, this was the night Whitley had said Caleb and the others were leaving to take the boat down to Boston to pick up guests in the morning, among other things. Maybe she should call the chief herself and make sure. She'd do just about anything to get her mind off the mess she left back at the inn.

She whipped out her phone and punched in the numbers.

"This is Chief Taylor. How can I help you?"

"Hello, Chief, this is Emily Parker."

"Well, hello. What can I do for you?"

"Did Colin already ask you to monitor that GPS transponder tonight—you know, the one you gave me?"

He cleared his throat. "You must be mistaken, you didn't get it from me."

That's right, no one was supposed to know that. "You're right, no, not from you," she said, playing along. "Are you tracking it?"

"No, sorry, I hadn't gotten the go-ahead from Detective Andrews yet."

"I have reason to believe the boat is headed out tonight, so if you could…"

She didn't want to bring Whitley's name into the investigation any more than necessary, and she had promised her she would do what she could to keep her brother's name out of it too, if that were possible.

"Sure, I'm on it," he replied. "Hey, isn't this the night of Colin's bachelor party?"

There was no reason to alert the police chief of the change of events in their personal life, but if Chief Taylor discovered anything from tracking that boat, she wanted him to know Colin would be interested in hearing about it. "Yes, that's tonight. But, please, he would still want you to call him if anything turns up."

"Sure will."

Emily hung up, standing under the glow from a streetlamp on Main Street. She glanced to the left, at the shops and restaurants all brightly lit, beckoning the tourists to come in and sample their wares. Looking to the right, toward the wharf, there were a few boats with lights shining from the cabins.

Would anyone be on the Hoosier Daddy? If they were planning to cast off tonight, likely one of those lighted boats was it. Maybe if she strolled by it, she could pick up some important tidbit of conversation.

She zipped her jacket and pulled the collar up around her neck before heading toward the bay. Passing several boats tied to the dock, she could see lights glowing down below on the Hoosier Daddy. She tiptoed toward it, hoping to hear something.

CHAPTER TWENTY-ONE
A Captive Audience

AS EMILY APPROACHED Eric Malone's trawler, muffled voices emanated from the cabin, but she couldn't make out what they were saying. She inched closer and, as she leaned toward the boat, something hard poked her in the back. She pulled up straight as her heart leapt into her throat. *Now what?*

She instinctively reached into her waistband, but her gun was not there. She hadn't brought it with her in the rush to get out of her room.

"Get on the boat," a harsh male voice demanded, his face so near the back of her head she could feel his hot breath through her hair.

"I'm not going—"

"It wasn't a request." He pushed, what felt like, the business end of a gun harder into her back. "Now, keep your mouth shut and get moving."

Her room at the inn didn't seem so bad at this

point—two men, both who loved her, fighting over which one would keep her. Would those two men, or anyone else, come looking for her? Probably not, at least for a while.

With the man sticking close behind her, Emily stepped over the gangway, as she was told.

"Down below," the man ordered.

She glanced over her shoulder. It was Caleb.

"I said move it."

An icy chill snaked up her spine. Of all the murder suspects, he hadn't been her first pick, hadn't seemed the most dangerous. What was he going to do with her?

Her gaze bounced around the stern, looking for something to grab to defend herself. There wasn't time to focus in the low light before he pushed her toward the door leading down to the cabin.

Thankful Maggie had planted the tracker earlier in the day, Emily trusted that Chief Taylor was keeping an eye on it. However, he couldn't possibly know she was on board.

Emily eased the small double doors open and descended the steps into the cabin. As she reached the bottom stair, Caleb forced her to the floor.

"Look who I found on the dock," he declared.

"What's going on?" Rosco growled. He and Eric had been the ones Emily had overheard on the boat.

Emily drew her knees up and hugged her legs, glaring up at her captor. What were they going to do with her?

Caleb pointed the handle of a screwdriver at her head, rather than a gun. "I caught this one snooping around."

"You couldn't have just scared her off?" Rosco barked. "Now what are we going to do with her?"

"I don't know," Caleb shrugged. "I didn't think that far ahead."

Rosco grunted. "The least you could have done was use a real gun."

~*~

Colin peered over at Evan, who was standing in the doorway to the bathroom, rubbing a towel over his hair and blotting his shirt. That man couldn't have chosen a worse time to show up. One more day and Emily would have been Colin's bride—but now? Colin's hands balled into fists at the thought. He wanted to deck that guy again.

Evan's intense gaze focused on Colin. Even from across the room, Colin could see a dark bruise growing under Evan's left eye and he wanted to knock that smug look off his face. Evan was probably thinking the same thing about Colin, but what right did that pompous Brit have to Emily now?

When Emily had discovered Evan's real name, she had wondered if they were even legally married. His death certificate would now be invalid, and Evan likely had no legal claim to Emily because he had used a false identity on the marriage license. That gave Colin little comfort after seeing Emily's reaction. The decision was clearly in Emily's hands and, before she ran off, she didn't seem too certain about which man she would choose.

"You two," Isabel said, pointing at each of the men,

"try to get along until she comes back. Don't make this any harder on her than it already is."

Evan crossed his arms defiantly. "I won't make any promises."

Colin said nothing, but propped himself on the edge of the bed. He ran his fingers through his wet hair, pushing it off his forehead, then he wiped a bit of blood from his lip.

The room was silent for the better part of a difficult ten minutes. But Colin couldn't stand it any longer. "How much longer do we wait?"

Isabel checked her wristwatch. "Let's give her twenty minutes. If she's not back by then, I'll call her and make sure she's okay."

"I'll call her now," Colin said, pulling out his phone.

"Wait, Colin. Give her some time to think things through," Isabel advised. "I think she just needs to be alone for a bit."

"It won't hurt to phone her. You could call and just say you were worried and wanted to make sure she was fine," Colin said.

"All right," Isabel replied. She dialed Emily's number and waited while it rang. "It's just going to voicemail. I told you, she wants to be alone. Give her that."

Colin nodded.

Evan huffed.

A few more minutes ticked by. "I'm going to call her myself," Colin declared. "This waiting is ridiculous." He dialed her number and it went to voicemail for him too.

"I say we go now," Evan asserted.

"As much as I hate to say it, I'm with Evan. I don't think we should wait any longer either." Colin rose to his feet and went to the window and peered out, toward the pool. "The temperature is dropping out there and the rain is starting to come down." He turned back to Isabel. "The weather is only going to get worse." Besides, he wanted to be the one to find her before Evan had a chance to swoop in like James Bond and be the hero.

Isabel glared from one man to the other and quirked one side of her lips. "All right," she conceded, as if they needed her permission. "Let's get the whole group together and make a plan. But, Evan, you can't be seen by them—you're dead, remember? Why don't you stay here and we'll check in with you?"

"Not a chance."

"She's right," Colin said. "If that gang knows you're alive, all of Paradise Valley will know soon too." Could Colin convince Evan to stay back so he wouldn't get anywhere near Emily? It was doubtful.

"We can find her faster if more of us are searching," Evan said.

Isabel moved close to Evan. "Colin's right, if people find out you're alive, then you disappearing for all this time will have been for nothing."

Evan's eyes narrowed as he stared at Colin, appearing to consider Isabel's advice. "Ten minutes."

"What do you mean?" Isabel asked.

"You search for ten minutes," Evan replied, "and if you don't call me and tell me you've found her, I'm out of here."

~*~

Isabel and Colin left Evan in Emily's room, with a promise to call. Even though it was better no one else knew he was alive, could he be trusted to stay there?

They called all their friends to gather in the lobby for an emergency meeting. Emily was missing, they were told, and they needed to find her.

Within minutes, everyone congregated around the fireplace and Isabel explained the situation—Emily and Colin had gotten into an argument and she took off to get some air. With the storm getting worse, they thought it was best to go find her and bring her back to the inn.

"That must have been some argument," Camille said glibly, staring at Colin's split lip.

He touched a finger to his lip, but did not reply. What could he say?

"Alex and I will scour the shops and restaurants up and down Main Street," Isabel stated.

Camille would go with her husband and daughter to search the streets, shooting off to the west from Main Street, which also housed a few shops and eateries.

Colin and Peter would search the shoreline and the wharf area, after Colin checked in with the police chief and asked him to have his patrolmen keep an eye out for Emily.

Maggie agreed to stay at the inn, in case Emily came back.

"I don't want to alarm you all," Isabel said, "but we have a wedding tomorrow and we can't have the bride catching her death of cold." Her gaze shifted to Colin and she gave him a little encouraging grin.

Colin breathed a laugh. He appreciated her trying to lighten the serious situation, but it did nothing to calm his nerves. Trying to get Emily to the altar felt like playing that silly Whack-A-Mole game. No sooner did he overcome one hurdle than another would pop up.

The small crowd began to disperse into their respective groups and Isabel moved next to Colin. She whispered to him that she was going to take Evan with them as soon as the others left, including him and Peter. "I'll explain what's happening to my husband first, then go and get him."

"You might as well," he muttered. He knew Evan was probably climbing the walls being stuck in the room, because that's exactly what Colin himself would be doing in the same situation—that is if Evan had stayed there, as he was asked.

"Let's go, Peter," he hollered across the lobby.

Peter and Colin stepped outside and headed down the driveway to the street. The wind was blowing and the rain had lightened to a sprinkle. Now, if it would only hold.

"Where to, boss?" Peter asked.

~*~

"You should have known better than to be poking your nose where it don't belong," Rosco barked at Emily, a scowl twisting on his face as he waved his gun at her. Apparently he preferred the real thing. "There's a lot of ocean between here and Boston. They'll never find your body."

Emily drew in a shuddering breath and her chest

tightened. He was right. She'd be making her way to the bottom of the cold Atlantic Ocean before anyone even knew she was gone from Rock Harbor.

Eric stepped closer to Rosco. "Let's think about this, man. We may be a lot of things, but we're not killers."

"That's not true, is it, Caleb?" Rosco arched a questioning brow at the young man.

Caleb's green eyes rounded. He tugged his ball cap off and raked his fingers through his shaggy brown hair. "Well, I…I had no choice. He would have ruined everything."

Just like I'm doing?

She scooted backward a few inches and rested against the side of the banquette, wishing she could crawl under the table and disappear.

"Who are you talking about?" Eric demanded.

The hairs on the back of Emily's neck stood up and an army of chills marched down her back. If Caleb had killed before, he easily could kill again. She could be next.

"Ben Kinney," Caleb mumbled.

CHAPTER TWENTY-TWO
Confessions

"CALEB, ARE YOU ADMITTING you killed Ben Kinney?" Eric glared at him and the blood seemed to drain from his face.

"Hey, keep it down," Caleb warned in a low voice, leaning closer to the other men. "Not in front of the hostage."

Even as fearful as Emily was, folded almost into a fetal position on the floor, her attention was riveted to the conversation.

Eric and Rosco both turned their gaze on her. "She's not telling anyone," Rosco ground out.

"Tell me it wasn't you," Eric groaned.

"Well, what did you want me to do?" Caleb shot back. "He found out what we were doing."

Eric grabbed Caleb by the arm. "But how could he have?"

"I don't know how, but he did."

If these guys knew it was Whitley who told Ben, would Caleb step in and protect his sister?

"He came to me at the inn one day," Caleb explained, "while I was working. He said I had to cut him in on our business, or else."

"The night he died?" Eric asked, jerking Caleb's arm.

Caleb yanked free. "No, the day before. I tried to act like I didn't know what he was talking about, but he wouldn't let up. He came back again the next night."

"What did you do?" Eric growled, worry lines forming around his eyes. He stepped closer to Caleb, speaking low, between clenched teeth. "Transporting drugs is bad enough, I didn't sign up for murder."

Emily listened intently to Caleb's confession, her heart pounding so hard she was afraid she would faint. Would she ever be able to tell anyone what she had heard? Not according to Rosco. And the fact that they were talking so freely in front of her confirmed they didn't plan to let her make it to shore.

"Hell, I didn't mean to do it, he just wouldn't leave me alone." Caleb scrubbed his fingers through his hair again and pulled his cap back on as his eyes nervously darted around. "Like I said, he kept pressing me about cutting him in on our business. I knew you guys wouldn't go for it."

"That's for sure," Rosco shot back. "I'm not splitting the haul with anyone else."

"Then he started in about my sister—how he was going to tell her what I was doing, how she followed him around like a lovesick puppy and he could get her to do whatever he wanted. He said he'd already gotten to second base with her and getting her in his bed wasn't far away."

Poor Whitley.

The movement of the boat on the waves was making Emily a bit nauseous. She raised her head and pulled in a deep breath. Her stomach settled a little as she blew it out slowly.

"He said if I didn't get him in with us, he'd have her any which way he wanted. Ughhh! When he started going on about my sister, I just lost it. I picked up the nearest thing I could get my hands on and smacked him upside the head."

Eric shook his head sadly. "Oh, man. This is going to come back on all of us—you know that, don't you?"

"Oh, don't get your panties in a twist," Rosco uttered with a smirk. "The boy didn't kill Ben—I did."

Rosco did it?

"You?" Eric gasped. His look turned from angry to nervous. Was he afraid of Rosco?

"I just let the boy think he did it, to toughen him up a bit," Rosco said with a rough laugh.

"I'm not a boy," Caleb bit back. "I'm almost thirty. And I did do it."

"Shut up about that!" Rosco snarled. "I can't have you going around telling people you killed Ben."

"Why not?" Caleb asked. "It's true."

"It's not true and if you say that it will screw everything up. I'm the one who did the deed, so I'm the one that earned the reward money. Don't get the idea we're gonna split it."

"What reward money?" Caleb asked.

Rosco narrowed his eyes. "You really don't know?

Or are you just playing dumb?"

"What are you talking about?" Caleb's eyebrows grew together into a nervous frown. "What money?"

"All right, all right, don't wet yourself. I believe you," Rosco said. "I've got this cousin in New York, see. He told me someone put a big bounty on that guy's head, fifty thousand Gs. I thought you might've heard."

Fifty thousand? Was Rosco's cousin planning to keep the rest of it for himself or was Rosco trying to pull one over on Caleb?

"He sent me Ben's picture on my phone and told me if I saw him I could make some real money," Rosco continued. "I guess someone else found him before me and tried to kill him but screwed it up."

The car crash?

"No, man," Caleb argued, shaking his head, "I don't know nothing about the money, but I am the one who hit him in the head with the side of my hammer, and he dropped like a ton of bricks."

"Naw. You might have knocked him out, boy," Rosco said, "but I stuck him with my knife, right in the heart."

That's what the medical examiner reported. The thought sent a wave of chills over Emily's body and she couldn't help but shiver. She pulled her knees up closer to her body and clasped her hands around them.

"I guess I should thank you for making my job so easy, boy."

"What do you mean by that?" Caleb asked.

Rosco turned toward him. "I followed the guy that night from the place where he was staying, then I saw him talking to you by those bushes next to the pool. I watched you clobber him and he went down, and I thought I'd lost my chance at the bounty money. But after you ran off, I watched him for a while, trying to figure out how I could spin it in my direction, somehow make it look like I'd done it before anyone else came wandering through there. Then he staggered to his feet and that's when I saw my opportunity to make that easy fifty thousand."

Caleb let out a sigh of relief and his shoulders dropped, seeming comforted at Rosco's statement, assuring him he wasn't a murderer after all.

Rosco's gaze turned hard on Caleb, his thick black eyebrows hovering over his dark brooding eyes. "So don't be getting no ideas about taking any share of that money."

"But how did he get on the deck to my room?" Emily blurted out before she thought it through.

Suddenly, all eyes were on her again. She cowered against the side of one of the benches and tried to wrap her hands around the table's leg to steady herself as the boat continued to bob.

"No one's talking to you," Rosco growled, wagging the gun at her.

"Yeah, Rosco," Eric said, eyeing him suspiciously. "I was kinda wondering about that myself."

"Jeez, that's simple. After I stuck him, I heard someone coming. So I dragged him over to the nearest deck and dumped him in the chair. Then I hid in the bushes 'til it was all clear."

"I wondered what happened." Caleb looked down at Emily. "So what are we going to do about the girl?"

"Emily," she squeaked, trying her best not to sound

frightened, but her high-pitched tone betrayed her.

Caleb frowned at her and tilted his head. "Huh?"

She drew a deep breath to relax her throat and glared at him square in the eye. "As long as you're going to kill me, you might as well know who I am." If she made some kind of connection with at least one of them, maybe she'd have a chance of getting out of this thing alive. What other options did she have? It was three men against her, and one had a gun.

The men shot questioning stares at each other, which did nothing to convince her she had succeeded to connect. She tried again.

"I'm Emily Parker." She forced herself to hold Caleb's gaze and her voice to stay calm, even though her heart was thudding hard and fast. "I'm getting married tomorrow—or, at least, I was."

"You shut up, woman, if you know what's good for you," Rosco said, his gun still on her.

She ignored him. How could things get much worse? She worked up a bit of a smile and turned her attention to Eric. "You met my fiancé, the police detective, didn't you, Mr. Malone? And my maid of honor, the FBI agent?"

"Police detective?" Eric mumbled. "FBI agent?"

"I told you to shut up," Rosco barked. "Boss, don't let her rattle you. Let's cast off before someone comes looking for her. We've been jawing long enough." Rosco turned his attention to Caleb. "You get us untied, boy, and I'll start the engines."

"No," Eric said sternly. "I want to know what you have planned for this woman first."

"That's easy. Wait 'til we're far enough out to sea,"

Rosco replied flatly, "then we'll dump her body." He said it like she was chum to be thrown overboard to feed the sharks.

Eric stepped closer to Rosco. "We're not killers." His voice sounded strained.

"You let her live, boss, and we'll all be spending the rest of our lives in prison," Rosco shot back with a snarl. "Is that what you want?"

"Of course not, but—"

"Well, if we don't get rid of her, that's exactly what you'll get. I ain't going to prison because of some skirt."

CHAPTER TWENTY-THREE
Chasing the Hoosier Daddy

CURLED UP ON THE FLOOR, Emily was paralyzed with fear as she listened to them quarrel, hardly noticing the motion of the boat now. She had never been this close to death with so little chance of being rescued.

"But her friends—" Caleb started to question.

"We don't have time to argue," Rosco growled. "We've got to get going before we draw those people down here looking for her. Otherwise, we won't make it to Boston on time, and you know what that means. The people we're working for don't accept lame excuses."

Eric cast a pitiful glance at Emily as the boat rocked. "It sounds like the wind is picking up and the rain is starting to come down. Are you sure you checked the weather report, Rosco?"

"I checked it—I ain't stupid. It said we were just

getting the edge of that big storm. It's turning eastward, out to sea."

"Maybe we should find shelter until the storm passes." Eric peered down at Emily. "We can take her with us until we decide what to do."

Rosco shook his head angrily. "No. We need to shove off now. You know they'll be expecting us in Boston just before sunrise. We have to board the passengers at nine, so we've got to get the cargo loaded while it's still dark. If we delay, we won't make it in time."

"Besides, it's too early in the season for a really bad storm," Caleb added, rubbing his arms nervously. "Isn't it, Rosco?"

"That's right."

Eric eyed Caleb, whose face had gone pale and uncertain, then he glanced up the stairs again, toward the stormy darkness. Eric laid a hand on Caleb's shoulder. "We'll be fine." His confident words did not match the expression on his face.

"I've got bills to pay, boss," Caleb muttered. "If we don't get this load, I'm gonna be in trouble, big time."

Emily thought of what Whitley had said about their mother living in a home and the expenses of that, for which Caleb was largely responsible. Was that what he was worried about? Or did he have other debt? Alimony or child support? She didn't really know much about his life.

"Ah, stop your whining," Rosco hollered. "It's just a little rain and wind. I've been sailing this ocean for the better part of twenty years. I know what I'm doing."

With her heart hammering in her chest, Emily

gazed at Rosco from her spot curled up on the floor. She could just imagine that he was thinking only about the fifty thousand dollars waiting for him. A chilling sense of fear continued to rattle her. It was clear they were going to drown her at sea, if they didn't shoot her first.

"You'd better go up there and get us out of here," Rosco told Eric, his gun still pointed at Emily.

"You're the captain," Eric snapped back.

Rosco shot him a cutting stare, then flipped the pistol around and handed it to Eric, grip first. "Then you hold the gun on her."

Eric reluctantly took the weapon and Rosco bolted up the steps. "Don't worry, Caleb," Eric said, glancing over at the young man, as he focused the pistol on Emily. "You tie her up while Rosco casts off. We'll be in Boston harbor before you know it."

~*~

Colin phoned the police chief. "This may sound stupid, but I've misplaced my fiancée. Do you think you could put out an APB on Emily and have your guys keep their eyes peeled for her?"

The chief laughed.

Colin was silent. He couldn't go into the details of his request.

"Oh. You're not kidding, are you?"

"No."

"So, she's really missing. How long?"

"Maybe twenty minutes."

"Mighty short time to report someone missing."

"I'm not officially reporting her, I'm just concerned

because of the weather and I need to find her. Will you help?"

"Funny," the chief said, "she called me about ten minutes ago to make sure I was monitoring that GPS tracker she had planted on the boat, 'cause tonight is the night they're supposed to go and pick up a load, remember?"

In all the furor over Evan, he had forgotten about the case. "That's right. Have you heard from her since?"

"No, I haven't. Sorry."

Colin sighed in frustration. His gaze flew toward the docks.

The chief cleared his throat. "Say, aren't you supposed to be having your bachelor party tonight?"

"Uh, that's been postponed," Colin replied. "I really need to find Emily." Would she have gone down to check on the boat?

"Did you two lovebirds have a spat?"

"Something like that." Colin glanced over at Peter, not wanting to have to explain about Evan and what transpired. "Have you seen any activity on the boat?"

The chief paused and Colin assumed he was studying the monitor. "As a matter of fact, it has moved a bit from the dock. They must have taken off for Boston a short while ago, but don't you worry. The search warrant came through and we'll be waiting for them when they get back in the morning."

"That's good to hear, but let's get back to Emily," Colin paused briefly, working to keep his words calm and coherent, caring more about finding her than about arresting the drug runners. "Chief, if I give you her cellphone number, can you track that?" Colin was anxious to find her.

"You sound worried, Detective."

Apparently he hadn't kept his voice as calm as he'd thought. "Can you track her?" he repeated, contemplating if they should start walking toward the wharf.

"Oh, we don't have any of that kind of fancy equipment in Rock Harbor. What would we need that for?"

"Do you have any connections at the Bangor Police Department, someone who could track it for you? I'm desperate here, Alvin." Colin cut a quick glance toward Peter, whose brows twisted into a suspicious expression.

Peter was a reporter after all, and Colin's statement of desperation had to be making his senses tingle.

"Whew! That must have been a humdinger of a fight, my friend."

"Do you, Chief?" Colin pressed.

"Sure, what's her number?"

Colin recited it to him. "Could you put a rush on it?"

"I'll try. What's the big hurry?"

"Knowing Emily, if she was thinking about the boat taking off from the dock tonight, she might have gone down to do a little snooping around."

"You figure she's on that boat?"

"She might be." He hoped he was wrong, but he wasn't taking any chances. "And if that's the case, do you have a police boat?"

"Eyah, I do," the chief replied. "It's moored down at the end of the dock. Are you thinking we should chase after the Hoosier Daddy? What if Emily's not on it?

Then we'll blow our morning drug bust. We've got to catch these guys, put a stop to the heroin they're bringing into our area. I'd want to know for sure she's on that boat before we go chasing it, especially with the storm out there."

"Then I'd better let you go so you can call the Bangor Police and get a trace on her phone," Colin said. "We need to know right away, one way or the other."

"I'll phone you back and tell you what they find."

"Thanks, Chief." Colin slipped his phone back into his pocket, trying not to make eye contact with Peter. "Let's head down toward the marina." Colin zipped up his jacket and took a few steps, expecting Peter to catch up with him.

"Whoa," Peter sputtered, grabbing Colin by the arm. "One freakin' minute! What's really going on here?"

"Let's talk while we walk. We're losing time."

As they hurried toward the docks, Colin explained that there had been a murder in town the day after the girls arrived. Because the police chief was just a young guy with no experience with murder investigations, he had asked for Colin's and Emily's help to find the killer.

"So instead of kicking back and enjoying the sights, you and Emily have been working a murder case all week?"

"Afraid so, only it seems it's also turned into a drug bust."

"Oh, man. And now Emily's in danger? How'd that happen?"

"Well, we got into an argument and she had to get some air, she claimed."

"I didn't want to say anything," Peter grinned, "but I saw that fat lip she gave you."

Colin touched his lip and winced. "This wasn't Emily."

"Then who?"

"It doesn't matter. We've got to find her."

Once they reached the dock, Colin saw the empty slip where the Hoosier Daddy had been tied. He looked around for any clues, anything that would lead him to believe she'd been on the boat, but there was nothing.

"Peter, a few of these boats have their cabin lights on. Maybe someone saw or heard something. You take that one," Colin said, pointing to a schooner a few slips away. "I'll take that old trawler down this way."

They split up and proceeded to question the occupants, but none of them claimed to have seen or heard anything. A middle-aged man was climbing out of a sports craft, stepping onto the dock, so Colin approached him, asking if he'd seen a pretty young woman with curly honey-blond hair, about five seven, a hundred and twenty-five pounds.

"Wish I had," he joked, "but no." He marched up the dock toward town.

"Now what?" Peter asked. "The rain is starting to come down pretty good."

Colin's phone rang in his pocket and he quickly pulled it out and answered it. "This is Colin."

"Hey, this is Chief Taylor. My friend at the Bangor Police verified that Emily's phone is on the same path as the boat, which means—"

"She's on the boat!"

"I'm afraid so."

"Now can we go after her?"

"Eyah, I thought you'd say that. Like I said, the boat's down at the end of the dock. I'll get one of my men and be down there shortly."

"Thanks, Chief." Colin stared out over the dark, choppy water as he tucked his phone away. "Emily's out there."

Peter put a hand on Colin's shoulder. "I heard. Tell me, what can I do?"

Ideas swirled around in Colin's head, trying to rush a plan together. "I'm going to have Isabel meet me down here, but you call your sister and tell them they don't need to search anymore."

"Are you sure? I'm happy to go with you."

"I know, Peter, but this is a police matter. It's best you take care of Camille and the others."

Peter patted Colin on the back a couple of times. "Good luck, buddy."

He began walking down the dock, back to the inn, his auburn hair darkening with the rain. He stopped momentarily, turning his head. "I want to hear about that fat lip tomorrow," he called over his shoulder.

"Yeah, that's not going to happen," Colin muttered to himself, waving a hand in the air.

He phoned Isabel right away and explained the situation. "Meet me at the far end of the dock, and have Alex and Evan go back to the inn and wait for us."

"Roger that," Isabel confirmed. "I'm only a few minutes away."

Chief Taylor met Colin at the police boat, wearing an opaque rain slicker, with his portable GPS monitor tucked underneath it. Alongside him was one of his men,

Officer Cantrell. The officer climbed aboard and started up the engine. "We'll be ready to cast off as soon as the rest of the parties arrive."

Colin turned back to Cantrell. "We're only waiting on one."

Before long, Isabel approached, the sound of her boot heels clicking as she marched down the dock. She struggled to hold onto her small black umbrella in the wind, and she was not alone. There was someone with her, someone taller, wearing a hat and coat and walking behind her. As they drew closer, Colin saw it was Evan.

"What's he doing here?" Angry, Colin pitched his chin toward Evan.

"I have as much right to be here as you do," Evan snapped back.

The chief stepped between them, facing Evan. "And you are?"

"Emily's husband."

CHAPTER TWENTY-FOUR
Pitching and Rolling

"EMILY'S HUSBAND, EH?" Chief Taylor's gaze slid over to Colin. "Sounds like an interesting story, but right now we need to catch that boat. Everyone on board!"

As fast as they could, the four of them poured into the police vessel. The officer untied her from the dock. "Squeeze into the control cabin and hold on," he yelled.

Chief Taylor checked the GPS monitor again as the boat backed out of the slip and pulled away from the dock. "We'd better get moving at warp speed, Cantrell, if we want to have any chance of catching up to them."

"Yes, sir."

Isabel moved to a rear corner of the enclosed area and held onto the metal railing that ran around the back of the interior. Evan took a spot beside her, and Colin went to the other corner and stood behind Cantrell, grabbing onto the bar.

Cooped up with Evan was the last place Colin wanted to be, but he didn't have a choice. He stepped up next to the chief, grabbing hold of a rack overhead to steady himself. He peered at the screen over the chief's shoulder. "Looks like we've got a lot of distance to make up."

"We'll do the best we can, Detective," the chief said. "I've become kind of fond of that feisty girl of yours."

Cantrell turned the forward lights on and gradually pushed the speed lever upward until they were away from the other boats, then he opened it up full throttle.

Colin gazed out over the dark water with a dreadful heaviness in his chest. *Hold on Emily—we're coming.*

The wind whipped at the boat and the rain was beginning to come down harder against the windows. The water was already choppy, with three- to four-foot-high waves slapping against the hull as the rescue boat cut through them.

"What does the weather report say?" Colin asked.

"I just got an updated report. It says the storm has taken an unexpected turn and is heading back toward land," the chief hollered, raising his voice over the wind and the roar of the engine.

Colin's gut tightened at the thought.

"Where are they now?" Cantrell asked.

The chief checked the monitor. "Looks like the Hoosier Daddy is just about to break the mouth of the bay. It's best if we can reach them before they hit open water."

"Chief," Cantrell's head turned toward his boss, "do

you think we should wait for the Coast Guard?"

"I wish we could." Chief Taylor sounded concerned.

Officer Cantrell checked the gauges again. "But what if—"

"Don't worry," the chief jumped in, seeming to know what the man was about to say. "The storm is moving pretty slowly."

The chief's gaze drifted to Colin. "But even at that, Cantrell is right. It could get real nasty out here."

Emily's image filled Colin's mind. How terrified she must be out there with those men. She was probably pretty confused too, considering what happened with Evan and Isabel only minutes before she ran off. He willed his eyes not to move in their direction, but he couldn't seem to stop his thoughts from going there.

What if those men had already killed Emily? Or dumped her overboard somewhere in the bay? They wouldn't need to wait until they were out at sea to do it. No. He had to stay positive. He shook his head, trying to let loose of the negative thoughts.

His gaze drifted out the window, to the dark waves and black sky, his eyes watering with emotion as he wondered about Emily.

"You okay there, Colin?" the chief questioned, studying him with concern.

The sting of embarrassment rippled through Colin's chest and up his neck, flashing hot on his face. He roughly wiped a hand over his eyes. "Yeah, it's just rain dripping from my hair. I'm fine." He didn't dare look over at Evan now, although he was certain he could feel the heat of the man's eyes boring into the side of his head.

Why did Evan have to show up now? Why couldn't he have just stayed dead?

"I've radioed for the Coast Guard," the chief announced loudly, "but they'll be about fifteen minutes behind us. With any luck, they can make up some of that time with their larger vessel."

Colin nodded at him, then his gaze went back to the ominous black water outside. The growing swells mirrored the emotions that were roiling inside of him. The boat continued to rise and crash against each angry wave in a jolting rhythm. "Looks like the waves are getting bigger."

"Eyah," the chief agreed, watching the GPS monitor. "Hopefully it won't be too long now. We're gaining on them."

Colin stared out the window again, his anxiety growing. He hadn't realized how tightly he had been gripping the grab bar until his hand began to tingle, having gone almost numb. He switched hands and flexed the fatigued one.

This rescue was taking too long. Each minute seemed like an eternity and the proximity to Evan was becoming unbearable. Would they reach Emily in time? How many times before had he almost lost her? Tonight, on the eve of their wedding, would this be the last time? Would he lose her for good, or would he be able to rescue her one more time? And if he did save her, would he then lose her to the resurrected ghost of her dead husband?

Evan's voice jolted Colin out of his thoughts. "What's the plan when we catch up to them?"

Chief Taylor turned toward Evan. "I'll use the bullhorn and order them to give up."

Evan shook his head. "Give me a gun. Come alongside the other boat and I'll jump across onto theirs before they know what's happening."

"You have no jurisdiction," the chief eyed him, up and down, with suspicion in his eyes, "whoever you are."

"I'll go," Colin declared. "I can handle these guys."

"She's *my* wife," Evan bit out.

"Not anymore!" Colin stepped nearly nose to nose with Evan, daring him to take a swing.

Isabel stepped between them. "Settle down. This isn't going to do Emily any good."

Colin took a step back and his gaze moved to the waves before them. Faint lights glowed in the distance. "Look! Up ahead!"

~*~

The boat was pitching and rolling on the waves and Emily fought the nausea. Caleb had tied her hands to a metal rail that ran around the dining area of the cabin.

She sat quietly on a banquette, trying to hear what Eric and Caleb were saying on the other side of the room. It sounded like Caleb was becoming more concerned about the growing storm and Eric was beginning to agree with him.

"All the money in the world won't do us any good if we're lying on the bottom of the ocean," Caleb said with a groan.

"Rosco assured me this boat can weather it," Eric

argued back.

Just then the boat pitched over a big wave. The men grabbed whatever they could reach and held on. Things went flying around the cabin.

Emily was ready to vomit.

As soon as the boat settled a bit, Eric flew up the steps to try to convince Rosco they needed to wait it out or turn back.

"Whitley really cares about you, Caleb," Emily said in the calmest voice she could muster. "Who'll take care of her and your mother if we all drown out here?"

Caleb released his death grip on the railing and took a couple of steps toward her. "You know my sister?"

"Yes. Sweet girl…and she's worried about you."

He briefly glanced over his shoulder at the steps, seeming to check to make sure no one else was in the cabin.

"You might spend a little time in jail for the drugs, but if you kill me, your life is over."

He stared at her without a word, but Emily could see in his eyes that the wheels were turning in his head.

"You didn't kill Ben Kinney, Rosco did. If you testify against him, I'm sure you can cut a deal and get your sentence reduced. Think of your mom and your sister."

He ran a hand over his face and dropped down onto the seat across from her, then he looked back toward the stairs.

"Eric doesn't seem like a killer, either," Emily said. "Don't let Rosco make this worse for you two than it already is." *Or for me.*

"But he's the one with the gun," Caleb argued.

"That's true, but he gave it to Eric, remember?" Was she making inroads with Caleb?

"But it belongs to Rosco and I'm sure he'll get it away from Eric if he needs to. Maybe I can do something to disable the engine." His gaze bounced around the cabin as if he was looking for anything he could use. "That would stop the boat."

"And leave us drifting in the storm," Emily said.

The noise from the engine decreased and the boat slowed.

Caleb nodded at her comment, not seeming to notice the change in speed yet. "I just meant temporarily, otherwise we'd be stuck out here on the ocean like a sitting duck."

"Who's a sitting duck?" Eric asked as he descended the steps.

~*~

"Is that them?" Chief Taylor called out, pointing ahead.

"I believe it is," Colin replied.

The chief got on the radio and checked in with the Coast Guard once more. "They're about ten minutes behind us," he reported.

"We can't wait for them," Colin shouted, his heart pounding in his ears.

"Colin's right, Chief," Isabel added. "We need to act now."

"We're closing in on them," Cantrell declared.

The chief checked the monitor again. "Looks like they're sitting still." His gaze flew to Colin. "Engine trouble?"

"Maybe they're reconsidering going farther out into the storm," Isabel surmised.

"We'll need to approach with caution, Cantrell," the chief said.

"Got it, Chief."

Cantrell pulled back on the throttle as they closed in on the Hoosier Daddy.

"It's go time." Chief Taylor's gaze went from Colin to Evan, then back to Colin. He pulled his pistol out of its holster and handed it to Colin. "I hope you know what you're doing."

"What about me?" Evan asked angrily, his brow dipping low over his eyes. He pulled a weapon out from under his coat and held it down against his thigh.

"I don't need your help," Colin snapped back, seeing Evan's gun.

"Don't be pig-headed, Colin," Isabel chided. "Take the help."

There was no way he was going to let Evan swoop in and play the hero by saving Emily. It was bad enough he was there at all. Colin wasn't going to give him the chance to steal her heart again—if her heart was still beating.

"Looks like there's no one on the bridge," Cantrell said, peering at the other boat through night-vision binoculars.

Colin tucked the gun in his waist and took them from Cantrell to look for himself. "That means either they're all below or another boat came by and picked them up, doesn't it?"

Chief Taylor pulled his hat off and scratched his

head. "The Coast Guard would have mentioned another boat in the vicinity." He flipped his hat back on, grabbed the binoculars from Colin, and took a look. "Cantrell, cut the engines and sidle up beside that boat."

"I'll do my best, sir. With these waves, I can't promise anything."

"Don't be a fool, Andrews," Evan argued. "Let me come along."

~*~

Rosco was close on Eric's heels as he descended the steps, a scowl on his face, seemingly because of Caleb's chatting with their hostage. As he unzipped his coat, his pistol could be seen stuck in the front of his waistband. Apparently he had retrieved it from his boss.

Caleb cleared his throat nervously. "Uh, we were talking about the storm, how it's getting worse."

"Captain Obvious," Rosco quipped and rolled his eyes.

"We decided to regroup and see what our options are," Eric explained.

"The weather channel's now reporting that the storm has shifted direction and is coming back toward land," Rosco said. "I think we should go for it, but Eric wants to wait it out or turn back. As much as I hate to say it, Eric might be right. We can't spend all that money if we're dead."

"That's what I said," Caleb pointed out.

A rumbling sound came amidst the battering waves and the howling wind, and something jolted the boat.

Rosco put a hand out to hush everyone and his other

hand went to the gun. His eyes squinted and he tilted his head to listen. "What was that?"

Colin? Hope leapt into Emily's heart.

Eric cocked his head and his gaze rose to the ceiling. "I don't hear anything but the wind and the waves crashing against the boat."

"No, it's something else," Rosco insisted.

The sound came again and the boat jerked sideways, like something hitting the vessel.

Rosco pulled the gun from his waistband and put a finger to his lips, cautioning everyone to be silent. He climbed the steps and pushed the door open.

CHAPTER TWENTY-FIVE
A Tragic Rescue

OFFICER CANTRELL HAD DEFTLY brought the boat up alongside the Hoosier Daddy.

With the gun in the pocket of his tightly zipped coat, Colin jumped from the police boat onto the Hoosier Daddy as the two boats banged together. As soon as he landed on the deck of the other boat, he pulled his weapon out, fighting to stay on his feet with the boat rocking and pitching in the storm.

The rain was now coming down in sheets. It would have been pitch-black if not for the illumination from the police boat and the dim lights coming from the cabin windows of the trawler.

He prayed Emily was still on board—and breathing.

A large wave pitched the boat high on one side and Colin lost his footing. He stumbled back to his feet and glanced over to the police boat, seeing the outline of several people watching him through the windows of the control house.

He pulled his attention away from them as the door to the trawler's cabin opened and a large, stocky man stepped through. With light coming up from behind him, Colin couldn't make out the man's features, but he did catch a ray of light sparking off a pistol as he raised his hand, and pointed it.

Colin knew what would be coming next, and there wasn't much time to do anything about it. He quickly drew his gun and fired. A flash of light emanated from the man's pistol just as the blast of gunfire sounded from Colin's own weapon discharging.

The dark figure dropped heavily onto the deck.

As Colin began to take a step toward the cabin door, a burning pain ripped through his chest. Colin had hit his target, but his target hadn't missed his mark either. He put a hand to the source of the searing pain and felt the warm and sticky-wet confirmation. He'd been hit.

He managed to stay on his feet, but stumbled down the steps.

"Colin!"

He heard Emily scream his name before everything went dark and he crumpled to the floor.

~*~

As Colin lay bleeding, Evan flew down the steps behind him, dripping wet, wearing only a shirt and pants. He must have seen what happened to Colin and launched into action. Eric and Caleb took a step forward, as if ready to pounce on the gun by Colin's hand, but Evan quickly scooped it up before they had a chance and he turned it on them.

Evan?

"The game's over, fellas," Evan said, looking as dashing as ever. "Now get those ropes off my wife."

Since being captured, the only thing that had consumed Emily's thoughts was trying to stay alive. She had pushed thoughts of Evan out of her mind and the sight of him again jolted her. As if in slow motion, Emily's gaze drifted down to Colin. Her fiancé was laying shot and bleeding on the floor, just feet from her—unconscious or dead, she didn't know—and the husband she thought was deceased was now calling her his wife. The enormity of the circumstances made her head swim, and she felt like she might pass out. She urged herself to keep it together.

"Sorry about all this," Caleb said as he untied Emily's hands. "I never wanted to hurt you."

Once freed, her choice was clear. It was Colin's name that came to mind as she heard the commotion outside the boat earlier. She ran to him now, and threw herself on the floor beside him. She didn't care what Evan thought at this point, her heart belonged to Colin.

"Colin?" She put a couple of fingers to his neck and felt for a pulse. "He's alive!" She leaned down and kissed his face, tears streaming down her own. "He's alive."

"We don't have time for that, love." Evan took her by the arm and pulled her to her feet. "The storm's a nasty one and I've got to get you out of here while I can."

"What about us?" Eric asked, standing beside Caleb.

"Yeah, what about us?" Caleb joined in.

"You two grab a life preserver for yourself and swim for it. The other boat's not far away. They'll be waiting for you, I'm sure."

"What about Colin?" Emily cried as she watched Eric and Caleb scramble up to the deck.

"I'll come back for him, but I've got to get you to the other boat first."

"No. Take Colin first. Then come back for me."

"But, Emily—"

"We don't have time to stand here arguing—just do it!"

Evan grumbled as he reached under Colin's arms and grabbed him around the chest. Colin moaned as Evan dragged him up the steps and rushed to strap an orange life vest on him.

Emily followed them up to the rear deck and held on to a railing as the boat rocked on the stormy waters.

The police boat was trying to maneuver to stay close to the Hoosier Daddy, but the strong waves were pushing it ten, or more, feet away. Isabel, Cantrell, and Chief Taylor were pulling Eric and Caleb up onto the boat when Evan hoisted Colin over his shoulder and jumped into the water.

As he swam, dragging Colin to the police boat while fighting the high waves, Emily realized why he'd had no coat or shoes on. After seeing Colin shot, he must have stripped off his coat and shoes in order to swim across to the Hoosier Daddy to rescue her.

But she wasn't going anywhere until she knew Colin was safely on board the other boat.

The chief and another officer pulled Colin up over the side of the boat as Isabel handcuffed Eric and Caleb to the railing that ran around the stern. Once Evan had gotten Colin into Chief Taylor's hands, he began the fight back to the Hoosier Daddy for Emily. The boats had now drifted even farther apart.

The officer ran to the controls and jockeyed the boat a little closer to try to close the growing gap. When Evan was within ten feet of the Hoosier Daddy, an enormous wave hit and pitched it on its side, throwing Emily into the water and pushing the police boat farther away.

"Emily!" she heard Evan scream as she slipped below the surface. She couldn't catch her breath, feeling herself going down.

She thrashed around in the dark, cold water, the crashing waves sucking her farther into their murky depths. She didn't know which direction was up, which way to go. Out of air and gulping sea water, she began to feel consciousness itself slipping away.

An eerie peace enveloped her and her mind began to quiet.

Just as she had chosen to succumb to her fate, and give herself up to the heaving waves, a set of strong hands wrapped around her and pulled. Before long, she broke the surface, spitting salty water and gasping for air. As she coughed and sputtered, an arm came across her chest, tightened around her, and she heard someone calling her name. It was Evan.

He swam for the police boat with his free arm, but

the high waves pushed them back toward the other boat. He pulled at the water again and again, his feet kicking furiously, trying to gain leverage, as he held Emily close.

After a fierce battle with the strong waves, they finally reached the police boat.

Evan groaned as he hoisted Emily up out of the water toward the waiting hands of Chief Taylor and the officer. They grabbed her and hauled her up onto the boat. When her feet had cleared the side of it, Isabel stood from where she had been tending to Colin, an expression of uncertainty on her face.

They set Emily down, motioning to Isabel to come, then they turned back for Evan, scanning the water.

"Evan!" Chief Taylor called into the wind as they surveyed the ocean below. "Evan, where are you, man?"

"Where is he?" Still sputtering the water from her lungs, Emily tried to scramble to her feet.

Isabel joined her at the side of the boat and draped a blanket over Emily's shoulders, then, almost tentatively, she slipped her arm around Emily and held her up.

The officer beamed a large flashlight across the water between the two boats. "I don't see him."

All Emily could see was the other boat drifting away as the ferocious waves beat against it.

"Evan!" the chief called again, but nothing. He turned to Emily. "I'm so sorry," he said, "but I don't see him."

"Find him!" she screamed. "You have to find him!" She couldn't just let him drown. He had risked his own life to save hers.

The officer swished the beam around over the inky black surface of the water. "I can't see him anywhere."

A huge bright light shone on their boat as the Coast Guard vessel approached. Chief Taylor ran to the controls to radio them, and, with Isabel's help, Emily followed him. The chief reported that they had lost a man overboard and they had another on their boat with a gunshot wound that needed immediate attention.

Chief Taylor glanced over his shoulder at Emily as the Coast Guard captain ordered them back to shore immediately. They would stick around a little longer and keep searching for Evan, but with the storm intensifying, they all needed to head back into the harbor.

"Roger that," the chief barked into the radio. "Cantrell!" he called out the door to his man who was still searching the waters. "Take us back to Rock Harbor!"

Emily shrugged out of Isabel's grasp and stumbled to the side of the boat, hoping to see some sign of Evan in the water, but there was none. The wind whipped her wet curls, plastering them against her face, but she didn't care. She slumped down on the deck and crawled toward the control cabin, coming to rest with her back against it, protected from the rain by a canvas overhang.

The officer brought the boat around and headed back to port. Her body shook as the boat's hull slammed into wave after wave as they raced toward the harbor.

In a dazed stupor, her gaze drifted around the stern. It was like she was watching a black-and-white movie in slow motion, everything in various shades of gray, thoughts slogging through her mind. Eric and Caleb were handcuffed to the railing, and they were getting pelted by the rain and wind. Isabel was now bending down, checking on Colin under a tarp they had placed over him to protect him from the elements.

Was he alive? Emily was so emotionally and physically exhausted, she couldn't even go to him. She was paralyzed by the fear that he might be dead…from a bullet he took trying to rescue her.

Slowly, her gaze moved to the side of the vessel, where Chief Taylor and his officer had lifted her over the edge and onto the boat. From where she sat, she couldn't see the water immediately below, but through the rain she could faintly make out the high rolling waves in the distance.

A bolt of lightning lit up the tumultuous waters for a second. Evan was out there somewhere. He had come back into her life for only an hour or so, and now he was gone again. She swallowed hard. Where would she be if he hadn't come back for her? Drowned?

An unexpected spike of anger stabbed her. "No!" She would be enjoying her bachelorette party with her friends, that's where. And Colin wouldn't be laying at the back of the boat fighting for his life either.

Her gaze floated over the murky waves and her anger subsided. Even though she wouldn't have been on the Hoosier Daddy if he had stayed dead, she had to acknowledge that Evan had likely given up his life saving hers. She shook her head sadly, burying her face in her hands.

Would the Coast Guard find his body? Would he wash up on shore someday? Could she even say for certain that he was dead this time?

"Emily?" Isabel put a hand on her shoulder and crouched beside Emily. "Colin is asking for you."

"He's alive?" She pushed her wet hair off her face

with both hands.

Isabel nodded with a smile, then stood, helping Emily up. "I think I've got the bleeding stopped, but we need to get him to a hospital quick."

More alert now, Emily was suddenly struck with the remembrance that her friend had played a part in Evan's deception. She narrowed her eyes, deciding that Isabel was the last person she wanted to talk to right now.

Emily began to step away, but Isabel grabbed her arm to stop her. "We're going to need to talk."

"We'll talk later." Emily pulled away. She needed to go to Colin. Isabel could wait—for a very long time if need be.

"All right then," Isabel conceded. "While you go over to talk to him, I'm going to make sure the chief radioed ahead to have an ambulance waiting for us at the dock. But, Em—"

Emily hurried to Colin, not waiting for Isabel to finish her thought. She dropped down beside him, her heart full of concern. His eyes were shut, his breathing barely detectable.

"Colin," she said softly, leaning down close to his face. "I'm here."

"Emily," he whispered, his eyes fluttering open.

Her heart leapt at the sign of life and she kissed the side of his mouth. "Shhh." She kept very near him, surrounded by the loud noise of the boat ripping through the rough waters of Frenchman's Bay. "Don't strain yourself, honey. Save your strength."

"I love you, Emily."

She tenderly brushed the damp hair off his pale

forehead as his eyes drifted shut again.

Would they make it to shore in time?

Blood stained his shirt and coat, and it was obvious he had lost a lot of it. Needing to be heard over the roar of the waves, Emily put her mouth against his ear. "No matter what, Colin, I want you to know that I love you more than any man I've ever known."

His eyelids raised slightly. "You think I'm going to die?" He started to chuckle but winced in pain. "You're not getting rid of me that easily."

CHAPTER TWENTY-SIX
Will They Say 'I Do'?

A COUPLE OF PARAMEDICS in bright yellow rain slickers stood on the dock waiting for the police boat to motor into the slip. Between the two men sat a steel gurney, with a sheet of thick plastic covering it, held in place by heavy vinyl medical bags, the edges of the drape flapping in the wind.

After retrieving Colin from the boat and loading him into the ambulance, they sped away to the hospital, lights flashing and sirens blaring. Helplessly watching the EMTs work, Emily had asked to go in the ambulance with him, but Isabel worked to convince her it would be better for her to go back to the inn.

"I'm sure Colin will be in surgery for at least an hour or two, digging that bullet out," Isabel said, "which will give you time to change into some dry clothes and rest for a while. You've been through quite an ordeal yourself."

"No, I'm fine," Emily replied, but she knew she was not. She was angry with her friend for the secrets she had kept. Maybe in Isabel's line of work they were an ugly part of the job, but it still hurt Emily deeply.

"Get some rest," Isabel said in a firm tone, "then I'll take you to the hospital."

Though she wanted to push back, Emily was too exhausted to argue any further.

~*~

After taking Isabel's advice, Emily gathered with her sister and friends in the small waiting room in the surgical wing at Rock Harbor Hospital. Following nearly three hours of surgery, Colin was doing well, the doctor announced when he came out to speak to those waiting nervously for him.

"We got the bullet out of his shoulder and repaired the damage. He's lucky it didn't pierce any vital organs. He's resting comfortably in post-op right now."

"Can I see him?" Emily pleaded.

"He's heavily sedated and he'll be unconscious for quite a few more hours. Why don't you all go home, get some sleep, and come back in the morning? He'll have been moved to a room by then."

"But I'd like to at least—"

"Emily, hon," her sister lightly grasped her arm, "let's do what the doctor said. You look exhausted."

"I'm fine," Emily lied again. She wanted to see Colin, know he was alive and that he was going to be okay.

Isabel put an arm around Emily's shoulder. "Your sister's right."

Emily shrugged out of her embrace, but Isabel continued. "Let's all get a good night's sleep, Colin included, and things will be better in the morning."

"In the morning," Emily gasped. "Oh no. Colin's parents!"

Susan's eyes widened. "What?"

"Colin's parents are supposed to arrive in the morning. They don't even know what's happened."

"Don't worry, Emily," Camille said, "you're the one who needs to rest. Maggie and I will make sure to greet them when they arrive and we'll explain everything."

"You just take care of you for a change," Maggie added. "Now *git*," she ordered, making a shooing motion with her hand.

Emily's shoulders dropped in exhaustion. She didn't have the strength to continue the debate. "If you insist." She hugged her sister and her friends, tears pooling in her eyes. "Tomorrow was supposed to be our wedding day." She huffed a hollow laugh and sniffed sadly. "But now..."

~*~

Emily slept soundly and didn't wake until almost ten. The bright morning sun streamed into her room, an encouraging sign that the storm had passed and things would be looking up.

She peeked over at the digital clock on the

nightstand. Surprised by the lateness of the hour, she shot out of bed and hurried to the bathroom.

Why didn't someone wake her up? She needed to get to the hospital to check on Colin. He was probably wondering where she was.

Hurriedly, she hopped in the shower. As the warm water cascaded down her back, the events of the previous evening flooded into her mind and replayed in vivid emotional color—being held captive and not knowing if she was going to live or die, remembering Colin lying on the deck of the boat, nearly bleeding to death, and Evan being swallowed up by the angry bay.

Finally, she turned off the water and stepped out, grabbing a fluffy white towel. As she wrapped it around herself, she caught a reflection in the mirror and did a double-take. This time, it was merely her own reflection staring back at her, but the night before, Evan had surprised her—no, shocked her—standing in the middle of her room when she left the bathroom, still damp from the shower.

His strong and dashing image filled her mind. For an hour or so, she'd had her husband back, but his brief presence had upended her life and put her in harm's way. In the end, he had given his life trying to save hers. Sorrow descended on her like a black cloud and hot tears poured out of her in sobs and groans, mourning his loss, yet again. She sat down on the side of the tub and cried until her legs were almost numb.

Her phone on the counter pinged, signaling she had received a text. She stretched to grab it and checked for a message. It was from Colin. He had taken a photo of himself with his phone, lying in his hospital bed, smiling into the camera, and had sent it to her with the message *Happy to be alive! Can't wait to see you.* She smiled.

His text had lifted her spirit. She splashed some water on her face and raked her fingers through her hair. Evan was gone again and she had mourned the loss, crying for him until there were no more tears to spill. She was ready to put his memory behind her, once and for all, relieved to know she wasn't losing her mind.

Emily took a critical look at herself in the mirror. She'd have to put on some makeup to cover the puffy eyes and slightly red nose before she saw Colin. She wanted to look her best for him, bring her brightest smile, and reaffirm her love for him, in case he had any doubt after finding her and Evan alone in her room.

Once she was dressed and ready for the day, she grabbed her jacket and headed for the door. Then she realized she did not have the keys to the rental car, so she phoned Maggie to ask for a ride to the hospital, which was located on the other side of town. It went to voicemail.

Emily phoned Camille and then Isabel, but both the same. Had they connected with Colin's parents yet?

Where was everybody?

There was a knock at the door.

Before opening it, Emily peered through the peek hole. It was her sister.

Worried, she pulled the door open. "Susan, is Colin all right?"

"Yes, he's doing well," she said with a smile, walking past Emily, into her room. "I just came from checking on him at the hospital. I even had a chance to visit with my husband a little."

"And Colin's folks, are they here?" Emily closed the door.

"Yes, Jonathan and Camille drove them to the hospital. Maggie and all the rest are there too. That's why I'm here, to get you."

"Sorry, I overslept. Why didn't you call and wake me up earlier?"

"We all figured you needed your rest, after what you went through last night, but I'm here now."

"Thank goodness, because Colin has the keys to the rental car."

"Shall we go? Your man has been asking for you."

My man. Those words stirred her heart. She couldn't wait to see him.

When they arrived at the hospital, Susan led Emily down the corridor toward Colin's room.

"This looks familiar," Emily said as she glanced around.

"It should. It's Brian's too." Susan pushed the door open and went in first.

Emily paused in the doorway, surprised that the place was filled with people—all her friends, Colin's parents, Ella McCormack, Whitley Donovan, and Chief Taylor. Her brother-in-law was in the bed next to Colin's, surrounded by his and Susan's children.

As Emily entered, they all quieted and turned, smiling at her and moving apart to make a straight shot down the middle, right to Colin.

On either side of his bed stood white wicker stands filled with the flowers she and Susan had chosen at the florist's shop a couple of days before. Colin had a boutonniere pinned to the chest of his hospital gown.

Propped up by several pillows, he flashed her a wide grin. "Morning, Babe."

Emily moved slowly to him, her gaze floating from face to face, awareness starting to dawn on her. She leaned down and kissed him softly. "What's all this?"

"What do you think it is?" Susan gestured toward the wedding dress hanging on a hook beside the bathroom door, an ankle-length sheath with long, fitted sleeves and a deep, square neckline, in the softest shade of winter white.

Emily sucked in a quick breath and her hand flew up to her chest. She looked at the dress, then back at Colin. "Really?"

He took her hand and kissed it. "Emily, will you marry me, today?"

"Today? But how?" Her vision blurred with happy tears.

"Easy-peasy." Susan laughed.

"What?" Emily blinked a few times, trying to hold the tears back.

"Mayor McCormack has agreed to perform the ceremony." Susan motioned toward Ella. "She's also a justice of the peace."

"She is?" Emily squeaked, her voice constricting with emotion.

"Now, I know she's not a minister, like you requested, but—"

"She's perfect," Emily cried, no longer able to contain the tears of joy. "But we forgot to get the marriage license."

"No worries, young lady. I brought the application with me." The mayor waved a paper in the air. "And I'll

301

be happy to walk it through the process on Monday, personally. After all, what's family for?"

"Family?" Colin questioned with a slight frown.

"Remember?" Brian said, "The mayor is my aunt."

"Funny how things work out." Emily drew a deep breath and tried her best to gain control over her tears. She turned back to Colin and squeezed his hand lightly. "I promised myself we would get married today, come hell or high water, but I never dreamed it would be like this."

Colin chuckled, then winced in pain and groaned. "We certainly got some of each."

Emily glanced around at all her friends, moving from face to face. "I don't know what to say. This is all so, so…"

"Wonderful?" Camille asked.

"Surprisin'?" Maggie chimed in.

Emily wiped a couple of stray tears from her cheeks, searching for the right word. "Overwhelming."

"Oh, now stop that," Colin's mother said, her eyes misting, "before you have us all blubbering."

"Everyone is invited down to the hospital chapel." Susan pulled the wedding gown off the hook. "As soon as we get the bride into her dress, the ceremony can begin."

"What about my shoes?"

"Got 'em," Susan assured her. "I snuck them out of your closet this morning when you weren't looking."

Isabel clapped her hands together a few times. "Come on people, let's get moving. We've got a wedding to put on. Can someone grab those flower arrangements?" She moved next to Emily. "I know

now's not a good time, but when you get back from your honeymoon, I hope you'll let me explain myself."

Emily wasn't sure how to feel. Isabel was her best friend, yet she had lied to her for years, had kept Evan's charade a secret, and who knew what else. But she did love Isabel—they were closer than sisters. Could she ever trust her again? Maybe Isabel had truly done it to protect her.

Emily nodded. "When we get home."

Isabel gave her a little smile before going off to help get the chapel set up for the wedding.

"It's really happening, isn't it?" Emily glanced down at Colin, still holding his hand.

"It certainly looks that way, Babe."

"Are you sure you're up to it? Going to the chapel, I mean."

"I think so."

"You think so? So the doctor hasn't cleared you to do this?" Emily pitched him a stern look.

"With help, I can get into a wheelchair and have someone push me down the aisle just as well as I can laying here."

Emily turned and looked at Brian, lying helpless in the other bed, one leg still in traction. He would have to miss the wedding because of his broken legs. "How about we have it right here?" she said. "Then Brian can be a part. He is family after all."

Susan beamed.

Colin nodded with a smile. "Great idea."

"It's settled then." Emily looked pleased with the new arrangement. "Now if someone can grab the mayor and get the fellas to bring the flowers back, I'll get into my dress and we can get this party started."

"Now, Emily," Camille stepped in, "do you have something old, something new, something borrowed, something blue?"

"Well, no," Emily replied. "I actually hadn't even thought of it. But those things—"

"Oh, we certainly can't have that," Colin's mother said, joining the group. "Here, Emily." She handed her a small black felt box. "I brought these for you. I thought you might like to wear them."

Emily slowly opened it and saw a beautiful pair of teardrop pearl earrings with diamond-crusted studs. "Oh, Carolyn! They're gorgeous." She hugged her in appreciation.

"They were my mother's and I wore them when I married Colin's father. So, there—something old."

"Can I get some help?" Colin moaned, trying to reach the drawer in his side table.

Maggie rushed to his aid.

"Pull out the drawer and hand me the black box in there."

Maggie gave it to him and he held it out to Emily. "This was going to be my wedding gift to you, Babe. Isabel was kind enough to get it from my room."

Emily opened it to find a strand of luscious pearls. "I love them!" She leaned down and kissed him. "Thank you, sweetheart," she uttered, looking deeply into his smiling eyes.

"And that takes care of somethin' new," Maggie said. "Now for somethin' borrowed." She handed Emily a white linen handkerchief with delicate hand-crocheted lace on the edges. "My granny made this for me when I

got married. So all you have left is to find somethin'
blue."

"Emily!" Whitley pressed her way through the
small crowd until she reached the bride. She lifted a
silver chain up and over her head and handed Emily the
pendant with the blue rhinestones that Ben had given
her. "You told me on several occasions how much you
liked this necklace and, well, after finding out who Ben
really was, I can't keep it. So there's your something
blue."

Caught off guard by the gesture, Emily looked
down at the pendant in her hand and then to Colin,
meeting his gaze. "Thank you, Whitley." She turned
back to the young woman and hugged her neck. "This is
wonderful. You don't know what this means. I don't
think it will go with my wedding gown, but I'll be sure
to wear it under my dress."

The girl grinned and seemed happy with herself as
she stepped away.

Emily fumbled with the pendant and slid the thumb
drive connector out, confirming it was exactly as she had
suspected. "I think we're set."

The men brought the flowers back as Emily and
Susan went into the bathroom with her gown. By the
time they came back out, everyone was in the room
waiting for the bride, making a center aisle for her.
Mayor McCormack stood on the right, beside Colin.

Emily slowly marched down the middle of the
crowd, holding a single white rose. Suddenly, the
wedding march began to softly play. Emily looked in the
direction of the music. It was coming from Molly's iPod,
and Emily flashed the girl a grateful smile.

She continued down the aisle, her eyes locked on her groom, and his on her. She glided to her place on the left of Colin, facing her guests, and took his hand.

"Wow," he whispered, his eyes lighting up. "You look so beautiful."

She smiled down at him and a happy warmth filled her, confident she had chosen the right man to spend the rest of her life with.

Mayor McCormack led Colin and Emily in reciting their vows. Maggie's borrowed hanky came in handy as a few joyful tears fell on Emily's cheeks, but she wasn't the only one in the room shedding them.

"Something must have gotten in my eye," Brian murmured to his wife.

"Me too," Colin's dad admitted.

"I promise you, Babe," Colin smiled up at his bride, his eyes moist as well, "'til death do us part, as long as we both shall live."

"Yes, as long as we both shall live." Emily leaned down close to him and whispered, "This couldn't be any more perfect."

"Now, who has the rings?" the mayor asked as her gaze danced around the room.

Colin's and Emily's eyes flew wide and they each shot an expectant look toward the other.

"Oh, no, the rings!"

THE END

Thank you so much for reading my book,
The Harbor of Lies.
I hope you enjoyed it very much.

Debra Burroughs

The highest compliment an author can get is to
receive a great review, especially
if the review is posted on Amazon.com.

Debra@DebraBurroughsBooks.com
www.DebraBurroughsBooks.com

Other Books

By Debra Burroughs

Three Days in Seattle, a Romantic Suspense Novel

The Scent of Lies, Paradise Valley Mystery Book 1

The Heart of Lies, Paradise Valley Mystery Book 2

The Edge of Lies, Paradise Valley Mystery Short Story

The Chain of Lies, Paradise Valley Mystery Book 3

The Pursuit of Lies, Paradise Valley Mystery Book 4

The Color of Lies, Paradise Valley Mystery Short Story

The Betrayal of Lies, Paradise Valley Mystery Book 5

The Lake House Secret, a Jenessa Jones Mystery,
Book 1

The Stone House Secret,
a Jenessa Jones Mystery, Book 2

Coming in paperback in February, 2015

ABOUT THE AUTHOR

Debra Burroughs writes with intensity and power. Her characters are rich and her stories of romance, suspense and mystery are highly entertaining. She can often be found sitting in front of her computer in her home in the Pacific Northwest, dreaming up new stories and developing interesting characters for her next book.

If you are looking for stories that will touch your heart and leave you wanting more, dive into one of her captivating books.

www.DebraBurroughsBooks.com

Made in the USA
Middletown, DE
25 October 2020